THE SOMALI CAMEL BOY

a novel

Nur Abdi

MAWEN**Z**I
HOUSE

We acknowledge the support of the Canada Council for the Arts for our publishing program. We also acknowledge support from the Government of Ontario through the Ontario Arts Council.

ONTARIO ARTS COUNCIL
CONSEIL DES ARTS DE L'ONTARIO
an Ontario government agency
un organisme du gouvernement de l'Ontario

Canada Council   Conseil des arts
for the Arts   du Canada

Cover art: m_pavlov/Vector paper cut background. Abstract origami wave design. Topographic illustration stock illustration/iStockphoto

Cover design by Sabrina Pignataro

Library and Archives Canada Cataloguing in Publication

Title: The Somali camel boy : a novel / Nur Abdi.

Names: Abdi, Nur, 1951- author.

Identifiers: Canadiana (print) 20190165189 | Canadiana (ebook) 20190165227 | ISBN 9781988449876 (softcover) | ISBN 9781988449883 (HTML) | ISBN 9781988449890 (PDF)

Classification: LCC PS8601.B35 S66 2019 | DDC C813/.6—dc23

Printed and bound in Canada by Coach House Printing.

Mawenzi House Publishers Ltd.
39 Woburn Avenue (B)
Toronto, Ontario M5M 1K5
Canada

www.mawenzihouse.com

In memory of my parents—Hibo and Isman Abdi

Author's Note

This is a story about a young Somali camel boy. In a way, it is also the story of his own society, a society riven by clan and subclan divisions, where people are more passionate about these groups than their nationality, their humanity, and even their religion. It is what makes them tick. It is what they fight for and die for. The end result: a decent and smart people fail miserably to govern themselves and take their position in the world.

Ali, the young camel boy and the main character in this novel, is only fifteen years old when an enemy clan kills his father and raids his herd of camels. He decides to go to the nearby town, where a government dominated by the enemy clan arrests him. Fearing for his life, he manages to escape from prison and flee all the way to Canada. But even in Canada, the demons of his clan culture still haunt him. He can't wait to go back home to fight the enemy clan and avenge the killing of his father.

1

LATE ON A HOT AFTERNOON, I was walking through an inhospitable scrubland covered with termite mounds and scattered acacia trees. The desolation of the place had already set my nerves on edge. Not a sign of life anywhere. Not even a small bird overhead. Then suddenly, in this bleak terrain, I heard a low rumble—an ominous sound behind me that got closer and closer. I wondered what it could be. Was some killer stalking me? If so, would I be able to fight it off with my stick? Would I be able to outrun it? My pulse raced. My heart hammered in my chest.

Unable to see anything at first, I stopped again and looked behind. And there it was, the one I feared the most, the one all men dreaded to come face to face with in a deserted landscape. A lion with a thick grey mane was trailing me just a short distance away. Only a patch of dry bushes and a narrow stretch of empty space lay between us; but the lion had yet to see me—its head was down and close to the ground, sniffing my tracks.

In a moment it raised its head and we locked eyes over some bushes. Both the hunter and the hunted weighed their options, during which a blink of an eye felt like a year. The lion leaped in my direction. I lunged towards the closest acacia tree and quickly climbed up. My feet kept slipping and one of my shoes fell off, but I managed to clamber up.

By the time the lion caught up with me, I was out of its reach up in the tree. It looked up at me, its mouth wide open, its knife-like fangs in full display. A man-eating lion so close! Too old to climb the tree and come after me, it let out one big roar after another as it circled the tree, going round and round.

Noticing the shoe that I had dropped, the lion sank its teeth into it. After chewing the shoe for a while, it spat out a mouthful of wet mangled lump. One more time, the lion looked up at me. Then it sat down in the shade of the tree and waited, knowing well that I had nowhere to go and would come down sooner or later.

My older cousin, Omar, had warned me about this journey and the risks out there. He had pleaded with me not to go alone through the treacherous land between the camel country and the town, Hargis. "It is no place for a young, unarmed camel boy to venture into," he said.

I didn't heed his advice and went on my way. I was in a hurry to go to town and nothing could dissuade me. My belief in fate and destiny got the best of me. And what a fate it turned out to be. I ended up crouching in the fork of two branches of a tree, a lion waiting for me on the ground. As if I hadn't had enough tragedies in my life already.

I was two years old when my mother died soon after she gave birth to my younger sister Asha. My father didn't live long either. Members of the Duki clan, our arch-enemies, had killed him in cold blood while he was out looking for a lost camel. They captured him and slaughtered him like they would an antelope. He didn't have a chance with an enemy who would never let a Sudi clansman go free and see the sun again. When I was told of his death, I cried for a long time. Even the sky wept with a damp drizzle that continued throughout the day.

Not satisfied with the blood of my father, the Duki struck again. They came back to take away the only thing I had in the world, inherited from my father. They took my herd of camels in a raid that they carried out in broad daylight. With my parents dead and my herd of camels gone, my homeland had nothing for me but tragic memories. I decided to leave it for good and take my chances in Hargis, a town far away. I had nowhere else to go, and nowhere else to make a living.

Before I embarked on the journey, I bid farewell to Asha, who was thirteen years old, and the only other person left in my immediate family. She was living with our aunt at the time and I went to their place. Fearing that we might never see each other again, she cried copious tears. I walked away before I cried too, and set out on this fateful journey.

Down below, the lion stayed put in the shade of the tree. If only it would leave me alone and look for prey elsewhere! But what if it sat there throughout the day and the oncoming night? Could I remain perched in a tree like a bird? How long could I stay awake on top of a tree? I could fall asleep and tumble down to the ground.

In a desperate attempt to force the lion to go away, I started pestering it. I pissed on it. I threw pieces of bark, twigs, and my other shoe at it, sometimes hitting it. The lion merely shrugged them off and roared in response.

The sun inched its way towards the western horizon. The scariest and longest day of my life was coming to an end. The night could turn out to be worse. It loomed large and a sense of foreboding took over me. The thought of hanging on to a branch all night long put a chill in my spine.

Soon, the sun dipped over the horizon and a short dusk followed. A moonless night began to spread its dark wings on the land. I looked around for any light or fire out there, any sign of a nomadic camp in the area. Not the slightest glimmer of light anywhere. It felt as if all the people on the earth had perished and I was the only one left behind.

At the far eastern skies, just above the line where the earth and sky meet, a flicker of lightning caught my attention. A deep rumbling thunder followed. Big dark clouds appeared out of nowhere and quickly spread and engulfed most of the sky, while flashes of lightning lit the earth. The wind started to blow with an unrelenting force. The trees swayed from side to side.

To brace myself for the violent change in weather, I tightened my grip on two branches. No matter what, I had to avoid tumbling down into the jaws of a hungry lion. It was no way to die. I had to defy the odds and stay where I was. But how long could I keep holding on to a branch in the midst of a violent rainstorm? Only divine rescue could get me through this predicament, and I started praying.

Even the monster lion needed a divine rescue. Rattled by the rainstorm, it got restless and agitated. It moved from one side of the tree to the other and back again. Then abruptly it ran off, jumping over bushes along the way. I could hear its roars getting fainter and fainter in the distance.

For a moment, I wondered what had caused its sudden departure. Did it detect some other prey and go after it? Did it go to seek shelter from the storm? Or had it just lost patience with a camel boy up a tree?

Whatever drove it away, my prayers had something to do with it. Not to lose any time, I climbed down in a hurry, picked up my stick and ran for my life. The lion could come back for all I knew!

As I rushed barefoot through the bushes, the rain splashed hard on my face. Some of the rainwater flowed into my mouth and gave relief to my dry throat and lips. The wind continued to gust as strong as ever and almost blew away my loincloth. More than once, I had to tighten it. Neither the rain nor the wind slowed me down. I kept on, sometimes running and sometimes walking. By the time the sun rose, the rain had stopped and the wind had died down, but there was still no sign of human presence anywhere.

A day later, I limped into the bustling streets of Hargis exhausted and desperate. For a young camel boy who had never seen a town before, what a scene! The white-walled buildings stretched as far as my bewildered eyes could see. Loud sounds reverberated from all directions. Waiters serving food and tea shouted their orders so loudly as if to announce to the whole world. Songs blared from every shop. Trucks roared along the roads, their horns louder than anything else.

In the streets, men walked in groups and exchanged heated arguments, while puffing on something that turned their breath into smoke. Young boys chased one another as they shouted their way through the crowds. Old men cursed them and shuffled along. The women strolled quietly down the street, dressed in long colourful blouses. Gracefully, they swung their hands back and forth, the aroma of incense trailing them.

A man who seemed in his twenties was selling broiled meat and steaming rice, handing out plates of the delicious-looking food to those who could pay for it. My eyes lingered on the food. My mouth salivated. My stomach growled. I had had nothing to eat for two days and wished I could get a piece of meat. But nothing was given for free in this town. Not even to a man dying of hunger. Only my clansmen could help me and I had to look for them and find them or I would starve to death.

I approached an old man sitting under a tree and exchanged greetings with him. I asked, "What clan do you belong to?"

"I am a Tuwi," the old man said. "And you?"

"I am a Sudi," I replied.

"You are a camel boy. What makes you come to town?"

"It is a long story. We all have our reasons that brought us here, don't we?"

"Yes, we do."

"I have just arrived here, as you can see, and I am looking for my clansmen in this town. Where can I find them?"

"The neighbourhood of the Sudi clan is not far from here. Go further east along this road," the old man pointed. "You will see a white two-storey building on the south side and a big mosque on the north. Your people are over there. You can't miss them."

I clutched my stick, tightened my loincloth, and set out as directed. To cross the busy road, I ran and dodged the speeding cars and trucks, which honked fiercely at me. A group of boys jeered at me. An old man with a white beard admonished them; then he gave me a shout. "Hey camel boy! Be careful and watch out. Those trucks could crush you into the ground."

Undaunted, I charged ahead until the white two-storey building came into view. I felt relief, knowing that my clansmen were close by. All I had to do now was to find my second cousin, who had lived in Hargis since he was a teenager. I had never seen him—he could have been walking beside me at this very moment or having lunch in the busy restaurant on the ground floor of the high building, where people were going in and out.

Outside the restaurant, I hesitated at first; then I stepped inside. A hot, thick smoke almost suffocated me. My nostrils flared; my eyes itched. I could barely see a group of four sitting near the door—an old man with an elaborate white headdress and three middle-aged men. After exchanging greetings with them, I asked, "I am looking for my cousin— Isman Hersi. Do you know where I can find him?"

"What is your name and which clan do you belong to?" retorted the old man with the headdress.

"My name is Ali. I am a Sudi clansman," I said.

"Recite your lineage," demanded one of the other men.

That was no problem for me and I started reciting the names of my forefathers: "Guleed, Mohamed, Farah, Hamud, Jibril, Abdi, Egal, Hussein, Ahmed, Hassan, Salah, Abdullah, Suliman, Saeed . . . " I went on until my eighteenth great-grandfather—the root of the Sudi clan. I had known the names of all my ancestors by the time I was five. No way could I forget the first lesson my father taught me.

"Are you the son of the late Guleed? The boy whose herd of camels was raided by the Duki clan about a week ago?" asked the youngest of the group.

"Yes, I am," I nodded. He turned out to be a relative of mine, a fifth cousin, and some of the ancestors I had just mentioned were his ancestors too.

"Sit down and have a cup of tea and a bit of food. Isman comes here in the evenings," he said. He called a waiter and ordered a cup of tea and two pieces of lahoh for me.

As soon as the waiter put the lahoh before me, I devoured it. Then I sipped the hot tea, barely listening to the conversation going on around me. I was about to drain the cup when the men stood up to go somewhere.

Twirling his moustache, the elder with the white headdress paused, focused his eyes on me, and said, "You will soon grow up to be a man, a real mature Sudi clansman. And a Sudi clansman takes his revenge. Always keep that in mind and never forget it."

He didn't need to remind me of something that had already been on my mind. The day I spilled the blood of the enemy would be the day when I had not only carried out my responsibility and obligation to my dead father, but also proved my manhood and made my clansmen proud. I was not going to let them down. No way! So I nodded to the elder without saying a word.

My fifth cousin also lingered for a moment to have a word with me. "Isman is probably at the livestock market," he said. "I will find him and we will see you in this restaurant in the evening. So just stay here and don't leave. Okay?"

"I won't leave," I promised.

"If you need another cup of tea, take these two coins." With that, he ran after the others.

I remained in my seat to keep my word and watched the comings and goings of the customers. However, not accustomed to sitting idly, I got bored and stepped out of the restaurant to go for a short walk, intent on returning before my cousins came back in the evening.

A block away from the restaurant, I came upon a group of men listening to news in front of a teashop. I could hear every word being said quite clearly, but the man relating the news was nowhere to be seen. I looked in all directions. I checked under the tables. Not a trace of him anywhere. Was he hiding somewhere and why? Or was there some kind of magic going on? I didn't know what to make of it. Taking a closer look, I realized that the deep voice of the newsman was blaring out from what looked like a small box. I turned to one of the men and asked, "Where is this man who is making all this talk?"

"You see that small box?" The man pointed with his stick.

"Yes."

"It is called *radio* and he is inside it," he said, doing his best to suppress a smile.

"What kind of man fits into that little box?" I asked.

"A small man with a big mouth," he said, his smile instantly turning to laughter that caught a lot of attention.

"Whatever is in that box, it isn't a small man."

"What is it, then?"

"A small devil," I said and walked away.

I went further into the town until I found myself on a street that seemed very strange to me. The men and women over there acted rather suspiciously. They didn't talk to each other like normal people; instead they communicated in hand signals or whispered to one another. Only later did I learn that it was the place where all the shady characters in town hung around to conduct their business. And it had a name, a special one. They called it Fucking Street. For a long time, I had no idea what the name meant.

Feeling uneasy, I turned around. But it was a bit too late. A tall, shifty-looking man bumped into me. It was no accident. Glaring at me, he said, "Camel boys sell their camels in town and have money. You have nothing, not even a senti coin. What is wrong with you?"

Without waiting for my response, he took off and crossed the street. It quickly dawned on me that he was a thief who had tried to steal money from me. Too bad, he targeted the wrong person and his snooping hand came out empty.

I was watching him disappear into a crowd when a young woman in a short skirt approached me and said in a low voice, "Hey, camel boy, you want to have a good time with a beautiful girl? Look at me. I bet you do. You can pay me five shillings to enjoy and taste the sweetest thing in the world. What do you say?"

Before I even figured out what the sweetest thing in the world was, a man close by whispered to me, "Camel boy, don't listen to her. She is no decent girl. She's a prostitute."

I panicked. Just hearing the word *prostitute* alarmed me. It was a word I associated with sin and immorality. Looking away from the woman, I took quick steps to get as far away from her as possible. I didn't stop until I had made my way out of the whole Fucking Street.

With the notorious street behind me, I took it for granted that there would be no more hassle. But just when I thought that I was out of the woods, two boys came along and started taunting me: "You ignorant, stupid camel boy, where are your camels? You lost them and ran away from your family? Here in town, we beat runaway boys like you."

Before responding, I had to know one thing, so I asked: "What clan do you belong to?"

"We are Duki," they said in unison.

The moment I heard *Duki*, every muscle in my body tensed like those of a cheetah about to snatch its prey. I clasped my stick tighter than ever. Duki boys had had the nerve to insult and threaten me. After what their clan had done to me!

The bigger of the two, a stout fellow with a scar on his face, stepped forward and we faced each other in the street. In an attempt to intimidate me, he screwed his face and knitted his brows. At the same time, he shifted his weight from one foot to the other, a clear sign that he intended to make the first strike. Not to give him that chance, I backed off a bit, swung my stick and hit him with all the force I could muster. The stick slammed on his chest and shoulder. He screamed in pain and staggered backwards, then retreated and hurried away as the people in the street burst into laughter. His friend also backed off in haste. The slick town boys couldn't handle the pain of a camel boy's stick.

It was time to go back to the restaurant. I had wandered into the streets and gone too far. The sun had just dipped over the horizon. The call to evening prayers sounded from the mosques, a part of my religion I had yet to practise. Not to lose more time, I hurried back to the restaurant, feeling bad about my failure to keep my word. My cousins were already there and waiting for me by the time I arrived. A bit nervous, I exchanged greetings with them.

"Where did you go?" Isman asked.

"Not far. I just walked off to the next street," I stammered. Brought up to be forthright and tell the truth, I always found myself stammering if I shaded it.

"Any problems in town so far?"

I shook my head and didn't say a word about all the hassle in the streets. The serving of dinner interrupted our conversation and our focus shifted to the plate of spicy liver and the big loaf of bread that came with it. Soon the spices put heat into our throats and bellies and we called the waiter for more water, a bucket of it.

After dinner, Isman took me to his home. He lived by himself, his family being away in the countryside. As we sat down in one of his two rooms, he looked at me and said, "You are a young version of your father. You look a lot like him."

I nodded and said nothing.

"He is in paradise. I know it," he went on. "He is just waiting for us to do something about his killing. We should never forget him and never let him down."

"I won't let him down. I will avenge his killing, you have my word," I said, making perfectly clear my intention.

"You have to be careful, though. Taking your revenge here in town is a bit complicated. There is the police and government and all that."

I nodded, understanding what he meant. Then, after talking briefly about life in town and its complications, we both fell asleep.

2

ISMAN WAS A SMALL LIVESTOCK broker who didn't have enough money to support me. Not to become a burden on him, I started looking for work the next day. It was a daunting task, in a town where job opportunities were as rare as the eclipse of the moon. I pleaded with busy store owners to give me a chance. I even stopped a man in the street and asked him for a job. "If you give me a job, I will work hard. I will work like a donkey," I told them all.

Weeks passed without any success. One day, I was sitting in desperation in the shade of a big acacia tree in front of the restaurant, looking back to a time when I had my father and my herd of camels and enjoyed a life free from worry and stress, when the shade of every tree was my home and the cover of every bush was my toilet.

The restaurant owner saw me and came over. After exchanging greetings with me—his name was Rashid—and complaining about the heat of the sun, he asked, "Did you have lunch today?"

"Yes," I said, ashamed of telling him the truth.

"You are still looking for a job?"

"Yes."

"Jobs are hard to come by here in this town."

"Indeed, they are."

"How about working in my kitchen? You will wash the dishes. You want that kind of job?"

"Yes, I want it," I said and didn't even ask him about the pay. This was a chance I couldn't miss.

The next day I toiled in a kitchen that was as hot as hell, while a mean assistant cook constantly badgered me about working faster. He talked to me in ways no camel boy would ever tolerate. But I restrained myself and ignored his insults. I had to keep this job and survive in this town.

For the first time in my life, I was earning money. After a few weeks, I had saved enough to buy a stiletto knife with a sheath. It was the only weapon I could afford. I tacked it onto my belt.

Only late in the evenings, when the restaurant closed, could I go out into the town. I walked the back streets and narrow alleys of Hargis in search of some lone Duki clansman. I couldn't wait to slit the throat of one of those people who had killed my father. Sooner or later, I had to do it. If not, the sickening image of my father's unburied body lying in the wilderness, a pack of hyenas ripping his flesh piece by piece like a sheep's carcass, would haunt me forever.

But, once in a while, I hung out with a group of my Sudi peers who worked in nearby teashops and stores. At night they would sit at a street corner and smoke cigarettes.

"Why don't you smoke with us?" they said. "You don't want to speak English?"

"Yes, I want to speak English," I said, excited about the possibility.

"See! Ali is a smart guy. Here is a cigarette. Go ahead and smoke it."

I had smoked a lot of cigarettes before realizing that they had played a trick on me and smoking cigarettes would not enable me to speak English or help me in any way.

I stopped smoking cigarettes and concentrated on my job, working harder than ever. After some time the owner promoted me to be a waiter. It was a job that brought me face to face with the customers. I served them with pride. They all belonged to the Sudi clan, which made things easier for me. Inside the restaurant it was always hot and stuffy, a thick smoke hung in the air. Not bothered by it, the customers came and ate while passionately arguing about the age-old conflict between us and the Duki clan.

"Do you think a time will come when we will live in peace with the Duki?" one of them asked.

"No. Never!" five others shouted back from different corners of the restaurant.

"When the sun rises from the west and sets in the east," one of the customers remarked, and they all laughed.

Once in a while, the arguments got out of hand and ended in shouting matches, but overall, listening to them was entertaining and enlightening and I soon became acquainted with all the regulars. My favourite customer was a very poor old man. I always called him by his real name, Koosar, but most people called him "the one-eyed man" because he had lost his sight in his right eye. Our people named every handicapped person by his handicap, no insult intended. The name of the deaf man was "the deaf," the blind man was "the blind," and the mentally-handicapped man was "the idiot."

A creature of habit, Koosar came into the restaurant every day at the same time, early in the morning, and sat at the same corner. As if he were hiding a secret or was ashamed of something, he often gave me his order in a low whisper. The order never changed. It was always a cup of hot tea. One day, I surprised him by serving him breakfast—a plate with two pieces of lahoh treated with fresh ghee and a cup of tea. Generosity being part of our heritage, I thought it was time I did something about that one cup of tea. "Don't worry about payment," I said. "It's on me."

Overwhelmed by my gesture, Koosar fell silent for a moment. Then, he started talking about his life. "Son," he whispered, "I haven't had breakfast since the British left town. The day we cheered loudly for independence, and hoisted that damn blue flag that miserably failed all our expectations, was the last day I had something to eat in the morning. I miss the British. They knew what a government was. I call it the good old times. I had a proper job as a translator and used to have breakfast every day. Now I sell dead people's clothes and consider myself lucky if I can afford a cup of tea in the morning."

Another regular customer, called Jiro, had a habit of saying outrageous things. He once claimed that he had a dream the previous night in which he was making love to the president of the country at that time—President Hamid. It became the biggest news; the people in town had nothing else to talk about that day. The police soon arrested him, and we all thought he would end up in jail for years. Luckily for him, the judge dismissed the case, saying that the law didn't apply to dreams. Jiro didn't stop there. Why stop when he had found a new way to insult any politician or president who didn't belong to his clan?

Seeing Jiro and Koosar every day made a demanding job tolerable. It was especially nerve-wracking in the mornings and evenings, when the customers all came to eat at the same time. During the intervening hours, there were moments to relax and chat with the few customers who dropped in for a cup of tea.

Two years had passed since the day I walked into Hargis, tired and hungry. I thought I had gotten accustomed to its way of life. I thought I had seen it all and nothing would surprise me in this town. Then came the day when my world turned upside down.

It was Wednesday morning and I started work a bit early, just after the break of dawn. As usual, I switched on the radio for entertainment and news. But the usual morning program wasn't on air. Not one item of news about the world, not one song about love and marriage. Instead, the radio continued to play sombre music without interruption. Something had happened in the country, but I had no idea what. There used to be border disputes with neighbouring Ethiopia once every few years, and I wondered if a conflict had flared up again.

Suddenly, there was some commotion in the streets. A convoy of military vehicles and armoured tanks appeared out of nowhere; it drove back and forth on the road outside. Jet fighters flew overhead scream-ing shrilly. At the same time, soldiers with grim faces appeared on the streets, their guns fixed firmly on their shoulders. We stared outside in amazement. Nobody had any idea what was going on. Nobody could explain this scary avalanche of military activities.

The music on the radio stopped and a nervous commentator asked listeners to wait for important news. A minute later, in a harsh voice, a speaker identifying himself as General Kahin came on the air. It turned out that the military had taken over the government and the elected civilian government was no more.

"President Ibrahim has been arrested, the constitution suspended, the parliament abolished, and any gathering of more than four people is prohibited," General Kahin declared, and added, "Any opposition will be punished severely."

From the farthest corner of the restaurant, Jiro wailed, "The sky is going to fall. The sun will never rise again. And you know why? The new military ruler is a Duki clansman. He will kill us all. He will shoot us one by one. And who can stop him? Nobody!"

The fate of every Sudi man in the hands of a military man, and not any military man but a powerful Duki clansman, evoked dire emotions in me, as dire as the world coming to a tragic end. If only I could survive long enough to avenge the killing of my father and to leave behind children.

3

It was a cool winter night when it all started. The people had gone home and slept peacefully. Meanwhile, in the wee hours of the morning, the military was on the move. The soldiers rolled out of their barracks and seized all government offices, from the House of Parliament to the offices of the lowest clerks. They broke into homes. They dragged the president out of his home and took him to jail, not even allowing him a few minutes to get dressed. The government ministers and members of parliament didn't fare any better. By the time the sun rose, even the political parties ceased to exist. The military closed the doors of the Tuwi party, the Sudi party, and the Duki party.

General Kahin, a tall dark man with restless penetrating eyes, had been only the deputy commander of the army a day earlier. But then the commander was killed when a mine exploded under his car. The next day, General Kahin led the military coup. Many people suspected that General Kahin had something to do with the death of the commander, who happened to be a Tuwi clansman. He got him out of the way to take over the government. And he didn't stop there. He continued to get rid of military leaders from the other clans, thus eliminating anybody who could challenge him.

General Kahin blamed the previous government for all the country's problems, including a long drought in the countryside, and proclaimed, "My government will solve everything. Life will get better in the country. It will start raining soon. There will be no more flu or sickness anywhere. We will cure everybody. I will form the most efficient government in the world; a government as efficient as a clock and as clean as a saint. It will be a government of what-you-know and not who-you-know."

But, he warned, "Nobody dare stand in our way. We are the military.

We only march ahead. We neither stop nor retreat. Anybody who stands in our way will be crushed like an insect or pest."

Almost everybody knew to whom the threats were directed. We, the Sudi, were the so-called insects and pests to be wiped out. We heard and took note.

No Sudi had ever expected anything good from a Duki. Not even their sheikhs preaching the Quran and the words of Allah. General Kahin had deposed the elected president of the country, President Ibrahim, for one reason only: he was of the Sudi clan. The age-old conflict between the two clans in the countryside was now being fought in a new arena.

It was still early that morning when supporters of General Kahin started to march in the streets. They were mostly Duki men and women showing their unwavering loyalty to their fellow clansman, carrying hastily prepared placards and chanting praises of the new government. The insults and threats began while they walked through our neighbourhood. It was a clear sign of the dangerous times to come. Like hungry lions, they were coming for the kill.

Inside our restaurant, the atmosphere was sombre. The customers, all of them Sudi, sat silently and ate their breakfasts. I could sense their jitters in their body language. Not one of them opened his mouth to share his thoughts. Why share, when they had the same thoughts on their minds? Their usual lively and spirited conversations had ceased, as they followed the news on the radio with grim faces.

Late in the afternoon, General Kahin formed his government and announced it on the radio. He appointed himself as the Supreme Leader of the country, his younger brother the minister of defence, a cousin the minister of the interior, his oldest son the minister of foreign affairs, another cousin the minister for finance. In short, a Duki clansman headed almost every branch of his new government. His proclamation about a government of what-you-know and not who-you-know had been empty talk.

In the history of our Sudi clan, we had never been in a situation where a Duki clansman determined our fate. Such a possibility never even crossed our mind. Before, there was always an elected parliament in the country, in which each clan was represented. Every clan felt safe that way. This all changed on that cold winter night.

Just after the radio announcement of what we soon called the Duki government, Koosar returned to the restaurant and sat quietly in his corner. I didn't get a chance to talk to him in the morning. I brought him a cup of tea without even asking him. I needed to discuss with him this Duki Military General who was going to rule us. I needed to talk to him about how we were going to survive under a hostile government. Koosar's appearance and demeanour gave away nothing, which made me all the more curious.

"What do you think of this powerful Duki clansman who is going to rule us? What do you think of this so-called Supreme Leader?" I asked him upfront without beating around the bush.

"It is too early to tell. We don't know much about him," Koosar replied in a low-key manner as if something was bothering him.

"Koosar, he is a Duki clansman. What else do you need to know about him?" I shot back.

"I want to see what he does."

"He already did a lot. He just formed a new government and almost all the ministers are Duki clansmen, some of them his family members."

"I know," he said curtly.

"And there is a lot more to come. He will start killing us. He will take his revenge on us, not once but a thousand times."

"Revenge about what?"

"About his cousins, two of them. You didn't hear it? We killed them in a clan war a few years ago. You think he will forget that or forgive us? No way!"

"Who told you about this?"

"The restaurant owner. Rashid told me. Most of our clansmen know about this. And mark my words! General Kahin is going to come after us to get his revenge. What are we going to do?"

"We have Allah," Koosar said instinctively, without thinking seriously about the danger we were facing.

"They have Allah too, the same one. So we have to get real and defend ourselves."

"You mean we have to start fighting?"

"We have to do something. Yes, we have to find a way to fight back," I whispered into his ear.

"There is nothing much we can do now. We can't fight him. He is going to use the military against us. A rush to fight is not a good idea. We have to wait. Maybe even give him the benefit of the doubt, and not judge him so early. He is a military man, remember. Perhaps that will make him transcend the traditional enmity between our two clans."

"Give him the benefit of the doubt! Since when did a Sudi give the benefit of anything to a Duki, or they to us?"

"All I am saying is: let us wait for a while and see what happens first."

"Koosar, we are talking about a Duki clansman here. He belongs to the same clan that killed my father and raided my camels, the same clan we have been at war with since the earth and the sky and everything in between were created. Don't let the military uniform deceive you."

"He is saying good things on the radio. He is saying that he will make the government more efficient and fight corruption and things like that. Let us see if he delivers his promises and keeps his word," Koosar argued back.

"And you believed him? You are a Sudi clansman and you believed what a Duki clansman says?"

"But he is a military man and he swore that he will serve all the people and defend the country. Doesn't that at least give you some hope?"

"No, it doesn't. I will never trust a Duki clansman even if he swore a million times to serve the country." I didn't budge, knowing that General Kahin would soon come after us.

Koosar didn't budge either and insisted on his wait-and-see-attitude. It didn't surprise me. Koosar sometimes defied our clan loyalties, a very unusual thing for any clansman to do. He had his doubts, of course, about a Duki clansman with so much power over him. But the fact that the Supreme Leader was a military man gave him some hope. He set himself up for a big disappointment.

General Kahin was once a camel boy who lived in the countryside like me. He herded his camels not far from the area where the Duki and Sudi clans used to wage attacks on each other every spring. In one of those wars, the Sudi killed several of his cousins. General Kahin had an axe to grind and revenge to take.

But what decided the future of young Kahin were not those wars. A devastating drought in the countryside changed his life for good. It was a year in which not a drop of rainwater fell from the sky and not a blade of grass grew on the land. As a result, his camels died one after another until his entire herd perished. Young Kahin had a decision to make about his life. He travelled to Hargis to make a living there just as I later did. The military recruited him and gradually, with his fox-like cunning, oratorical skills, and devious tactics, he worked his way through the ranks to become one of the highest commanders in the military. On the way his clan gave him all the assistance he needed.

The Duki camel boy was now the supreme leader of the country. He could do whatever he wished. Nothing was beyond his reach. The army and the police stood ready to carry out his orders. And he held the fate of his arch-enemy, the Sudi clan, in his hands. For the first few weeks, the Supreme Leader didn't take any action against us. No Sudi clansman was arrested or killed. I didn't know what to make of this. I had expected him to start settling scores with us straight away. Was he busy setting his traps? Was this the calm before the storm?

One morning, just as I came to work, there came breaking news on the radio. I stopped and steeled myself for some bad news. But it turned out not as bad as I feared. It told us how the Supreme Leader had established friendly relations with a country called Russia. Throughout the day, the government radio had one program after another about Russia. It couldn't stop talking about this big brother they had found and something they called communism. They called the Russians the shining star of the north and the white angel on earth. It was as though they had stumbled on another Duki clan in a foreign country, who were just like them but with white skin. During those radio broadcasts about Russia, two words always came up: *capitalists* and *proletariat*. After listening to them for some time, I figured out that the capitalists were the bad guys, the proletariat the good ones.

The talk about the capitalists and the proletariat continued for three days until there came new breaking news on the radio. Every customer in the restaurant fell silent. This could be the start of our nightmare.

Indeed, it was. The government had executed eight men in the middle of the night. Among them were the previous president, two of his ministers, and five former members of parliament. They had been taken from jail to face a firing squad. In a single night, the Supreme Leader had wiped out all the Sudi politicians. Their bodies were not even given back to their families.

It didn't end there. Ten more Sudi clansmen were arrested two days later, among them our beloved chief, seven former officials in the military, and two businessmen, all accused of working secretly with American capitalists. They were tried, found guilty, and executed.

The Supreme Leader had drawn his sword out and no Sudi in town was safe. He had killed the most prominent Sudi men; now he was coming for the rest of us. The enemy who had snuffed out my father's life and raided my herd of camels could arrest me any day and subject me to a hail of bullets, before I even had a chance to take my revenge on them.

Our clan felt impotent and powerless. Never before had a Duki clansman killed so many of us and got away with it. Never before had we failed to retaliate against such deadly attacks. I resorted to prayers and called upon Allah and the Prophet to save us. I even invoked the names of the Prophet's close disciples and pleaded with them to come out and take a stand, to intercede for us. This was no time to be neutral.

The day of the executions of our chief and other Sudi men was sunny and clear. Thousands of Duki flocked into the national arena to watch the killing. For them, this was a dream come true. On the radio, an announcer reported the scene, describing it vividly and with excitement. The ten victims were tied to wooden poles and stood side by side in a horizontal line. They wore a white sheet wrapped around their waists and a blindfold. More than thirty armed soldiers stood ready to shoot them. As soon as they got the order, a roar of rattling gunfire ensued.

Having heard the report on the radio, I stepped out of the restaurant and looked up at the sky for any sign of heavenly disapproval. The sun didn't turn red. No storm loomed over the horizon. And no calamities fell on those who had the blood of innocent Sudi men on their hands. Time passed like on any normal day. Disappointed, I went back into the restaurant to get on with my work.

Five days later, more breaking news. The government had arrested fifty-five Sudi schoolboys. It called them "young capitalists" and accused them of having engaged in a conspiracy with American capitalists. They weren't involved in any conspiracy. All they had done was organize themselves to clean a graveyard in their neighbourhood. If they had conspired with somebody, it wasn't with American Capitalists; it was with the dead bodies in the graveyard.

In the middle of the night, they were snatched from their homes one by one. The court found them guilty, just as we expected. The judge sentenced twenty of them to death; fifteen, who were older than sixteen years of age, were sentenced to fifteen years in jail. The younger boys got ten years.

Late on that day, Koosar came by the restaurant carrying a papaya and proceeded to his favourite corner.

Skipping the usual greeting "salam alaykum," I asked him, "Koosar, what are capitalists?" Having heard the word too many times, I had to understand exactly what it meant.

"Capitalists are the wealthy people in Europe and America. They are the people with the money," Koosar said.

"But are these capitalists in Europe and America terrible folks? I mean, are they the most vicious criminals ever, the worst of the worst?"

"Not necessarily. They are just like other people except that they are richer. The only thing is that there are those who don't like them. That is all."

"Who doesn't like them?"

"The Russians."

"So that is it? That is where the Supreme Leader learned this thing: just call your enemy a capitalist, and then shoot him in the head?"

"Yes, indeed. The Russian tactics serve him quite well. He took a page from the book of communism." Koosar shrugged his shoulders and started slicing the papaya. He gave me a piece. I noticed that a lot of the customers in the restaurant were eating papayas as well. Apparently there was a craze for papaya in town.

"Why are so many customers eating this fruit today? Are they giving it away for free?" I asked.

"There is nothing else in the food market and it is cheap."

"And why is that? What happened to the other fruits?"

"Communism happened to the other fruits. It's one other lesson General Kahin learned from communism. But this lesson is not about killing people."

"What is it about, then?"

"It is about controlling prices. The Supreme Leader asked for a list of all the fruits that are sold in the country. To fix the prices of fruits. But papaya wasn't in the list. Somehow, they forgot to include it. And you know what happened then?"

"No."

"Every farmer decided to promote and sell the only fruit not on General Kahin's list. That is why there is only papaya in the market. No other fruit. And it is cheap."

A customer complaining about the service in the restaurant suddenly screamed. I scrambled to my feet to take his order. Too pre-occupied with the Duki government, I almost forgot about the customers I was supposed to serve. The cranky customer whined for a while; then he ordered only a cup of tea. To shut him up, I served him the cup of tea quickly.

By the time I was done with him, Koosar had already left. I stood at the door and watched the people in the street for a while, wondering when the Supreme Leader would strike again and arrest another group of Sudi clansmen.

I knew that I couldn't stay safe for long and that worried me. If they arrested our schoolboys cleaning a graveyard, how could I be safe and survive under this government? The killing and the arrest of every Sudi man brought the danger one step closer to me.

To beat the odds and stay alive as long as possible, I had to watch my words. I had to make sure that no stranger was within earshot when talking about the government and the Duki clan. To say anything about the Supreme Leader posed the greatest risk. We had a secret nickname for him—Big Mouth. In fact, Koosar came up with the nickname and for a good reason. The Supreme Leader wouldn't shut up for a moment. Every day, he made speeches on the radio, one after another. Without saying anything meaningful, he just blabbered and kept rambling on with a lot of nonsense, sometimes bragging and praising himself, and sometimes bullying and blustering. He certainly deserved the nickname, a valuable Sudi secret that enabled us to talk about the Supreme Leader and get away with it. Unfortunately, the government later found out about it and arrested five Sudi clansmen for saying "Big Mouth." How they found out, we had no idea. But we knew one thing for certain: it was no longer safe to say the nickname.

If only I had accomplished the two things I set out to do the day the Supreme Leader took over the government. I owed it to my dead father. I owed it to my clan. I touched the stiletto knife on my waist belt just to make sure that it was still there.

4

As usual, business slowed down after the breakfast rush hour. I was chatting with a customer when somebody tapped me on the shoulder. I turned around, a bit apprehensive that a policeman might have come to arrest me. Luckily, my worst fears didn't come true and I sighed with relief. An innocent-looking man from the countryside was standing behind me.

"You are Ali?" he asked in a low voice.

"Yes."

"I am the cousin of your brother-in-law, Yusuf, and I have a message for you from your sister. Can I talk to you in private?"

"Sure," I said and followed him out of the restaurant.

"Your sister, Asha, wants you to go and visit her," the man said, relaying his message as soon as we were outside.

"Did she give you any reason why I should go there and visit her?"

"Yes. It's about marriage. She says it is about time you make a family."

"Do you know if she has a particular girl in mind?" I probed, obviously excited.

"Yes, there is a girl, a real Sudi country girl related to my wife. And if I were you, I would go now to marry her."

His mission of relaying the message completed, he bid me farewell and walked away, not even sitting down for a cup of tea.

It took me a while to absorb the good news. My sister Asha was handing me an opportunity I couldn't miss. Other than avenging the killing of my father, nothing else was more important to me than marrying a girl, making a family, and leaving behind children.

Not to lose any time, I approached the restaurant owner straight away and asked him for a one-month leave from my job without pay. He had no objections. In fact, he encouraged me to get married. And so did most of my clansmen.

Early next morning, I hurried to the truck station to catch the first truck leaving for the countryside. I paid the driver a ten-shilling fare and hopped into the open back of the truck with thirty other passengers.

When it was time to go, the engine of the truck failed to start and sputtered. Spitting curses, the driver tinkered with the engine. After five attempts, it came to life and the truck inched its way through the narrow, crowded streets and out of town.

The driver had been chewing qat all morning. He obviously wasn't in his right mind, and the passengers watched him with alarm, afraid that he might get into an accident or hit one of the jaywalkers. "The road is for the trucks, you walking moron!" he screamed at a jaywalker and threw an empty can at him. Luckily, the truck made its way to the outskirts of town without any mishap. Only then did the driver calm down, and the truck picked up speed.

At first, none of the passengers spoke; it was quiet and boring. Somebody had to say something. And lo and behold, an old man on my right turned to me and asked, "What clan do you belong to?"

"Sudi," I said.

"I am Tuwi," he said. "Why are you leaving town?"

"To marry a girl in the countryside."

"It must be your first time."

"Yes, indeed."

"I married four times and have three wives now," he smiled, proud of his accomplishment.

"Married four times! You must have liked it so much," I said in jest and reciprocated his smile.

"It is a good thing. I enjoyed them all, even the one I never wanted to happen, when I married my sister-in-law after my younger brother was killed in a war between two Tuwi sub-clans," he explained, a sad tone creeping into his voice.

We both fell silent for a brief moment out of respect for his fallen brother. Then I said, "Marrying a woman who used to be your sister-in-law, that is really something."

"Yes, it is; but I had to do it. I had to be the stepfather of the children my brother had left behind and take care of them."

"That is nice of you," I agreed with him, and added, "But your first night with a woman who used to be your sister-in-law. That must have been challenging."

"It sure was."

"How did it go?"

By now, our conversation had attracted the full attention of the passengers, some of them having that devilish smile on their faces that says: Yes, we'd also like to hear it.

The old man collected his thoughts for a moment, and then said, "It was late in the evening when a Sheikh solemnized our marriage and left us. Alone together in the house, I summoned all my courage just to touch her. And she certainly didn't make things easier for me. I touch her leg and she says, 'your brother touched that leg.' I touch her breast and she says, 'your brother touched that breast.' I touch her cheek and she says, 'your brother touched that cheek.' She missed no chance to remind me that she had been the wife of my brother as if I did not know."

"She was testing you. Just to see if you are man enough and brave enough to be her husband," I opined.

"Maybe you are right. But I have got news for you. I proved that to her. You know how I did it?"

"Yes. I can't wait to hear that."

"I grabbed her butt and said, 'I bet my brother did not touch here.' She never mentioned my brother again," he concluded with a triumphant smile.

Two other men chipped in and shared with us the stories about the first nights of their marriages. The stories entertained us for most of the journey as the truck roared along an unpaved dusty road. Late in the afternoon, we arrived at a small hamlet of about ten cottages, a few of which were teashops. I had a cup of tea in a noisy teashop and a glass of camel milk. Then I set out towards my sister's village on foot. It was not very far from the hamlet, and I trudged along a terrain with dense bushes. Rabbits and antelopes made quick dashes from one hideout to another, and birds chirped all around me. Eagles hovered in the sky above.

I reached the nomadic camp just before it became too dark. As I approached it, a girl came out from one of the huts and walked past me, making her way towards a small forest, most probably to collect dry wood to make fire. She stole a quick glance at me and turned away the moment our eyes met.

The evenings were always the time of day when nomadic camps hummed with activity. Young girls brought the sheep and goats back home, before night descended on the land. The bleating of hungry little lambs and mother sheep filled the air. In front of their huts, women stood pounding millet with heavy wooden columns, their babies strapped on their backs. The mothers busy in a race against the setting sun to prepare their dinners, the babies' cries fell on deaf ears.

It was more than four years since I last saw Asha, but I recognized her the moment I set my eyes on her. She had grown up into a woman, and was married with children. She was cooking food in front of her hut, her baby boy sitting beside her. We hugged each other and exchanged warm greetings. Even the baby got into the spirit and seemed happy to see his uncle.

My brother-in-law, Yusuf, joined us a short time later. It was the first time we met, and he didn't disappoint me. As we sipped tea together, we talked about the new Duki government and what it meant to the Sudi clan. Asha soon interjected with: "Ali! Let us talk about you. You are here to marry a girl. What do you say if we go to the girl's father tomorrow night to ask for his daughter's hand in marriage?"

"That is fine with me. That is why I am here," I agreed.

Late in the evening, after we had our dinner of rice with camel milk, I left them and went to sleep in a shelter close by, which was furnished with a mat and pillow. After watching the stars for some time, I fell asleep.

When I woke up in the morning, my two cousins, Omar and Musa, were sitting beside me. What a surprise! They came to lend me a hand in the marriage. After the warm greetings and a long happy conversation, they went to work to make arrangements for my wedding. They approached the bride's family and set up a meeting between two groups of men; they cooked lamb with rice; and they asked a sheikh to solemnize the marriage.

Early in the afternoon, just after lunch, a distant uncle of mine opened the meeting inside a cozy nomadic hut with a few funny anecdotes to create a friendly atmosphere. At the right moment, he made his move and addressed the issue that had brought us all together. "Father Hassan," he said, "we are here to ask you for your daughter's hand in marriage for our boy Ali."

The girl's father didn't make a long speech. He seemed to be a man of few words. He expressed his love for his daughter and what she meant to him, and he concluded by saying, "I bless Ali with my daughter and wish them a happy marriage."

The dowry money, four hundred shillings wrapped in a cloth, was handed over. The sheikh solemnized the marriage with a verse from the Quran. In his conclusion, he blessed us with a happy marriage and many children, particularly sons.

From the moment the Sheikh concluded his blessings, I was married to a girl I knew nothing about. What did she look like? What kind of person was she? I couldn't wait to see her.

My sister and mother-in-law worked out an arrangement in which I could meet her for the first time. Late in the evening, my older cousin, Omar, accompanied me into a dome-shaped hut. Inside sat two girls. I was married to one of them, but which one? The tall shy girl whom I had seen the previous day or the shorter one with the ever-ready smile?

"Good evening, girls," Omar started with an informal greeting.

"We hope it will be a good evening," said the short girl.

For a while, we indulged in a casual back-and-forth conversation, during which the tall girl barely said anything. She just stole quick glances at me a few times. She must be the one, I thought, and felt proud of my sister, who had chosen her for me. My cousin and the other girl soon did the right thing, bid us farewell, and left.

Alone with her, I wondered at how marvellous she looked. She was beauty at its best—the angelic face, the bright lively eyes, the soft voice tinged with tenderness, the grace and the innocence. Could all that be real or was I having a fancy dream? It all seemed too good to be true. Just to make sure that this was no dream, I pinched myself, my finger-nails digging deep into my left arm. The pain jolted me, leaving no doubt that this was all real. I had to pull myself together and talk to her.

"What is your name?" I blurted out.

"I don't have a name," she responded coyly as she fed the fire with pieces of wood to keep the flames going.

"What does your mother say when she wants to call you?" I asked.

"Don't you think you should have known my name before you married me?" she said, still tending to the fire.

My sister had told me her name, but I had forgotten it. How could I have been so careless? An awkward silence ensued, and I feared that she might think I was a dimwit who had nothing to talk about. Desperate to say something, I asked, "Where did you get water for your camels and sheep in the winter?"

"Are you thirsty and need to get water from there?" she responded, her face beaming with a smile laced with a bit of sarcasm.

I had asked her the wrong question. I had to do better than this. I needed to take charge and talk like a camel boy. "You know what?" I said, "You are not as beautiful as I thought."

"Too bad, I disappointed you. But here is the thing, you are not the only one who's disappointed," she shot back with all the self-confidence only a beautiful girl could muster.

"What is that supposed to mean?"

"It means I was expecting a handsome and smart guy too."

And so the conversation went on, a camel girl and a former camel boy talking tough like two adversaries and courting each other at the same time. I never told her the truth and put my feelings in words. I never admitted the reality and said, "I am lucky to marry you," or, "You are beautiful." And neither did she.

It was about time I made my move. Embracing her, I pulled her up close. I started caressing her shoulder and arms. One touch on her right breast and we both felt the heat. My restless hand kept moving down her chest, past her navel, to that little hump just above her centre of femininity. I stopped there. There are places you don't touch a Sudi girl.

To take her to the next stage, I began to undress her. She responded by gently slapping my hands. Nothing serious. But all along, I knew it wouldn't be easy. Like all the other girls in the country, she had undergone the traditional practice of infibulation—a part of her clitoris and the inner labia had been cut off with a razor, the outer labia scrapped from inside and stitched up together, leaving only a small opening for menstrual blood and urine to pass.

A formidable barrier lay ahead and I knew it; a barrier specifically set up to prevent sexual intercourse before the wedding night. But I was in no mood to wait and went ahead. My attempts failed miserably no matter how much I tried. I had a better chance of threading a needle in a dark house than consummating sexual intercourse with her. I had to wait, but not for long.

The next night was the wedding night. The celebrations for one of the most important nights of my life started early. Fatima—for that was her name—came and joined us a little late. The minute she stepped into the hut, the drumbeat of a loud country dance went wild. The women in the village cheered with shrill and high-pitched sounds. Excited children ran around the house, laughing, clapping, and singing.

Sitting next to me, Fatima kept biting her lower lip. She was in pain, and I felt sorry for her. Earlier in the evening, the barrier to prevent pre-marital sex had come down. An old woman had taken care of it with a razor, and Fatima looked different. Gone were the expressive smiles, the twinkling eyes, the beaming face, and the clever evasive answers to all my questions.

To entertain us, the guests swapped jokes the whole evening. But they couldn't stay too long into the night and left, one after the other. The night ultimately belonged to me and my bride.

The minute we were left alone in the house, we looked at each other, saying more with our eyes than we could ever say in words. The light in the hut dimmed. The last piece of wood was burning. Without engaging in any foreplay, I started to undress her. She feared that sexual intercourse would cause her more pain. Feeling sympathy for her, I said, "I won't hurt you. I will never do that. But it is our wedding night and we have to consummate our marriage."

"I am a bit scared," she whispered, but finally she relented. As she felt the penetration, she put a piece of cloth in her mouth, sank her teeth into it, and closed her eyes. Every move I made, her muscles twitched and her body quivered. After a while, she relaxed and even enjoyed to some extent. It certainly didn't hurt as much as she feared.

Within days, she had recovered from the genital operation and we enjoyed our new marriage together until it was time for me to return to town. Before she could join me, I had to rent a house, buy furniture, and make a home for her.

The day I was to return to Hargis, I woke up early and drank the camel milk served to me by my wife. Then I dressed, making sure that the knife was firmly tacked to my belt on the right side. Bidding farewell to my sister was the hardest part. She feared for my safety from a government that was out to get any Sudi man. "I lost our father and I don't want to lose you too," she said and started crying.

I braced myself for dangerous times ahead, a bit worried, but by no means scared.

5

It was past midnight when I arrived back in town. The streets looked deserted, all shops were closed. Not a person was in sight, not even a cat in search of a mouse. The few security lights beside the road stood lonely, flickering and emitting a weak pale light. Hargis looked like a haunted place.

In the frightening silence, I heard a sound. Down the road, a man was running towards me, having just turned a corner. Obviously, someone was chasing him. The man stopped, threw himself in the midst of a group of homeless men sleeping beside a wall. Two policemen turned the same corner in hot pursuit and came to a stop. The man they were chasing could not be seen anywhere. It didn't occur to them that he was right there, among the homeless men, pretending to be asleep.

"Did you see a man come running here?" one of them asked.

"Yes, he ran in that direction," I lied, pointing down the road. "He just disappeared into that street corner." Somehow, I felt that the man being chased was a Sudi and I had to help him.

"Why are you walking the streets at this time of night?" the other policeman asked, as though there were some kind of curfew in town.

"I just got off from a truck," I said.

"Where did you come from?"

"From the countryside."

Without further questions, they scurried off in the direction I had pointed.

The moment the sound of their footsteps died down, the man raised his head and looked around like a scared rabbit. Seeing it was safe, he stood up and stepped over a sleeping man, careful not to wake him.

"You must be a Sudi clansman," he said to me without greeting me or thanking me first.

"Yes, I am. How do you know?"

"You protected me from those stupid policemen. I am a Sudi too."

"Why were they chasing you?"

"I refused to bribe them."

"Bribe them about what?"

"About nothing."

"About nothing?"

"About being a Sudi. They wanted me to pay them a hundred shillings or they would put me in jail. I didn't have that much money and ran."

He made his escape by hurrying off in the opposite direction. I also resumed my walk, still thinking about his story. The policemen had demanded a bribe from him simply because he was a Sudi.

As I walked in the empty street, a lone figure appeared in the distance. Who could that be, I wondered. I could tell that he was a man walking in my direction and smoking a cigarette. A chain of smoke trailed him. If he turned out to be a Duki, it would be a precious opportunity: the two of us in the middle of the night in a quiet empty street. He would have smoked his last cigarette. I pulled the knife on my belt a bit closer.

As he approached me, I noticed that his thick moustache and full beard covered almost half his face. Just before he passed me by, I engaged him with a greeting, after which I asked him promptly, "What clan do you belong to?"

"I am a Tuwi clansman," he said and shuffled along to wherever he was going.

Disappointed, I resumed my walk towards the restaurant. There had been peace between us and the Tuwi clan for some time. I had no reason to kill a Tuwi clansman. So I pushed the knife back and continued walking.

From the eastern horizon, rays of light began to illuminate the sky. Dawn was breaking. Not enough time to go home and get a proper sleep. So I decided to take a short nap inside the restaurant before starting my work there in the morning.

Arriving at the restaurant, I knocked on the door; one or two of the dishwashers would be around. They couldn't afford to rent a house and slept here at night. Nobody opened the door. I knocked harder and shouted their names until Abdulla finally opened it. He whined about being woken up at such a late hour. I ignored him and put five chairs side by side to sleep on them.

Not an hour had passed before a loud scream woke me up. "Guys, Guys! Get up, get up! Get ready for a new day!" It was the assistant chef, screaming at the top of his voice as though the restaurant were on fire.

We all woke up and went to work. Soon the kitchen was buzzing with all sorts of activities. Food sizzled, flames howled, and water boiled. The early customers trickled in and gave their orders. They had two choices for breakfast: plain lahoh with goat liver or lahoh treated with ghee. A cup of hot tea went with either choice.

Happy to see me back, customers greeted me with firm handshakes, "Congratulations, Ali! Now you are a married man. Now you are a big deal and have responsibilities. Our heart-felt blessings to you."

I basked in all the attention and moved from one customer to another until Koosar, my old friend, came in.

"Hey Ali, you look great. The new wife must have been pampering you."

"What did you expect? She is a country girl," I shouted back.

"Good for you. These country girls are the real thing, unlike those in town," Koosar remarked.

"Koosar, you have a problem with these girls here in town?" someone asked jokingly.

"Yes, I have a problem with them. They are like the boys," Koosar responded.

"Like the boys?"

"Yes, like the boys. They've lost their femininity."

"Koosar, what are you having for breakfast? The usual cup of tea?" I intervened.

"No, I want a complete breakfast—a plate of liver and two pieces of lahoh."

A complete breakfast! Either I didn't hear him right or Koosar had stumbled upon a fortune. Just to make sure, I cupped my ears and asked him again, "Did you say breakfast?"

"Yes, a breakfast, Ali. Hard to believe, isn't it?" Koosar smiled, enjoying my reaction of disbelief. He knew quite well the thoughts going through my mind.

I promptly served him his breakfast to talk to him about something more important than food, and I asked, "So, what happened while I was away? What was the government up to? It seems a lot has happened and things have gotten worse."

Koosar had his mouth full and took his time. Swallowing what was in his mouth, his Adam's apple bobbing, he cleared his throat and said in a low voice, "You are right. A lot has happened. For one thing, police agents are everywhere, especially in our Sudi neighbourhood. You can't escape them. They watch us all the time, even when we are peeing. The government has assigned one of those snakes to our restaurant and he is always here."

"In this restaurant?" I whispered in alarm.

"Yes, he just sits there, all day long. You might as well employ him to work in the restaurant."

"These snakes used to come and go."

"This one is as permanent as the tables in the restaurant."

"Is he here now?"

He scanned the room and quickly spotted the man.

"You see the restless-looking tall guy sitting near the door?"

"The one wearing the white shirt?"

"Yes, that's him."

"How did you know that he is a government agent?"

"What else would bring a Duki clansman to our restaurant? When he started coming every morning, we began to suspect him. And when he arrested one of our men, he showed his true colours. Look at him now! He is moving to another chair. He must have set his sights on somebody."

The man walked over to a short chubby fellow in a brown shirt, sitting by himself. He parked himself beside the guy and struck a conversation with him while we watched.

"What's he going to say to the man?" I asked Koosar, incredulous that this was happening right in front of our eyes.

"He could say anything. Two days ago, he started a conversation with another unsuspecting man. It ended with an arrest. The agent put handcuffs on the man and took him away."

"And why did he arrest him?"

"The agent said the government is dominated by the Duki. The man said nothing, just nodded. The agent arrested him there and then."

"A nod? That was the crime that got him arrested?"

"Yes. He agreed with him that the Duki government dominates the government. That nod sealed his fate."

"But that is the truth. They own this government as they own their camels."

"Ali, the truth is no longer about facts. It is about who is telling. Whatever the Supreme Leader and his Duki clansmen say is the truth, no matter what."

"Even if they are lying?"

"Yes."

For a moment, I was lost for words. What would they do next? Who was safe now? Finally, I said, "We have to do something about that man the agent is talking to. We can't watch him fall into a stupid trap." Determined to warn the Sudi about the snake he was talking to, I made my way towards their table and interrupted them. "There is a woman outside the restaurant who wants to see you. Can you come over for a few minutes," I said to the Sudi. Without asking any question, he stood up and followed me. We stepped out of the restaurant, and I turned to him.

"You are a Sudi, aren't you?" I asked.

"Yes," he replied, surprised not to see any woman outside.

"There is no woman here and nobody is waiting for you. I just called you to warn you. Do you know the man you were talking to?"

"No, why?" he asked.

"He is a government agent and a Duki. I guess you know what that means?"

"I sure do."

"Stay away from him. If he asks you a question, don't give him an answer, not even a nod. Pretend you are deaf or dumb or something."

"Thanks for the warning. I shouldn't be talking to him at all," he said, and with a nervous grin on his face, returned to the restaurant. But this time he sat as far away from the secret policeman as he could.

My mission accomplished, I returned to Koosar's table and asked him, "What should I do if this agent comes to me with his nonsense?"

"Beat him at his own game. Tell him what he wants to hear. Tell him a bigger lie than the one he is peddling."

"Like what?"

"Tell him that the government is the best," Koosar said and smiled.

I always respected Koosar's ideas, but I decided to take a pass on this one. No way was I going to lie and say something good about their government. Instead, I decided to keep my distance from the guy and have nothing to do with him.

But the agent didn't take the hint. He wasn't giving up. Every time I brought him his cup of tea, he would try to initiate a conversation with me. I rebuffed him time and again, sometimes pretending to be too busy. But he continued nagging me. He wasn't taking no for an answer. One way or another, he would come up with something to get me. One afternoon, as I brought him his cup of tea and put it in front of him, he said, "I never heard you singing the popular government song."

"What government song?" I asked.

"The one that says, 'The Supreme Leader is the Father of the Nation and the bravest man on earth.'"

"I can't sing," I said.

"Why?"

"I lose my voice whenever I sing."

"You lose your voice when you sing this particular song or all songs?"

"All songs make me lose my voice," I said, and tried to move on.

"Did you go to a doctor?" he asked.

"Yes."

"What did he say?"

"He said it is incurable. I have to live with it."

"I am praying for you."

"Don't waste your time. It won't work."

"Why do you say that?" he asked, surprised.

"If a prayer was going to help me, the prayers of my clansmen would have helped me. They didn't. So what makes you think yours will help?" I said and turned to a real customer who was calling me.

The next day, I told Koosar about this. He smiled and asked, "And is that true? Do you lose your voice when you sing?"

"No, it was something I came up with just to shut him up," I said. "But can you see the stupidity of it? I am looking for an opportunity to stab him to death to avenge my father, and here he is talking to me about singing a song."

Koosar thought for a while, then he said, sounding serious, "I know that you have to avenge your father, but here is the thing: do it the right way and at the right time. To kill and be killed is not the right way. That is suicide."

6

Koosar was right. I had to be careful. One way to accomplish my objective would be to follow the agent into some dark alley and kill him there. Nobody would see anything. No policeman would arrest me. So far, such an opportunity eluded me. The man always left the restaurant early, before sunset, like a coward who feared the darkness of the night. Only one night he did stay with us until it got dark. I excused myself from my work and went after him. I trailed him from a distance and watched him strolling down the main street. He knew he was safe in the Sudi neighbourhood as long as he remained on the main street with its security lights. I waited for him to take a turn into a dark backstreet. He didn't, and continued walking on the main street until a police car came from behind and stopped for him. He entered and they drove off.

For months, the only good news I heard was Fatima's pregnancy. Other than avenging my father's murder, nothing else could make me as happy and fulfilled. I even convinced myself that the baby would be a boy and came up with a name for him. I called him Dagaal, meaning "a fierce fighter." I expected nothing less from my son.

Not to miss his birth, I sent a message to my wife to join me in town. I had already rented a small house and it was time we lived together as a family. A week later she arrived and I welcomed her at the truck station. Through the crowded streets, we walked together towards our new home, a small house with one bedroom, a living room, a kitchen and a bathroom.

Having never been to a town before, Fatima was overwhelmed by the buildings, and all the hustle and bustle in the streets. Her excitement didn't last long though. Soon the daily busy routine of a housewife took over. Most of the time she stayed at home alone; sometimes, she met up with other wives in the neighbourhood. They would sit together outside their doors and chat about their lives.

Every day I left my wife at the break of dawn and returned late in the evening when the restaurant closed. Fatima waited for me and never went to bed before me. She waited for that knock on the door. One night, the familiar knock on the door never came.

Fatima suspected that something had happened to me and my life could be in danger. She knew quite well that I would never stay away from my home for a whole night. Early in the morning, she rushed to the restaurant, where they broke to her the awful news. "The police arrested your husband yesterday and he is in jail," they told her.

The wretched day had started like any other day. After the breakfast rush hour, business had slowed down as usual and I was bored. A few customers were left, and one of them saw me yawning and laughed. But to the police agent who was stationed in the restaurant, this was no laughing matter. It was the opportunity he had been waiting for. He finally found an excuse to put me away. Jumping up from his seat, he came over and arrested me on the spot.

"What is this about? What have I done?" I asked, outraged, as any innocent person would be.

"I don't have to explain to you. You will know everything at the police station," he snapped, and snatched the knife from my waist and put handcuffs on me.

"Hold on! What's the problem? Why are you arresting him?" Rashid, my boss, asked. Two customers also stepped forward and tried to intervene.

"Shut up. Or I will call more policemen and arrest you too," the agent bellowed, as he pushed me out of the restaurant.

Along the way, I pleaded with him once again, "At least, tell me what I am arrested for!"

"You insulted the Supreme Leader," he replied.

"Insulted the Supreme Leader? Who insulted him?" I asked.

"You."

"When? Maybe you mistook me for somebody else."

"No, it was you."

"I don't remember saying anything about the Supreme Leader."

"It is not what you said. It is what you did."

I tried to remember what I had done. Nothing came to mind that could be construed as an insult to the Supreme Leader.

At the police station, they registered me and put me in a prison cell. It had no windows and felt like a deep hole in the ground. All I could think of was my mortality. I expected no mercy or justice from our sworn enemy. They might keep me in jail for a long time or stand me before a firing squad. If only I had acted in time and taken my revenge!

As I wallowed in my failure, two policemen came barging into the cell. One of them, the younger of the two, kicked me hard on the back a few times, saying, "You are the brave guy who dared to insult the Supreme Leader, aren't you? Go ahead and open your mouth again. Go ahead and try to act out the nickname your clan gave to the Supreme Leader. Let's see it."

"I wasn't acting out any nickname. I swear that is the truth," I said.

"And you think we will believe you? You people will never tell the truth."

They continued kicking and punching me, their boots and truncheons slamming me on my chest and hips. Every part of my body ached and I felt dizzy. I was barely conscious when they left me. "We'll be back," they said and slammed the door shut.

Bruised and bloodied, I lay on the concrete floor as still as a dead body. An intense pain plagued every part of my body from my scalp to my toes. But despite the suffering and torment, something finally clicked in my mind, and I recalled that I had yawned just prior to my arrest. That was my crime; that was what he was talking about. I had to tell the policemen about what had really happened and I started shouting at the top of my voice. "He got it all wrong! The policeman arrested me for nothing. I was just yawning! Just yawning and nothing else. I didn't open my mouth to act out any nickname."

No response. The truth didn't make a difference to the Duki government.

Meanwhile, Fatima had arrived at the police station. When she heard my screams, she broke down and sobbed. Eight months pregnant, she could hardly walk long distances, but she had managed to come. She pleaded with the policemen in the station to let her see me.

At first, they told her to go away and made fun of her. "What is in there, in that big stomach of yours? A wicked Sudi baby boy?" But she persisted and stood her ground until they relented and brought her to my prison cell.

The moment she saw me, she started crying. "Why did they arrest you? And what have they done to you?" she asked.

"I yawned," I said.

"So?"

"They say I opened my mouth to demonstrate the Supreme Leader's nickname—Big Mouth."

"Everybody yawns. Why is your yawn different from that of other people?"

"Don't worry about me. I will be all right. The important thing is you and the child inside you. You better go back to the camel country to stay with your family. Without me, you can't survive in town."

"And leave you here in jail? I don't know what to do anymore. How can a person be arrested for yawning? What is this world coming to?" she screamed, tears flowing down her cheeks.

"For the sake of our baby, please go back to your family. Don't worry about me. I will get through this," I implored her and tried to reason with her.

She continued crying until a policeman came in and told her to leave.

For three days, nobody else visited me in jail, not even Isman, my second cousin. I understood their reluctance. Anybody who visited me could become a target. On the third day, Koosar came. The threat of the security forces going after him didn't deter him. Neither their firing squads nor their jails intimidated him.

Koosar went from office to office, not sure who to talk to until a corporal walking by recognized him. Koosar was well known in town as the peddler of used clothes.

"Have you come to sell your clothes here?" the corporal asked.

"No, I came to see a prisoner," Koosar replied.

"Who is that?"

"Ali, the camel boy. He was arrested three days ago."

"It is too early to sell his clothes," the corporal snickered, meaning I was not dead yet.

"Who said anything about his clothes? I came to see him," Koosar shot back.

The corporal took Koosar's defiance in stride and even helped him to see me. The moment Koosar set his eyes on me, he started shaking his head. "I can't believe they arrested you for yawning," he said. "What next? Coughing and sneezing to become a crime?"

He railed against the Duki government. I warned him to lower his voice: "It's not a good idea to come and visit me. They will go after you too," I whispered.

Taking a quick glance at the policeman standing near the door, Koosar said, "Son, don't worry about me. What can they do to a man who sells dead people's clothes for a living that will make him worse off? Arrest him? Put him in jail? None of that will make me worse off. Why? Because I am right there, at the lowest rung of life. And when you are there, you are there. It can't get worse. It can't get lower than this."

"Koosar, you shouldn't say things like that. They are after anybody who belongs to our clan, rich or poor," I reiterated.

"I will be fine. It is you we are all worried about. Our clan has hired a lawyer to defend you."

"Do you think a lawyer will help me against them? I don't think so."

"We will see. They pretend to be a government. They pretend to have courts like normal governments. Let's see if he can do something for you."

Koosar would have stayed with me for hours had they not told him to leave. On his way out, I could hear the corporal picking on him again.

"We will let you know when you can take away his clothes," he said and laughed with his fellow policemen.

Koosar ignored them and walked away.

7

THE POLICEMEN INTERROGATED ME WITH beatings every day, except on Fridays. Apparently, they would keep on torturing me until I admitted guilt or died. It was a painful, harrowing experience. But despite everything, I refused to admit guilt.

Then, one day, four policemen barged into my cell early in the morning. They pushed me out and took me outside into the back seat of a police car. The doors had barely banged shut when the driver gunned the car down the main road westwards. On the way, people stopped to catch a glimpse of the condemned person inside the car. A speeding police car always caught their attention and put fear into their hearts.

Soon we reached the large, looming National Security Court, which had decided the fate of our beloved chief, the previous president, our schoolboys, and hundreds of other Sudi men. The mere sight of that place knocked any sense of hope out of me. I was taken into the building through a back door. Inside the court, I was told to sit down on a chair. I slumped upon it, my hands still cuffed together. Two armed security officers stood in a show of vigilance behind me.

The multitude of people in the court surprised me. Not one empty chair. They had all came to watch my case. They stole glances at me and whispered to one another. Why these people, mostly strangers, were interested in my case, I had no idea. Perhaps a case stemming from a mere yawn had stirred curiosity in the town.

Among the audience, however, I recognized some of my Sudi clansmen—my cousin Isman, Koosar, Jiro, and Rashid. Their presence meant a lot to me. Their concern for me showed in their pale anguished looks. I greeted them with a nod and they nodded back.

On the other side, I recognized the agent who had arrested me; he had a broad smile on his face. Next to him sat the government prosecutor, Captain Abdulla, a tall strong Duki clansman. Notorious for his ferocity and excesses in courts, he was one of the most feared and hated men in the country.

Not far from me, a man wearing a suit stood up and approached me. He exchanged greetings with me and told me that he was my lawyer. He returned to his seat without saying much. It was the first time I had seen him, his requests to contact me beforehand having been rejected by the authorities.

A door flew open, and the judge, a high-ranking military officer, made his way towards the bench. He looked straight ahead without a glance to his right or left. At the same time, somebody shouted an order for everybody to stand up. All complied; even old Koosar jumped to his feet.

The judge sat down cautiously as though worried that the chair might collapse under him. He had a good reason to worry. His weight and the weight of all those stars and medals on his shining starched uniform could become too much for the chair. Luckily, it didn't collapse or give way, and he sat safely.

Without a word of greeting to anybody, he turned to me and said: "Are you ready to admit the crime?"

"Admit what crime, Judge? I committed no crime. I just yawned," I answered promptly.

"Did you open your mouth?"

"Yes I did."

"Ah!"

"How else can one yawn, Judge? Can a person yawn with his mouth shut?" I asked, ready to face this powerful judge with the simple truth.

He glowered at me, apparently incensed by my response. After shuffling the papers on his table into some order, he said to the prosecutor, "Go ahead and present your case."

The prosecutor leaped up from his chair and sauntered towards me, straightening his necktie and clearing his throat along the way. He was about to ask me his first question when my lawyer intervened. He had something to say.

My lawyer approached the bench and said, "Judge, I would like to put forth a motion, before anything else."

"What motion are we talking about?" the judge asked, surprised.

"As a member of the Military Council under the Supreme Leader, have you not already approved the prosecution of my client?"

"Yes, I have," the judge replied, looking impatient.

"This means that you believe my client is guilty."

The judge merely nodded.

"A judge has to be impartial. But you have already endorsed my client's prosecution. You already believe that he is guilty. You cannot be impartial. I think then you should recuse yourself from this case. That is my motion."

"Who says I can't be an impartial judge?" the judge replied.

"The law."

"I am the law!" the judge asserted with indignation.

"You are the law?"

"Yes, I am. Who makes the law?"

"The Supreme Leader."

"That is right and I represent the Supreme Leader in this court. We make the law. In other words, we are the law. It is that simple."

The lawyer had nothing more to say and, shaking his head, sat down.

Once again, the judge instructed the prosecutor to proceed. Captain Abdulla marched towards me, holding me with his gaze. Nobody could intervene now. Nobody could stop him this time. Like a lion seeing a prey at a short distance, he was ready to jump on me.

"Do you support the government?" he asked, firing his first question.

"Yes," I lied with a clear conscience.

"Have you ever been to an Orientation Centre or joined the demonstrations supporting the government?"

"No."

"So how can you claim that you support the government?"

"I am a waiter at a restaurant, working every day of the week, from dawn till late in the evening. I couldn't find time to take part in the demonstrations supporting the government."

"You couldn't find one hour to show support for the government?"

"No, I couldn't."

"And you know why?"

"I just told you why—I was busy doing my job."

"No, it is not that. It is because you are a capitalist."

"I am a capitalist? Like the rich people in Europe and America?"

"Yes."

"Wait a minute! If I am rich, where is my money?"

There was muffled laughter and murmuring in the court.

"You are a stupid capitalist. Stupid capitalists have no money. You are not even smart enough to keep your mouth shut. Instead you keep opening it as wide as you can to act out that disgusting nickname that your people have given the Supreme Leader."

"I was not opening my mouth. I was just yawning," I repeated for the twentieth time, if not more.

"Why?"

"I don't know. Why do people yawn everyday?"

"Because they are sleepy."

"So was I."

"In the middle of the day? Nonsense! People get sleepy and yawn in the night before they go to bed."

"Allah can make you yawn anytime of the day," I said. By invoking the name of Allah, I knew I couldn't go wrong. He wouldn't dare to challenge that statement.

"Allah has better things to do than get involved with your mischievous activities. And talking about better things, do you know the name of our Supreme Leader?"

"General Kahin."

"Do you know him by any other name?"

"Yes, the Supreme Leader."

"Any other name?"

"No."

"How about a nickname?"

"The president has no nickname."

"Come on! Tell us the truth. I am talking about the one you and your people use."

"The new one?"

"Yes," the prosecutor smiled.

I knew one thing for certain: if I uttered the Supreme Leader's real nickname that our clan had given him, Big Mouth, it would be all over for me. It would be the firing squad. The audience in the court seemed to be holding their breath.

"So what is that nickname?" the prosecutor boomed.

"The Father of the Nation," I said promptly. It was one of the Supreme Leader's favourite titles, which I had heard on the radio all the time. To do a little kissing up wouldn't be bad for my case.

"Is there any other nickname of the leader that you know of?" The prosecutor pressed on, not giving up.

"The Father of Wisdom." Also from the state radio.

"Any other nickname?"

"The Father of Success."

"Any other nickname?"

"The Father of Education."

"Any other nickname?"

"The Father of Victory." I could have gone on the whole day.

The prosecutor was obviously disappointed; his attempt to lead me into a trap had failed. But he didn't give up and moved on. He reframed the question and asked, "Do you know any nickname of our leader that does not start with the word 'Father'?"

"Yes," I said without hesitation.

Again, the audience became still, fearing the worst.

"What?" the prosecutor asked.

"The Great Leader," I said and dashed his hopes.

He asked me the same question again and again, and each time I came up with one of the hundreds of the Supreme Leader's favourite titles: the Great Orator, the Great Teacher, the Great Philosopher and so on.

"I have nothing more to ask, Judge," the prosecutor said and swaggered back to his seat.

The judge, stirred from his slumber, turned to the defence lawyer and asked, "Do you want to cross-examine your client?"

"No, Judge," my lawyer said without even standing up.

"In that case, you can go ahead, prosecutor. Call your witness," the judge instructed.

The prosecutor jumped up from his chair and was back in action again, calling to the witness stand the guy who had arrested me. He had barely settled down when the prosecutor asked him, "What do you know about the accused?"

"I know a lot about him. And you were right, captain. He is a capitalist. He is a dangerous man and a sworn enemy of the government."

"How did you come to know these facts about him?"

"The way he served me in the restaurant. His actions revealed the truth about him. He wasn't a waiter. He was a ticking time bomb."

"Can you be more specific?"

"One day I ordered a cup of tea. He kept me waiting for that cup of tea for ten minutes. That was the first signal that tipped me off. It was the red flag about his anti-government sentiment."

"Did he give you any reason why it took him so long?"

"No, he didn't. But I figured out myself. He was dead set against the presence of a government officer in the restaurant. He was playing hard ball with me. He hated me and would do anything to get rid of me. That is why he never served me properly."

"Anything else he did that showed his subversive activities?"

"Like any cunning criminal, he changed his tactics frequently. For example, another day he served me tea and there was no sugar in it."

I couldn't take this anymore and jumped on my feet and shouted, "That is not true! I always brought him sugar with the tea. I always served him well in the restaurant."

Furious, the judge rapped his gavel on the bench to restore order. "Sit down and don't make any more outbursts, or I will announce the sentence right now. Do you hear me?" he bellowed. The stifling heat inside the court contributed to his irritability and soured his mood.

I took his warning seriously and sat back on the chair. With order restored, the prosecutor resumed his questioning.

"Has he done anything else to sabotage the government?"

"Yes," my accuser said. "As days went by, he became more brazen in his actions. One day, he served me black tea when I had ordered a cup of tea with milk. It was a part of his plan to sabotage the government."

"Black tea?"

"Yes, Captain, black tea."

"You've done a good job of collecting valuable information about his every move. Anything else he did?"

"Once he served me lunch. But he didn't bring the soup with the lunch. Without the soup to wash it down, I almost choked to death. Indeed, it was what he wanted. But I survived, thanks to Allah."

"When you finally decided to arrest him, what had he done?"

"This time, he aimed for the top, setting his sights on the Supreme Leader. He opened his mouth wide, a demeaning, cowardly act, to demonstrate that stupid nickname that he and his people have given the Supreme Leader."

"How about his claim that he was just yawning? What do you think of that?"

"He would say anything to cover his crime."

The prosecutor turned to the judge. "Judge, I have no more questions." He returned to his seat, beaming like a triumphant warrior. He was proud of the way he had presented all the crimes I had committed: tea without sugar, lunch without soup, tea without milk, delay in serving, and yawning.

The judge turned to my lawyer and asked, "Do you want to cross-examine the government agent or do you want to take a pass on him as well?" At the same time, he started cracking his knuckles, which sounded as loud as gunfire.

My lawyer didn't respond and remained on his seat. He waited until the judge was done with his fingers.

"I ask you: do you want to cross-examine the officer or not?" the judge repeated, raising his voice.

"Yes, Judge, I will cross-examine him. As soon as you are done with your fingers. You cracked seven of them. Only three more to go."

"Go ahead. No need to wait."

The lawyer didn't move until the judge had cracked his last knuckle. Only then did he stand up and approach the government agent. For a minute or two, they stared at each other like two warriors about to engage in a fight. Neither of them blinked or looked away.

"Let me get this straight," the lawyer said, the frown on his face matching his tone of incredulity, "Do you really believe that my client was a threat to the government just because he delayed in serving you a cup of tea for a few minutes or that he served you tea without sugar by mistake?"

"Mistake! That was no mistake. That was an intentional act of defiance to a government officer and thus a potential threat to the country," the agent argued back.

"Did you ask my client to bring you some sugar when you found out that there was no sugar in the tea?"

"Yes, I did."

"And did he bring it to you?"

"Yes he did, but I had to wait another ten minutes."

"Over the times you visited the restaurant, how many times did you order a cup of tea?"

"Thousands of times."

"And out of those thousands of times, how many times did he forget to put some sugar into your cup of tea?"

"Nobody forgot anything. This was a premeditated intentional act. And I don't know how many times. I didn't count them."

"Could it be only one or two times?"

"I don't know. I don't keep records."

"When you ordered tea with milk and Ali served you black tea, you said it was part of a plan to sabotage the government."

"That is right."

"What does black tea have to do with sabotaging a government? I mean, how does that work? Does black tea explode like a bomb?"

"Let me explain. A government officer orders a cup of tea with milk. You serve him black tea. That is an act of defiance. It is where terrorists and saboteurs start their games. It is what they do before they join the big leagues of terrorism and start throwing bombs and grenades."

"Did you tell my client about his mistake and ask him to bring you some milk?"

"Yes, I did."

"And my client did bring the milk to you, didn't he?"

"Yes, he did after a while."

"And you don't know how many times Ali served you tea without milk out of the thousands of times you ordered tea because you don't keep records."

"Yes."

It was at that moment that a miracle of miracles happened. The judge yawned, a big one, as big as that of a camel after a long winter night. To me, it was no normal yawn. It was a message from Heaven. I had to do something or say something. I jumped on my feet before the judge even had time to close his mouth and shouted: "That is all I did. Do you see that? The judge yawned just as I did the day they arrested me!"

My loud reaction caught everybody in the court by surprise. Some people suppressed their laughter by putting their hands over their mouths. At first, the judge looked embarrassed, but he soon recovered and came swinging at me. "Shut up, you idiot! And don't make any more loud outbursts in my court, or else." His face was twitching in a fit of temper. For a moment, an awkward silence and a state of suspense prevailed in the court, until my lawyer cleared his throat and spoke.

"Judge, you just yawned. It is okay," he said, "there is nothing wrong about that. It comes naturally. We can't help it. But how would you feel, Judge, if somebody arrested you for that now, just as my client was arrested? You were not alluding to any nickname of our Supreme Leader, or making fun of him, or anybody else for that matter. You were just yawning like all other human beings do when they get sleepy or bored or tired."

"No more talking about my yawning," the military judge barked angrily. "One more word about that, and I will stop the proceedings and render my judgment!"

The lawyer heeded the warning and turned his attention towards the government agent in the witness stand.

"So a cup of tea without sugar or milk, or a late arrival of soup is a conspiracy against the government? Is that what you are saying?"

"Yes. Besides, I know when somebody is thinking about engaging in any conspiracy against the government before he even acts on it."

"You can read minds?"

"Yes."

That claim created a buzz in the court. The Duki clansmen who were present nodded their heads in agreement. All the Sudi looked at each other in disbelief.

"What an extraordinary talent you have here! You must be a genius, a superman, if you can read minds," the lawyer sneered. "Let's put your talent to the test . . . " he scanned the courtroom. Pointing at Koosar, he said, "Can you tell us what is now on the mind of that old man at the very back seat? What is he thinking about now?"

"He is thinking about the good and useful projects the government is carrying out in the country," the agent answered promptly. He didn't even waver or hesitate for a moment. He felt confident that Koosar had no option but to confirm his statement. Nobody could do otherwise.

But Koosar had always been unique and different. Would he remain true to himself? That was the question on my mind and on the minds of all those who knew him.

The lawyer asked Koosar, "Is the agent correct? Were you thinking about the useful projects the government is carrying out in the country?"

"No," Koosar replied.

A small commotion erupted in the courtroom. The defiance in Koosar's answer was obvious. The judge hit the gavel on the table and glared at Koosar. "What were you thinking about, then?" he asked in an aggressive tone.

"I was thinking that when the whole universe was created, which one came first at the very beginning of time—day or night?" Koosar responded, not the least intimidated.

The judge looked confused. The creation of the universe was probably the last thing on his mind. Pinning his hope that he might get a better response the second time, he asked, "What were you thinking before that?"

Without missing a beat, Koosar replied, "I was thinking whether chicken legs are hind legs or forelegs."

"Chicken legs? Why were you thinking about chicken legs? You work in a chicken farm or something?" the judge asked, his face twitching with anger.

"No."

"Where do you work?"

"I work in the streets of this town."

"And do what?"

"I sell dead people's clothes."

"Dead people's clothes?"

"Yes."

"Get out of my court!"

"What is wrong with selling dead people's clothes? Is it not a job, Judge?" Koosar stood his ground.

"Take him out of the court," the judge ordered the policeman who was standing beside him, adding, "He is not a normal person. He is a devil, pure and simple."

The policeman went over to Koosar and started pushing him out of the courtroom. But Koosar didn't go quietly and shouted at the top of his voice, "Why is my job so upsetting to the judge? If he has another job for me, I will take it."

My lawyer watched Koosar being pushed out. Then he turned and walked slowly towards the witness. He asked, "Now that you have dismally failed to read minds, here is one simple question: do you sometimes yawn?"

"Me? Yes."

"Do you sometimes sneeze?"

"Yes."

"Do you sometimes belch?"

"Yes."

"Do you sometimes hiccup?"

"Yes."

"Do you sometimes cough?"

"Yes."

"Do you sometimes break wind?"

"No."

"No?"

"I don't know."

"You don't know?"

"I don't know what you are talking about."

"You know very well what I am talking about."

It was at that moment when the prosecutor jumped on his feet and shouted, "Objection! If the lawyer doesn't drop that question and asks it one more time, he will find himself sharing the prison cell with his client. Who does he think he is, and who does he think he is talking to?"

I felt that my lawyer and clansman needed support. I had to do something to take the pressure off him. I jumped on my feet as well and screamed at the top of my voice, "Objection! Everybody breaks wind. Why doesn't he admit it? Who does he think he is? Some kind of an angel?"

The judge stopped playing with his whiskers and glared at me. He said nothing at first, just took a big breath. Then in a booming voice he said, "First of all, ignorant criminals like you don't object to anything. They have no say in my court. They just sit there until they are sentenced. Second of all, what do you know about angels?"

"Nothing much. Do they also . . . ?" I trailed off.

"Then shut up and don't make any more outbursts in my court. The next time you disrupt the court, I am going to order the policemen to cut your tongue and push it through your throat. That will shut you up for life. Do you hear me?"

"Yes," I said and sat back on my chair. The judge's warning was dire. I took note of it and started praying to Allah to intervene and make the government agent fart at that very moment, one for the ages, one for the sake of justice, one loud enough and powerful enough to shake the earth and knock down everybody to the ground.

Next, the judge directed his anger at the lawyer and reprimanded him for asking such a question. "The objection of the prosecutor is upheld," he shouted. "Your question denigrates a government officer. It is an attack on his honour as a person and an attack on his clan as well."

Scratching his head, the lawyer said, "Judge, I asked the question because I wanted to make sure whether the government officer who had arrested my client for yawning could differentiate yawning from intentional opening of the mouth. Whether, like all human beings, he experienced yawning, and coughing, and sneezing in his daily life and would recognize when others do the same. The fact is that what occurred in that restaurant on that day was just one of those biological phenomena that all human beings experience in their daily lives. My client yawned that day, just as you yawned yourself a short time ago, just as we sneeze, cough, belch, and yes, break wind every day. Nothing less and nothing more. It was not an act to malign anybody, or to destabilize the government, or to refer to some nickname. And if Ali goes to jail because of this, he should not be the only person to go to jail. We all have to be found guilty and sent to jail because we all yawn."

The judge had been looking at his watch for some time, as though in a hurry to go somewhere. When my lawyer had finished speaking, the judge suddenly cleared his bench, looked up, and declared, "It is time for the court to reach a decision. It is time to end this case."

"But, Judge, I have not called my witness," the lawyer protested. "He is a customer who was there at the time when Ali yawned and the policeman arrested him."

"There is no need for that witness," the judge stated bluntly. "The police agent witnessed the incident and that's enough." In the courtroom full of expectant faces, the judge took a piece of paper from his pocket and read the sentence. "I find the accused guilty of maligning the Supreme Leader and find him guilty of engaging in anti-government activities. So I hereby sentence him to ten years in jail."

The instant I heard the verdict, I jumped on my feet and screamed, "Ten years! Allah Akbar! For yawning! Allah Akbar! Is that your justice? Allah Akbar!"

"Shut up or I will change my mind and give you the death sentence!" the judge shouted back as he walked out of the court.

In less than two hours, it was all over. The judge had barely left the room when the same four policemen who had brought me to the court quickly surrounded me. They dragged me out of the court and into their car.

8

THE POLICE CAR SPED TOWARDS the prison where I would serve my sentence. On the way, the judge's last words kept echoing in my mind. Ten years, in which I would have no chance to see my wife and child. Ten years, in which I would have no chance to avenge my father. A sense of hopelessness and despondency took hold of me. But I knew that it could have been worse—a firing squad. At least, now, I had a chance of coming out of jail alive after ten years.

Meanwhile, the four policemen in the car were sharing jokes. One of them told a story about his cousin who had married a woman twenty years his senior. They laughed like this was the funniest thing they had heard. In response, another one remarked, "Come to think of it, the longer a fruit matures, the sweeter it tastes. I have been there myself. You have to taste it to believe it." More laughter.

We approached an impressive building at the northern edge of town, its gleaming white walls reflecting the sun's rays. Birds chirped on the surrounding trees. It looked like a house with a large courtyard, but the high fence and the armed prison guards perched on towers gave the game away. Just as I gave an inner sigh of relief that I had not been taken to the notorious Dark Cave prison, a sergeant met us at the gate. He loudly ordered me to get out, then grabbed me by the collar and took me to a bare room where five other prison guards were waiting for me. They stripped me and I stood naked before six men.

For no apparent reason, the sergeant screamed something. Almost simultaneously, the five prison guards started beating me up. The scream had obviously been a command. They hit me mercilessly in every possible way. They kicked me with their big boots, punched me on the face, and slammed their truncheons on every part of my body. All the while, the sergeant kept screaming what sounded like encouragement. Just as I thought they would beat me to death right there and then, the sergeant stopped screaming. The beating came to an end. Later, I learned that the beating session was called "Political Orientation," which was delivered to every political prisoner.

The sergeant threw a prison uniform at me and told me to put it on. Then he told two of the guards to lock me up in a prison cell. The two guards pushed me and dragged me through a dark corridor until we reached a door. They opened it and pushed me in.

It was a small room with two small beds, one of which was occupied by an inmate. He sat up on his bed as soon as we entered and stared at me with intense curiosity, like someone who had not seen another human being in a long time. He had a shaggy beard and grey hair, and I suspected he was younger than he looked. I greeted him with a nod, and he reciprocated.

Without saying a word, I sat on the empty bed. I needed time to rest and recuperate. A fierce headache and an aching back and hips were tormenting me. My fellow inmate let me take my time and waited. He had probably gone through the same experience as I had.

After a while, my pain had eased and I felt a little better. It was time to engage my fellow prisoner. At first, we spoke in generalities, the kind of small talk people make when they meet for the first time. But I had to know which clan he belonged to, for I could only trust my clansmen. Encouraged by the way he talked, I took the initiative and asked, "Which clan do you belong to?"

"I am a Sudi, and you are?" He spoke eagerly and awaited my response.

"I am Sudi too." I smiled, relieved to be sharing the cell with a fellow clansman.

From there on, we chatted earnestly like two brothers who hadn't seen each other for a long time. He had a lot to say. Before the Duki government threw him into jail, he had been a seaman and worked on board ships that took him all over the world. He had visited many foreign countries. His extensive travel experiences, his lively nature, and his penchant for telling stories were a boon for me.

"You won't believe why I am here," the seaman said. "I came from

England to take my vacation of four weeks here in our country. The last day of my vacation, I was ready to fly back to England when one of those government thugs knocked on my door—you know those with the blue uniforms? I think they call themselves the Blue Angels."

"I know them. They are no angels. They are the attack dogs of the Duki government."

"Yes, that is it. He was one of those attack dogs. I opened the door and this moron is asking me which clan I belong to. I told him. Then he says that I need to come with him to a place called an Orientation Centre. 'Why?' I asked him. 'To hear a speech that will cleanse your brain,' he said. 'I have no time for that. I am travelling to England and I am too busy,' I said. 'Your brain has to be cleansed before you go anywhere,' he said. 'My brain is cleansed,' I replied. 'Where did it get cleansed?' he asked. 'In my mother's womb,' I shot back angrily. 'Brains are only cleansed in our Political Orientation Centres,' he said. 'My brain is just fine and I am not going anywhere,' I insisted. 'You are a capitalist, I know the likes of you!' he shouted at me and arrested me."

Under different circumstances, I might have found his story funny and laughed it off. But it was no laughing matter and I asked him, "Where did they try your case?"

"In a place where they certainly didn't serve justice. In a place where Hitler would have felt at home," he said in a sad tone.

"Were you expecting justice from that court?" I asked, somewhat bemused.

"Of course, I was. Shouldn't we?"

"I guess you've stayed too long in foreign countries and forgotten the way we do things here."

"What did I forget?"

"You forgot that a Sudi clansman never expects justice from a Duki. Not now. Not ever. That is the way it has always been."

"So there is no hope of getting justice here in our country?"

"There is. It is justice that has nothing to do with courts. You take a gun or a knife and make our own justice," I said and added, "Let me tell you something. They killed my father, raided my herd of camels, and put me in jail now for yawning. And did I ever expect justice from their court? No. Never!"

"Sorry to hear that they killed your father."

"They did. Some five years ago. I should have avenged his killing by now. But sooner or later, it will happen."

"The problem is, they have all the power. They are in control of the military, the police, and the whole government."

"I know, but that won't stop me."

"By the way, did you say you are in jail for yawning?"

"Yes. Hard to believe, isn't it?"

"A yawn? Why?"

After telling him my story, a wry smile flickered on his face and he said, "Ten years for yawning! Unbelievable!" His crime no longer seemed so frivolous. He shook his head. Later, whenever the seaman saw me yawning, he would smile and say, "Ten more years in jail!"

Our conversation continued until late into the evening when they switched off the lights. The prison cell suddenly became pitch dark. It was time to go to sleep, or so I thought. I had no idea that we would soon have company. In the darkness, armies of bedbugs descended upon us. An enemy as dangerous and calculating as the Duki was out for our blood. No way to escape from them. They bit us hard. They sucked our blood, and we could do nothing about it. We moaned and cursed.

With every sting, the seaman let out a scream; then he reminisced about the good times when he used to live in a comfortable life in ships and foreign countries. "How can a person sleep in a place so infested with bugs?" he screamed, desperate and feeling helpless. "I've been to Antwerp, I've been to Rotterdam, I've been to Los Angeles, Liverpool, New York and every major city in the world. I have never seen anything like this."

In the morning, when the first rays of the sun poured through the small window below the ceiling, the bedbugs disappeared. They knew their time was up and made a quick retreat into their hideouts, the multitude of cracks in the walls. Not one of them went astray or fell behind.

I thought we would have a peaceful moment and get much-needed sleep, but then came a loud banging on the door. Startled, I turned to the seaman and asked, "What's that?"

"The prison guards. They are waking us up. They want us to get ready," he said, and jumped out of his bed.

"Ready for what? Are we going somewhere?"

"Yes, we are going."

"Where?"

"They will tell us later."

It didn't take long before a tall prison guard with a big red eye entered our cell and looked around, presumably checking that everything was in order. He saw the two of us sitting on our beds. What else did he expect?

A young boy followed him into our prison cell and put a small tray on the floor with two dry loaves of bread and two hot cups of tea. This was our breakfast, our first meal of the day.

"The food here is useless," my companion said. "It's unfit for human consumption. Not even the dogs in Liverpool would eat this food. You know what they would do?"

"No," I said, not even interested in what the dogs in our country would do, let alone those in Liverpool.

"They would take a sniff and walk away from it."

"Maybe the dogs in Liverpool are not as hungry as we are."

"I am telling you, if the United Nations knew what we are eating, they would have called an international meeting," the seaman opined.

"International meeting about what?"

"About the infringement of our basic human rights."

I listened to the seaman half-heartedly, not fully understanding what he was talking about. The United Nations and his talk of human rights meant nothing to me. I had heard the name of the United Nations from the radio a few times; but I never thought they could do anything for me. So without saying anything, I just chewed my bread quietly and washed it down with the hot tea.

Just as we finished our breakfast, the tall prison guard arrived with another guard, and they ordered us to go with them.

The first chance I got, I asked the seaman, "Do you know where we are we going?"

"I think we are going to the downtown area to work there."

"Work! What kind of work?"

"We will collect trash from the streets."

Sudi clansmen never collected trash from the streets or did any other dirty job. Any one of us who worked in those jobs betrayed his clan and dishonoured us. Doing such a job was abhorrent to me and I found myself in a dilemma. Lowering my voice, I said to the seaman, "Are you okay with sweeping the streets. I am not. Who do they think we are? Ruri clansmen?"

"Be sensible. You are not a Sudi now," the seaman whispered back. "You are a prisoner. You belong to no clan. And if you refuse their orders, you know where they will take you?"

"They will take me to the Dark Cave?"

"Yes."

It came down to a choice between going to the Dark Cave or sweeping the streets. As the seaman reminded me, the Dark Cave meant certain death. And so I had to swallow my pride for the time being and do the cleaning. But I barely did much the whole day. I picked up papers here and there when I saw the prison guards watching me. I also kept lowering my head out of shame, and avoided eye-contact with the people who passed us.

"Have you ever swept streets when you were in those foreign countries?" I asked the seaman when he came closer to me.

"I was a seaman, not a janitor," he responded, a bit upset.

"How about the prison guards in Liverpool and Rotterdam? Do they force their prisoners to sweep the streets?"

"No, they don't. The prisoners in Liverpool have rights. Nobody sweeps the streets of Rotterdam and Liverpool anyway."

"So how do they clean their streets?"

"Machines do those jobs for them. Machines sweep the streets. It is not like here," he said in a sour mood. To show his disgust with the job, he kicked a barrel full of trash. The barrel almost turned over, and some of the trash spilled back into the street. The prison guard with the big red eye came over and said to him, "Don't do that again, understand?" and then punched him so hard that he staggered and almost fell to the ground. Regaining his balance, the seaman went to work and put all the trash back into the barrel. There would be no more talk about Liverpool and Rotterdam for the rest of the day.

To witness the attack on my sub-clansman and fail to do anything made me feel ashamed. I bit my lower lip in frustration. If only the assault happened under different circumstances. As an act of support for my clansman, I stopped collecting the trash. It was the least I could do for him. I just moved around from one location to another until the end of the day when they took us back to the prison.

Back in the prison cell, two dishes of maize with milk were waiting for us. It was our dinner after a long day. By then, the seaman had recovered from the hit he had suffered from Red Eye, as we called the prison guard. My companion's only concern at the moment was our dinner.

"Who can live on this kind of low-value tasteless food? No fruits, no vegetables, no vitamins? Nothing," he fumed in disgust.

Not interested in his talk about the prison food, I quietly ate my meagre dinner.

The seaman got the message and said, "Am I talking too much?"

"No, you are not," I responded.

"Then, what is the problem?"

"We just have to talk about things more important than food. That is all."

"Like what?"

"Like those foreign countries that you have visited and the people over there," I said. The more he had told me about them, the more interested I had become.

"What do you want to know about these countries?"

"Everything. I want to know about their people—their beliefs, their way of life, and what makes them tick. I want to know how they govern themselves, and if they have presidents like the Supreme Leader."

The seaman's face beamed with a big smile. It was what he liked to talk about most and he didn't hesitate. "First of all, they don't have presidents like the Supreme Leader. Forget about that. They have good elected leaders, democratic leaders, who serve all their people in a just and fair way. What else were you asking?"

"About their way of life, their beliefs, and what makes them tick," I reminded him.

"Where should I start? I have a million things to say about that."

"You can begin from wherever you wish. I am all ears. I am listening."

"The first thing you have to know, Ali, is that people in these countries have different cultures and they are different from us."

"In what sense?" I inquired.

"For one thing, they are curious people. You can't believe how curious they are. They want to know everything about everything. They are always looking for answers and won't rest until they solve all the mysteries of the world. They have to know what causes diseases; why some objects float and some sink; why some products dissolve in water and others don't; why some creatures fly and soar into the heavens and others can't. They want to know what is beneath the ocean and what is up there on the moon and the stars. They even want to know about the sex lives and the sleeping habits of snails and lizards."

"The sex lives of lizards! Did you say that?"

"Yes, they call it science," the seaman continued. "It's how they accumulated knowledge and reached the level of progress and development that they have. And not only do they do their research for the sake of knowledge, they also work hard. They have great work ethic. They always want to improve their living standard and make tomorrow better than today. It's not in their culture and tradition to sit passively and watch the world go by, dismissing everything as God's will. They don't say 'Inshallah' and leave it to some higher power to come to their aid. They take matters into their own hands and make it happen. They don't accept poverty as God's will. They don't accept sickness as God's will. They don't accept hunger as God's will. They take charge and do something about it. Time is too precious for them to waste sitting under trees and in front of teashops drinking tea and chewing qat all day long and talking about the fighting prowess of this clan and that clan. In fact, they don't even belong to clans; they live as free individuals under a democratic government that serves them all. It is a society of free individuals, not of clans like ours is."

The seaman had said more than I expected. I could hardly keep up with him. But before I addressed the important issues, I had to get something out of the way. I said, "You know what I always wanted to know?" I asked him, trying hard not to laugh.

"No," he said.

"The sex lives of lizards and snails! What did they find about that?"

As much as I tried, I couldn't help laughing. I quietened down after a while and even apologized. But the whole idea about the sex lives of lizards and snails sounded hilarious to me. No matter how much the seaman justified it, the significance of that subject eluded me.

"You can laugh all you want," the seaman responded, sounding disappointed. "To know something about the sex lives of lizards and snails is important. It is a part of knowledge. It is part of science. And science is what led these countries to progress. It is what made it possible for them to reach the moon."

I still had my doubts that anything good could come from learning about the sex lives of those slimy creatures, but I let it go. He had raised in his long monologue other important issues.

"Are you telling me that the people in Europe and America don't belong to clans? How can that be possible? How can they live without belonging to clans?" This one point had struck a chord in me.

"Trust me, there is no Duki clan or Sudi clan in their countries," he stated firmly.

"Then how can they identify one another?"

"They have names, family names, and addresses. They don't need to belong to clans for identification."

The notion that somebody could live in this world without belonging to a clan defied everything I had ever believed. Without clans, how could they feel safe? How could they deal with one another? How could they know the roots of a person and whether he was a friend or a foe? Out of the many questions I had on my mind, I chose the one that would expose the defect of this strange idea.

"How can you survive if you don't belong to a clan? I mean, who can you depend on for security and protection?"

"You can depend on the government and the police. The government has the duty to protect its citizens," the seaman said without any hesitation.

"A government like ours?" I shot back.

"No, not a government like ours. I am talking about a government that believes in the rule of law; a government that prosecutes criminals and leaves innocent people alone; a government that represents all the people."

"Okay, let me ask you this. If a man is killed and leaves no son or brother behind, who is going to avenge his killing if the dead man didn't belong to a clan?"

"The government takes care about that. But it is not about revenge. It is about serving justice. The government makes sure that the killer pays a price for his action. It makes no difference whether the dead man leaves behind a son or not."

"How does the government make him pay a price?" I probed.

"By punishing the murderer. They have real courts and good laws to administer justice. Not like the court that convicted us, but real and just courts."

"How about when somebody raids your camels and takes them away from you? Can a government do something about it?"

"Yes. They have laws against robbery and theft. They have laws against all crimes and a punishment for every one of them."

"Do they have a law against yawning?"

"Come on! Don't be ridiculous. We are talking about democratic, free people. Their constitution protects their freedom, a constitution that is as dear to them as their Bible. Nobody can take away their freedom. They value it more than anything else. They cherish it and die for it."

Apparently, the seaman knew what he was talking about. Some of the things he told me about the people in Europe, America, and Canada sounded a bit strange, but overall what he said about these foreign countries left a lasting and positive effect on me. As I rolled into my bed I said to the seaman, "One day, we will make a government as good as that of those foreign countries. But we have to get rid of the Duki government first."

And so it went. Every night, after they locked us in our cell, we indulged in talk about those foreign countries. Then we tried to go to sleep under the assault of the blood-sucking bedbugs. Fighting off these creatures kept us awake for hours, sometimes until dawn. And every day, the guards took us to town to do their dirty work, except on Fridays, when they gave us a break and we stayed in our cells. Sometimes, they even allowed us to meet our loved ones. The seaman looked forward to the moment when he could see his wife and children.

I expected no visitors. My wife had gone back to her family in the countryside. One day, however, I had a visitor. A prison guard took me to a room near the prison gate to see him. And what a pleasant surprise it was to see Koosar, my old friend and fellow clansman! Koosar scrambled to his feet, his smile melting away all the wrinkles on his face. We shook hands and, after quick exchange of greetings, we sat face to face on two stools.

At first, we had a small talk about my life in jail. Then Koosar informed me about the steps the Duki government had taken against our clan. He said they armed and encouraged the camel-herding Duki clansmen to attack the Sudi. Their hostile actions were not limited to the countryside. In the town, Sudi businessmen had lost their trade and contracts, and were forced to give up their businesses to the Duki. Hearing all this, I became despondent.

Koosar tried to cheer me up. "Son," he said, "Remember one thing: the forces of injustice and darkness only win in the short term. In the long term, they always lose. Have you heard about Hitler?"

"I think I heard his name somewhere, probably on the radio. But I don't know much about him," I said.

"He was one of the worst leaders who walked on the surface of this earth. He started a world war. He caused the death of millions of men and women. A lot of suffering and mayhem everywhere. But by the time the war ended, he was defeated and disgraced."

"You think the Supreme Leader will end up like Hitler? Defeated and disgraced?" I asked, desperate for a glimmer of hope.

"No doubt in my mind," Koosar said and added, "Let me tell you the story of another terrible leader, Wilwal, who once ruled a country with an iron fist. You know what he used to do?"

"No," I said, eagerly waiting to hear the actions of this other monster.

"He used to force men to have sex with their mothers."

"That is horrendous. What kind of man would do such a thing? How could he even think about something like that?"

Koosar fell silent for a moment; then he said, "Power is a dangerous thing that corrupts the soul of some people. It makes them confident that they can never do wrong. It makes them believe that they are always right, even when they kill thousands of innocent people. Without shame and without guilt! But eventually time and human tenacity for freedom defeats even the most powerful."

The prison guard moved in our direction and we stopped talking. He signalled the end of the visit. It was time to take me back to the prison cell. I said goodbye to Koosar, and the prison guard led me back to my cell.

Back in my cell, I found the seaman excited, a big smile on his face. He must have heard some good news, I thought. And sure enough, it turned out to be the best of news. The prison guards told him that his prison sentence was coming to an end. He would be released from prison in three days. The seaman thought that he had at least five more months to serve and the news had caught him by surprise.

"Congratulations!" I said. "That is good news. What are you going to do when you leave here?"

"Get out of this country. What else?"

"But you will return one day."

"I don't think so."

"Never?"

"Not as long as the Duki government is in power."

"I understand. But what will you do in these foreign countries? Work as a seaman again?"

"That is the only thing I know. I will go to Liverpool and look for a new company and a new ship to work on."

On the eve of his release, the seaman couldn't have been more cheerful. The seaports around the world beckoned him. He yammered away late into the night about what he would do in Rotterdam, Antwerp, Liverpool, and New York. At times, he would pause and look back on the years he had served, and all the abuses he had suffered, the time four soldiers beat him with a whip until he cried like a baby, and the day they arrested him, when his daughter followed him sobbing.

On his last day in jail, he woke up early. Uncharacteristically quiet and reserved, he had too many things on his mind. He couldn't wait to travel to faraway countries, to disappear into the strange lands and high seas of the world. He felt safer there than in his own country. The dangers of the stormy seas would not stop him. And when it was time to go, he rushed out of the prison cell as soon as one of the guards opened the door, barely saying goodbye to me.

"Hey, don't forget me when you go to Liverpool," I shouted after him. "Write to me! You know where I am. You know my address."

"I will do that. But what do you want to know about Liverpool?" he shouted back as he stepped out of the prison cell.

"I want to know what more they have found out about the sex lives of lizards," I said, and then laughed for a long time. I was missing him already. I sat back on the bed and waited for another day in jail to take its course.

9

THE DAY DIDN'T GET ANY easier afterwards. The prison guards took us to town; but this time, we had to work at a government construction site, carrying heavy bricks up a steep ladder. We sweated. We got exhausted. But all that paled in comparison to my feelings of shame and guilt when I learned what kind of building we were constructing. It would be a Political Orientation Centre, one of those notorious places where the government claimed to cleanse brains. It hurt even though I had no choice. Cleaning the streets no longer seemed like such a bad thing.

In the evening back in the cell, there was no other inmate to keep me company. It would be a long night. There would be no stories about Liverpool and Rotterdam, no more gripping sea adventures to listen to and pass the time. And the bedbugs would have no one else to attack. They would sneak upon me from all sides and suck the blood out of me.

On the third day, however, soon after dinner, there was a click on the door. Two prison guards opened it and pushed a new inmate in.

"Welcome to Hilton Hotel," one of the guards said as he took the handcuffs off the new inmate. They laughed at their own joke while I gawked and rubbed my eyes in disbelief. The new inmate was no stranger. It was Jiro. Fate had once again brought us together, this time in a prison cell. It didn't surprise me that Jiro had ended up in prison. He had a habit of saying the wrong thing at the wrong time.

The instant the guards closed the door behind them, I said, "What did you do this time, Jiro? I hope you didn't say that thing again." I should have greeted him first. I should have allowed him to settle down; somehow, I couldn't help myself.

"Say what thing? What are you talking about?" Jiro mumbled in a low trembling voice. He was in a bad shape, with bruises all over his body.

The screaming sergeant and his team had put him through their Political Orientation and clobbered him with their truncheons.

"I am talking about your dreams. Did you have a new one?" I asked.

"No, I didn't." He looked around. "I need to go to the toilet first. My bladder is bursting open."

"The bucket is over there," I said and pointed.

Once Jiro relieved his bladder, he came back and lay down on his bed, still in no mood to talk. He kept moaning and feeling his bruises. Jiro, the hell-raiser, the man who couldn't wait to shoot his mouth on every subject, had nothing to say. Not a word. I felt sympathy for him and let him take his time.

After a while, he sat up on his bed and said, "I didn't have any dream this time. I did nothing. They just arrested me."

"You did nothing?" I asked, a little doubtful that he was being frank with me. "They must have accused you of something?"

"They accused me of not sleeping. That is why I am here."

"Not sleeping?"

"Yes, not sleeping. Hard to believe, isn't it?"

"I don't get it."

"Let me explain. One day, I was in the restaurant with Koosar and that old devil was taking cheap shots at me."

"What kind of cheap shots?"

"You know, about that dream I once had. He asked me if I had had it again. He was just teasing me. I should have just said no to him. Or even better, I should have kept my mouth shut, knowing that the Duki police agent was there listening. But I didn't. I took the bait and said, 'Are you out of your mind? I don't even sleep these days. I stay awake all night long.' And the next thing I knew I was under arrest."

"For what?"

"I told you. He arrested me for not sleeping. He said I was busy conspiring against the government and that is what kept me awake all night."

How ironic to arrest Jiro for not sleeping. I shook my head, flabbergasted by what I was hearing. They should have arrested him for anything else, but not that. I smiled somewhat sadly and finally asked him, "Didn't they know who you are?"

"What do you mean?"

"I mean: didn't they know what you could do in your sleep? Didn't they know that you are more dangerous and pose a greater threat to them asleep than awake at night?"

"Probably not."

"Instead of putting you in jail, they should have paid you money for not sleeping."

"You think so! You think they should have paid me money for that? Let me tell you something," Jiro hissed, a bit irritated. "My harmless dreams were nothing compared to what the Duki clansmen are doing these days. Do you know that no Sudi wife is safe from them?"

"What are you talking about?"

"Didn't you hear the rumours in town?"

"I am in jail, I am not in town."

"He is crazy about our wives."

"You mean, the Supreme Leader?"

"Yes, and he isn't the only one."

"But it could be only rumours. You think it is true?"

"Nowadays, the rumour is the truth. There is no difference. The truth went underground and only comes out in the form of rumours."

"The Supreme Leader has three wives and he wants more?"

"It is not about sex."

"Then what is it about?"

"It is psychological—to humiliate us, to take away our pride. They are fighting us not only with their guns but also with their penises. A Sudi clansman went to a government office to get a permit to build a fence around his home. The officer told him to bring his wife to him or he wouldn't sign the papers."

For a few minutes, I was lost for words. Then I said, "They used to take bribes in the good old-fashioned way. They used to take money."

"No longer. These days, they take bribes with their dicks."

I stood up, then sat down and stood up again. Unable to stay still, I paced the small cell in anger, going round and round like a cornered lion. I never thought I would see the day when such a violation could happen to a man, more so to a fellow Sudi clansman. I would rather lose my life than lose my wife to another man. There are things so outrageous that they should never happen in this world. This was the ultimate insult, a direct challenge to our manhood.

I stopped and faced Jiro. "What happened to our clan? What happened to us?" I said. "What happened to the sons of our wise men and heroes—Ina Egare, Abdi Dhagah, Waran Ade, Danbioogan, and Abdi Warabe? In our past, nobody has ever looked at our women this way and gotten away with it! How did we get to this stage?"

"You'd better lower your voice. They could hear you outside," Jiro cautioned.

I ignored his warning and continued: "This is unbelievable. The Sudi clan can't protect their wives. Do you know, in the past even the horses of the Duki clan would tremble and pee when they saw us?"

"Not really."

"You know nothing about our history, Jiro."

"I know our history. I only missed that part about their horses peeing at the sight of Sudi clansmen," Jiro said and giggled.

I looked away, disappointed. The man who had taken on presidents in his sleep didn't measure up to my expectations.

"How widespread is this? I mean, how many of them are engaged in this kind of thing?" I asked him.

"More than you can imagine. They tell each other about their conquests of Sudi girls and wives. They flaunt their sexual prowess. Just before they arrested me, a powerful commander, closely related to General Kahin, forced his way to the house of a Sudi clansman, abducted his wife and married her. And when the husband complained, he put him in jail."

I never thought I would hear something that appalling and immoral. How could that even be possible? How could a man marry a woman already married to another? What religion allowed him to do so? The religion of the Russians and communists?

Not knowing what else to do, I just kept gazing at the ceiling until the prison authorities switched off the lights and immersed the cell in total darkness. It was a long night, one with a lot of nightmares. Jiro didn't get much sleep either. The bugs kept him awake. He covered his entire body from head to toe with a sheet, but that didn't help. I could have told him.

In the morning, the daily routine started as usual with our meagre breakfast. Then we boarded the truck and were taken to the downtown area. Jiro sat next to me, but we didn't exchange a word during the whole trip, the awful stories he told me still on my mind.

As the truck approached our destination, I turned to Jiro and said, "About those despicable acts of the Duki men that you told me last night, I have to take a stand today. One way or another, I have to say something that needs to be said. I can't remain silent."

"And what are you going to do?"

"I am going to show them that we are men too, just like them, with two testicles as big as theirs."

"What exactly do you have in mind, Ali?" Jiro asked, sounding worried.

"Just wait and see," I said and looked away.

The truck came to a halt at the Duboto intersection in the eastern downtown area. The prison guards jumped down and issued orders, "Get down! Hurry up, we are working here today."

It was a busy street and people paused to watch us curiously. I didn't move and waited for the other inmates to go first. I had decided to be the last one out. As I hit the ground, I was naked from the waist down. My shorts had fallen to the ground, two steps away from me. While on board the truck, I secretly tore my shorts from the front all the way down until they were barely holding together. I planned to bare myself and face the prison guards and the public with my private parts in full display.

Having done so, I opened my mouth in fake surprise. Then I smiled nervously to create the impression of complete innocence. If they discovered that my actions were deliberate, I could end up in the Dark Cave.

The reaction in the street was varied. Some people laughed as if the sight of my naked genitals were a joke. Others looked away, horrified or embarrassed. As for the prison guards, their reactions at first were disorderly and chaotic. They just milled around confused and angry, uncertain how to handle a naked prisoner. One of them ran to the sergeant who was in charge to report. Meanwhile, the other inmates giggled like teenage girls. Jiro could not help laughing. The laughing and giggling stopped when the Duki sergeant approached. He looked at me, knitting his eyebrows in disbelief. He could have come a bit closer, but he stopped about ten steps away from me.

"What is this?" he shouted at me after a moment's silence.

"This is my penis. What were you expecting, sergeant?" I said loudly.

"He was expecting a vagina?" A homeless man in the front of the crowd shouted.

The sergeant ignored the comment and retorted, "I know it is your thing. But I am not asking you about that."

"Oh, you mean about the rest. These are my testicles, the two of them, sergeant," I said and pointed at them with my index finger. "Every man has two testicles and only two. Nobody has more than two, sergeant. The Sudi have two; the Tuwi have two; the men in Liverpool have two; the capitalists in America have two; the communists in Russia have two; the white men have two; the black men have two; the yellow men have two. Which makes us all equal. Do your people have more than two testicles, sergeant? Do the Duki have three or four testicles? That, of course, will make you better than us."

"Every man has only two, you fool," the sergeant fumed, his eyes looking past me and a spray of saliva shooting out of his mouth.

"So what is the problem, sergeant? Do some people have special ones?"

"Shut up and answer my question. Why are you naked? That is what I want to know, not how many testicles you have. I don't care how many testicles you or the man in Liverpool has."

"Oh, you are asking me about my nakedness," I said, feigning to misunderstand him.

"Yes, I am asking about that, you idiot!"

"My shorts got torn into two when I jumped from the truck, right in the middle. I threw them over there. I can get them back, but they are of no use now."

The sergeant took a quick look at the torn shorts. He seemed to be struggling to come up with a solution about me. Finally he walked up to the front of the truck and ordered the driver to return to the prison and bring back a pair of prison shorts. The trip to the prison and back would take at least half an hour. He had to wait with this embarrassing situation of a naked prisoner under his supervision.

In the street, a big crowd had gathered; people couldn't get enough of me and continued to stare. Girls giggled and laughed their hearts out. Children pointed their fingers at me. Women shyly covered their eyes with their hands, some of them clandestinely peeping between their fingers. The smiles on their faces betrayed them. The men looked at me with dismay, perhaps resenting the fact that male genitals were being exposed not at their best, in broad daylight, to the opposite sex.

All the while, I stayed close to the Duki sergeant, my nakedness in his face, as it were. If he moved away, I followed him. If he turned away, I walked around him to stay in his sights. There was no escaping me. I wanted him to take a good look at me and be able to say: there goes a man like me.

An old homeless-looking Sudi woman pushed her way through the crowd. She was well known in town, having degenerated into some kind of madness when her husband took a young woman as his second wife. She approached me cautiously, a big frown etched on her face. "Son, what is wrong with you?" she asked.

"Nothing," I said.

"Are you Sudi?"

I nodded.

She winked at me and turned to the sergeant. "You must be a Duki, sergeant," she said.

"Yes, I am," he retorted. "What do you want?"

"I knew you would be a Duki. I can see it from your swagger. I can see it from the sarcastic grin on your face. Now, sergeant, your clan has all the power in the country. You are the big bosses now. You can do whatever you want. We all know that. So what are you trying to prove here by showcasing a naked Sudi prisoner in the streets?"

"You are a crazy woman who doesn't know what she is talking about," the sergeant dismissed her angrily.

"Yes, I am a bit crazy. But you know who is crazier than me? A sergeant who strips the prisoners of their clothes and parades them in the streets naked."

"Nobody stripped him of his clothes," the sergeant shot back.

"Then why is he the only one naked, sergeant? Is this the new policy of your government? Marching naked Sudi men in the streets? He is a man like you with as much manhood as any other man. Look at him!"

"His manhood means nothing to me. In fact, I will take it away from him."

"And what does that mean, sergeant?"

"It means that he will have no more testicles or a penis to show to all the people in town. I will cut them off. He will never be able to claim that every man has two testicles. There will be exceptions. He will be an exception."

"How dare you talk that way or even think about something like that? And if you cut it from him, what will you do with it? Give it to your mother!"

"No, I will give it to you. You are the one who got crazy when you could no longer get it from your husband!"

She kept hurling insults at him until a policeman arrested her and led her away to a police station.

The sergeant didn't calm down. He was still furious and agitated. Like someone possessed, he walked back and forth in the street, his eyes looking away into the distance. Suddenly he stopped to lash out at me: "I will make you pay a heavy price for your stupid nakedness. Never again will you play that stupid game with me. Never again can you claim that you are equal to other men."

The crowd in the street was getting out of control. One of them threw a question at me. "Who took your wife from you?"

I should have ignored him. Instead, I took the bait and shouted back, "Men who have no respect for other men because they have power; men who think they can get away with anything because they have power; men who forgot what other men can do to them."

"Shut your big mouth and don't say anything." The sergeant confronted me once again, wagging his finger at me.

Finally the prison truck roared back into the street with a new pair of shorts for me. It had taken more than an hour. Meanwhile, the sergeant had had enough. The street was too crowded with people to do any cleaning. He probably also feared that some of the prisoners might use the cover of the crowds to try and escape. He threw the replacement shorts at me and instructed the guards, "We are going back. We can't do much today. Make sure all the prisoners are on board the truck."

On the way back, the mood of the guards was grim. They snapped at us without provocation. No doubt, things would be difficult when we returned to the prison. There would be retribution, and everybody knew who would bear the brunt of it.

Even Jiro was upset with me. "Why did you do that? Did you have to go that far and bare your genitals to the whole town?" he whispered into my ear.

"Who went too far?"

"You!"

"You dreamed of making love to the president of the country and I am the one who went too far?"

"All I am saying is that you put your life in danger unnecessarily."

"I don't call that unnecessary! I call it something else."

"What do you call it?"

"I call it standing up to abuse. I call it confronting the enemy even when you are down and out. I call it doing what you can to protect our honour."

The short conversation between us ended when the truck passed through the prison gates. The truck had barely come to a stop when the guards started issuing orders. "Get down! Get down!" they screamed. We got down quickly and they herded us back to our cells.

I had not been long in my cell when two guards came for me. I was not surprised. Just as I expected, they took me to the office of the prison director, the powerful man who ruled the prison, a man feared by the inmates and for good reason.

The director, sitting behind his desk, was a bulky man with plump cheeks in a country where most people were thin and tall. I wondered what he ate that made him so big and fat. He was a simple soldier when the Supreme Leader led the military coup and seized power. Then, he got promotions, one after another. He was the cousin of the Supreme Leader after all. That gave him the right to get whatever he wanted.

The director ignored me at first and I just stood there before him with the guards beside me. My eyes lingered on the four empty chairs in the office, two of them in front of his desk. As if I had a chance of sitting on them! Suddenly he looked up, focused his eyes on me and said, "You are a Sudi, aren't you?"

"Yes, I am," I replied.

"And you are in this prison because you insulted the Supreme Leader?"

"I insulted nobody. Not the Supreme Leader. And not anybody else."

"You opened your mouth as wide as you could in a restaurant full of people. Did that happen?"

"I yawned. That is what happened. That is why I am in jail."

"I bet you made that claim in the court and nobody believed you. So what makes you think that I will believe you now?"

I didn't respond and remained silent.

"What did you do before you worked in the restaurant?" he asked. My file was in front of him.

"I was a camel boy."

"And what happened to your camels?"

"I lost them," I said.

"Did you look for them?"

"I did. I couldn't find them."

"How many camels did you lose?"

"Sixty."

"And what were the marks on your camels?"

"A cross on the neck and a cross on the hip. Have you seen them?"

"Have I seen them?" he replied, his face beaming with a smile that had sarcasm written all over it.

"Yes," I responded and stared back at him.

"What do you think?" We both knew that a Duki clansman would neither admit seeing my camels nor give them back to me.

Once again, I didn't respond and remained silent.

Like a python going for the kill, he suddenly inflated himself. Then he snarled at me as though in attack mode and said, "Forget about your camels and tell me why you committed this second crime. Why did you take off your shorts and get naked in the middle of the town?"

"I didn't take off my shorts. They got torn by accident," I replied calmly.

"And you think I believe that nonsense?"

"But that is the truth. You have to believe it," I said and looked out through the window.

"Now hear me," he said, wagging his finger. "You have committed another crime. This has to stop. And the only way to accomplish that goal is to send you to the Dark Cave. I think the judge should have sent you there in the first place. They will take care of you there, believe me. They know how to deal with criminals like you. You will be sent there soon, in a few days. Until then, you will remain in your cell." He signalled to the guards to take me away.

The guards took me back to my cell, where Jiro was anxiously waiting for me.

"What happened? What did the director say?" he asked as soon as we were alone.

"Not good news. They will take me to the Dark Cave. And you know what that means," I said and threw myself on my bed.

"Did he say when they will take you to the Dark Cave?"

"In a few days. They take the prisoners in groups. I guess they are waiting for more inmates to go with me."

"This is not good news. It is what I feared. Do you now regret posing yourself naked in the centre of town?"

"Not a bit."

"Maybe you don't know much about the Dark Cave. It is a slaughter-house. They kill people there. Nobody comes back alive from there."

"Maybe I will escape before that happens."

"You can try, but it is risky."

"I am ready to face any risk and you know why?"

"No."

"Because escape is my only option. And when you have only one option, you have to take it."

I had already formulated a plan in my head. One more day of forced labour in town and I would make my move.

"If they capture you, you will be a dead man. You know that?" Jiro said.

"Don't worry. A man who is already wet should not be afraid of water," I said calmly.

10

It was going to be a long night. Who could fall asleep when faced with the prospect of the Dark Cave? I stayed awake all night. The bedbugs swarmed all over me, but they didn't hurt this time. Somehow, my body had become numb and lost all feeling. After what seemed to be an eternity, dawn finally broke and rays of light poured in through the small window.

Jiro woke up early and we stared at each other. No greetings, no good morning, and no wishes for peace. Greetings meant nothing at this point, nothing more than empty words. My fate depended on whether they would take me out to town that day or not. If they left me behind, it would be all over for me. Something that I had hated before turned out to be my saviour, my path for survival.

The prison guards banged on the door in the morning. I started praying. Not for paradise and its pleasures. Not for forgiveness about my past sins, but just to go to town with the other prisoners to sweep the streets. The fact that they didn't impose on me extra security boded well. It was an encouraging sign.

But, first, we had the meagre breakfast as usual. Then two prison guards, Red Eye and another fellow, opened the door and told us to get going. I had never been so eager to go out with the other prisoners and collect trash from the streets of the town. It was as if nothing had changed. My prayers had been answered. Nobody stopped me; nobody treated me differently. The daily routine unfolded as it always did. "So far so good," I said to myself and hurried towards the truck before anybody else.

The truck stopped at Salahlay Street in Hargis and we went to work. Garbage needed to be collected near a food market, and I worked harder than ever. I toiled like my whole life depended on it. And it did. The prison guards were happy. This was the calm before the storm, the suspense before the action. All the while I weighed the situation and waited for the moment the guards were distracted. The slightest chance and I would go for it.

Jiro stayed away from me, fearing that he would be accused of conspiring with me and having known all along about my plan. Good for him. He had to follow his instincts and do what he had to, to survive. I moved towards the end of the street to put some distance between me and Red Eye, the devil in the uniform. To outsmart him wasn't going to be easy.

Suddenly I saw Koosar coming towards me, two second-hand shirts thrown over his shoulders. He often hustled his goods in this part of town. Just to see him at this critical moment gave me a sense of comfort and encouragement. Koosar always brought out the best in me. He flashed a smile, showing the gap where his two front teeth were missing. He appeared as cheerful as always. No amount of hardships and trying times would ever put Koosar down.

"How are you doing, Ali?" he asked, when he was close enough.

"Not good," I mumbled in a low voice.

"What happened?"

"I have to escape now. I know it is risky, but I have to go. They will kill me if I don't."

Koosar had nothing more to say. He sensed that this was no time to ask for details. He passed me, exchanging greetings with Jiro along the way. Then he turned to Red Eye to try to sell the shirts to him.

Koosar's audacity never ceased to amaze me. Of all the people in town, he wanted to sell second-hand clothes to a prison guard on duty. And not any prison guard, but Red Eye himself.

"You want to buy this shirt? It is cheap and good," Koosar recited his familiar sales pitch, showing Red Eye one of the shirts.

Red Eye looked at Koosar but said nothing. He had been standing watching inmates collecting trash for about two hours. Bored, he just yawned.

"Hey, watch out, soldier," Koosar yelled at him. "That is a serious crime. Our people go to jail for what you just did. Sometimes, they even lose their lives and face the firing squad for that simple yawn. Now, do you want to buy this made-in-England shirt? It is the real thing."

"A good man took out your right eye. If you don't go away and get out of here, I will knock out the other one from you!" Red Eye bellowed.

"First of all, you yourself have no eyes to brag about. Second of all, do you know what I did to the man who took out my right eye?" Koosar countered, not the least intimidated.

"Cried and begged him for mercy?"

"No, men like me don't cry. I stabbed him and he almost died."

"What clan do you belong to?"

"Clan! Clan! Can we talk business? I am selling good shirts here. A wealthy man—may his soul rest in peace—used to own these shirts, a man who never bought low-quality clothes. Look! Made in England, not Taiwan."

By distracting Red Eye, Koosar did for me the greatest favour. He gave me once-in-a-lifetime chance. I took a few quick steps further towards the end of the street, pretending to look for trash to collect. Then I made a mad dash, turned the street corner in the blink of an eye, and almost knocked a young man to the ground. I melted into a crowd of shoppers. Then I slowed down, took off my prison shirt, threw it into a trash bin, and kept walking. A pair of shorts was all I was wearing. But so were the manual workers all around the town in the baking sun. I took brisk, long strides to get as far away from the guards as possible, and headed towards Koosar's shack.

Thanks to the fat prison director's mistake in threatening me with the Cave, I got back my freedom and my life. He had imposed no extra security upon me. What was he thinking? That I would just wait for the day when they beat me to death in the Dark Cave? I continued walking, feeling proud and victorious, until I reached Koosar's shack, located in Shacktown, in the eastern outskirts. The shack was locked and I waited for him in the shade of a big tree nearby. Boys were playing soccer in an open space not far from me.

While watching the boys, I wondered if Koosar had succeeded in selling the shirt to Red Eye. Just the thought of it made me smile. It would be a miracle if he pulled it off.

It was after sunset when Koosar returned home. The moment we saw each other we started laughing. Then Koosar unlocked the door and let me in.

"When did you get here?" he asked. "Your escape was in the news at noontime and police are looking for you everywhere. I saw them in the restaurant twice."

"I came here straightaway," I said.

Inside the one-room shack, two small mats lay side by side. One mat served as the bedroom, the other, the living room. I sat on the living room mat. Not the least bit worried about the risk of hiding a fugitive, Koosar welcomed me warmly. When he realized that I was starving, he decided that he had to do something.

"I will go back to the restaurant, speak to the owner, and get you something to eat," he said and hurried off.

An hour later, he returned with a dish of goat meat and rice. My cousin Isman, whom I hadn't seen since my day in court, was with him. We greeted each other warmly and discussed family matters for a short while. We soon got on to the current situation in the country and the Duki government's unrelenting attacks on us.

Two days ago, Isman said, late in the evening the Special Forces had rounded up thirty-seven Sudi boys from the streets. They put them in a truck and took them to a desolate area west of town. There the boys were ordered to get down and made to stand shoulder-to-shoulder some distance from the truck. When they were arrayed as ordered, the soldiers opened fire. Like dry leaves dropping from a tree, our boys fell to the ground on top of each other. Some of them died instantly; others struggled for a moment, gasping for their last breath in life. Their blood, still warm, flowed from their dead bodies and soaked the parched soil. A soil desperate for moisture and rain got the blood of our people instead.

"Then what happened?"

"The soldiers dug a large pit and dumped the bodies inside."

"How come you found out all this? Has one of the soldiers talked and told the story?"

"No, one of our boys survived. He pretended to be dead and hid among the dead bodies. When the soldiers were gone, he got up and escaped."

We became silent, each with his own thoughts about the misery of the Sudi. After a while, Koosar packed up the plates and spoons and took them outside to wash. When he came back in, Isman stood up to go home. Just before he stepped out, he turned around and said, "Have you heard about the birth of your son?"

"No, I hadn't heard. I'm happy to hear it," I said, though I couldn't help wondering in what kind of world my son had been born. If only I could see him and hold him in my hands. A father and a son not knowing one another, how wrong and disappointing! But somehow, I felt confident that he would grow up to be a fighter for his clan and his family. And Allah forbid, if they killed me, the Duki had still to contend with one more man in the family.

But for now, I had to make a decision about what to do next. To stay too long in Koosar's shack didn't seem right. Something could go wrong. The police could find where I was hiding. I had to go.

I turned to Koosar. "What do you think I should do? I don't want to stay here more than a night or two. My presence here in your place isn't good for you. It could endanger your life."

"Son, there won't be any problem." He became thoughtful, then added, "For a few days, at least. And what will you do? You will do what all the other Sudi men have done who escaped from this government. They went abroad: Europe, America, Canada, Australia and many other places in the world. You can do the same."

"You want me to flee? You want me to go all the way to Europe? Before I avenge my father? Only a coward would do that, Koosar," I argued vehemently. I couldn't help feeling both sad and angry.

"It's not fleeing. It's a tactical retreat. It is what you do in a war sometimes," Koosar argued back. "You will avenge the killing of your father at the right time. This is not the right time."

"When is the right time?"

"When our clan starts to fight back."

"And when will that be?"

"We don't know yet. But it will happen one day. That is for sure."

"How far away are these countries that you want me to go to?"

"That is not really important. You know why? These airplanes can take you and bring you back in hours from the farthest corner of the world."

To run away went against everything I believed in. How could I live with myself afterwards? But to stay was also foolhardy. They would capture me and kill me. There were no good options. I thought long and hard about the difficult choice that I faced. In the end, I decided to go along with Koosar's suggestion. I could come back when the time was right, as Koosar had pointed out.

In the morning, when I woke up, I was alone in the room. Koosar had already left. As usual, he would have gone to the restaurant early in the morning for his cup of tea. I looked around his shack for any food. He had nothing much there, only a jug of water. I drank some water and went back to sleep until noon.

During the day, Koosar did what he had always done. He hustled his second-hand clothes in the streets. But he had one more thing on his mind that day. He secretly searched for information about the routes taken by those who had escaped. He closely worked with Isman and they sought advice from some Sudi clansmen. They did it all in a discreet way, careful not to tip off the government spies who seemed to be everywhere with their long ears and sensitive noses.

In the evening, he returned with a bundle of new clothes for me, two pants and two shirts. Isman, who didn't accompany him this time, had bought the clothes. But something else drew my attention the moment I opened the door to him. The sweet smell of camel meat wafted into the room. Having had nothing to eat all day long, I ate the food quickly and was munching the last piece of the meat when somebody knocked on the door. I stopped chewing and looked at Koosar. Who would come to see him in his shack at night? A woman who visited him at night? The ghosts of the dead people whose clothes he sold? Or a policeman who had come to arrest me? Koosar scrambled to his feet and went to the door. He opened it slowly. A woman wearing an all-white dress, the traditional sign of mourning, stood in the doorway. She had come to sell him a large bag of clothes belonging to her late husband.

Koosar quickly negotiated with her the prices of the clothes, without even a word of condolence to her. To him, death was something normal, as routine as his cup of tea in the morning. It was his business and his life. He struck a deal with the widow and she left.

The image of the widow in white lingered in my mind. If I fell into the hands of the Duki government, my wife would wear a similar dress. Just the thought of it convinced me that I had made the right decision to leave the country. I looked at Koosar and said, "I am ready to escape to a foreign country. Just tell me what to do."

"Yes, let's talk about that," Koosar said slowly, scratching his short grey beard. "Many of our clansmen have already been through this. You will do the same. You walk out of this town on a dark moonless night until you reach Gebel. Gebel is only twenty miles west of here. From there, you can find a truck that will take you to Djibouti."

"And when I reach Djibouti, then what?"

"There is a community of Sudi clansmen there. They will help you. They know what to do and how to work out a means for you to go to Europe, Canada, America or whatever other country they find for you."

"So, first I have to go to Djibouti?"

"Yes."

"I don't have money to pay the fare for the truck. Can I walk to Djibouti?"

"No, you can't do that," Koosar said. "Djibouti is too far. I have some money for you. Your cousin, Isman, collected it from our people."

I decided to leave right then. There was no reason for me to stay any longer. It was eight o'clock in the evening, and a dark cloudy night, the best time to walk through the crowds in the streets. Later at night in deserted streets I would be conspicuous and an easy target for the police.

It wasn't easy to bid goodbye to Koosar. I said to him, "I will miss you. Allah willing, we will see each other one day. I know we will. One way or another, I will find my way back to this town. Nothing can keep me away. I have a debt to collect, a debt of human blood."

I stepped out of the shack, feeling guilty that I couldn't bid farewell to my cousin Isman as well.

With the utmost caution, I moved through the back streets and dimly lit areas of the town, avoiding security lights and bright spots. Like a wild animal, I sought refuge in dark places, among the shadows of trees and buildings. Anyone in the street could blow the whistle on me. So many enemies to watch out for: the ordinary policemen, the multiple government agents, the fanatical dimwits who called themselves the eyes and ears of the government, and above all, the ordinary Duki clansmen.

I walked briskly through the downtown area. The crowded streets soon gave way to quiet neighbourhoods in the western outskirts of the town. I didn't slow down and kept walking until I was out of the city, at around midnight. On top of a hill, I stopped to take one last look at Hargis. A thick mist had descended on it, yet the lights still glittered from one corner to the other. An exceptionally bright light started blinking as though saying farewell to me. My eyes welled up, and I felt a lump in my throat. I turned around and went on my way.

Danger lurked all around me—poisonous snakes, wild animals, long thorns on the ground, and sharp twigs. Foxes howled and hyenas wailed in the distance. I kept handy the two simple weapons I carried, a wooden club and a small knife Koosar had given me. Despite all the danger out there, I still felt safer here than in the open spaces and the roads where I could come face to face with the police.

I embarked on a long journey and left behind everything I had ever known, for an unknown future. Just the thought of it made me uneasy. Would I ever again see my wife, my son, my sister, my cousins, and Koosar? Would I succeed in coming back to my town? More than anybody else, I thought about my dead parents, remembering the days I used to enjoy the company of my father and how it all ended after Duki men killed him. I should have done something about it and shed the blood of his killers. How long could I live with this sense of failure?

For a few long hours, I trudged along the dark and dangerous terrain. Finally, I came across an open grassy land. Burning firewood and lights could be seen here and there, an obvious sign of settlements in the area. I decided to stop and rest for a while. The moment I lay down beside a thick bush, I fell asleep.

Sometime in the morning, the bleating of sheep startled me. I stood up and looked around. The sun had already risen and sheep were grazing nearby, a teenage girl wearing a white skirt tending them. I approached her, exchanged greetings, and asked her how far it was to Gebel. It turned out that I only had to go over a hill to the west to reach it.

The moment I reached the hilltop, Gebel came into view. I hurried down and made my way into the small town. Its streets buzzed with all sorts of activities. I slipped into one of the teashops for a cup of tea and something to eat. Every fibre of my body yearned for food and rest. The short nap among the bushes hadn't helped much. I sat down and before I realized it, I yawned. I looked around me, alarmed that I couldn't act in time and prevent it. Luckily, nobody came to arrest me. This time I got away with it.

A waiter came to serve me and I ordered my favourite breakfast: two pieces of lahoh treated with ghee and a cup of tea. I ate it in haste, drained the cup of tea, and bolted out. Lingering around or striking a conversation with the people there was out of the question.

In the streets, the autumn winds were blowing hard. It whipped up the fine dust in the streets and made it hard to see. To avoid breathing in the dust, people covered their faces with a piece of cloth. I did the same. The autumn winds gave me a reason to hide my face from lurking government agents. I got help from where I least expected.

I walked around a bit and quickly found the truck station. Three men and two women stood there. They were having an animated discussion about the price of maize and how it had soared.

"The trucks to Djibouti, do they leave from here?" I asked them.

"Yes," said a middle-aged man with a large bushy moustache, before resuming his conversation.

I sat quietly on a tree stump a few steps away from them.

I hadn't waited long before the truck roared into the empty station, fully loaded with bags of coal and passengers. It had barely stopped before the driver jumped out and asked, "Are you guys going to Djibouti?"

"Yes," we all said.

"Okay, you have to pay me the fare, fifteen shillings per person."

One by one, we paid him the fare. After shoving the money into his pocket, he instructed us to get on board. I squeezed myself tightly between an old man with a long beard and a heavy-set woman, who made no attempt to accommodate me. I could hardly breathe, let alone move my arms and legs. We thought it might get better once the truck was on the road. It didn't. For hours, we suffered silently. In an attempt to make the best of a bad situation, some of the passengers tried to entertain the rest of us by telling stories. When the stories held our interest, we felt a little better. Other times we didn't.

The truck went humming all day with no end in sight. It was as if we were going to the end of the earth. A road full of cracks and potholes made things a lot more difficult for us. Whenever the truck went over one of those potholes, we would get tossed into the air, only to land on the hard sacks of coal. We moaned and grunted. We cursed. We feared getting thrown overboard and screamed at the driver. He ignored us and kept on. He was driving too fast on a road full of cracks and potholes.

Beside the road, the land looked bare and unforgiving. Not a drop of rain had fallen on it for years. Not a single living creature could be seen anywhere. Only a dry leafless acacia tree appeared in the distance once in a while.

The sun began to set and a difficult day came to an end. We expected the night to be even more difficult. It would definitely be a long one. No chance that we would get any sleep. In the limited space, the passengers huddled together and slumped over each other. Even the few women among us had had enough and let themselves fall into the arms of strangers, their breasts and cheeks pressing against the faces of men too tired to care.

The distressing night, the night from hell, continued with no end in sight. It proved to be longer than any other night I had ever lived through. Just when I had lost all hope, a ray of light finally appeared over the horizon and the sun rose. If only the truck stopped somewhere! If only we could get a chance to stretch our arms and legs for a moment!

Around noontime, our prayers were answered. A small town came into view ahead of us. They called it Addeh. Those who knew the area told us that the Djibouti border lay only a few miles beyond Addeh. The end of a gruelling journey was finally in sight.

The driver parked the truck in front of a restaurant in an old brick building. He had barely switched off the engine when all the passengers tried to scramble out. Some of us collapsed in our first attempt. We could barely stand up. We limped and staggered into a warm inviting restaurant where roasted meat and tea were served. Any kind of food would have been good enough and tasted delicious to me at the time. For half an hour, I munched the meat and washed it down with hot tea.

We had barely finished the food when the driver told us that it was time to go. He was determined to leave as soon as possible and ordered those who had legal documents to get on board the truck. The rest of us he couldn't take any further. The truck had to cross the border and go through Djibouti immigration. This was a surprise to me. I had no clue what legal documents meant, let alone those required at the border. And so I found myself left behind in the middle of nowhere. I didn't know what to do. Certainly, I couldn't stay in Addeh for long. The authorities in this small town would soon find out about me. Desperately I approached one of the passengers left behind like me and asked, "What are we going to do? How are we going to reach our destination?"

"Djibouti isn't far from here. We have to walk and sneak into the country under the cover of night. That was my plan all along," the man, who was about my age, said.

"Is it easy? You think it will work?" I asked.

"Hopefully, it will work. I and some others are hiring a guide. You can join us, and pay a fee. If not, I don't know what to tell you. You can go back to the place you came from."

The guy didn't mince words. He was as blunt and tough as they come. I thanked him and joined the group; the fee was ten shillings. Going back was definitely not an option for me.

The guide was a tall slim guy with broad shoulders. After pocketing the money, he took us to an empty spot behind the restaurant to talk to us about the venture ahead. "I will be walking in front of you," he said, sounding like a warrior giving a pep talk to his fighters before attacking an enemy.

"Follow me and keep up with me. No talking, no noise, and above all else, no smoking. If you hear or see anything suspicious, don't run, because you can't outrun them. Just lie down, take cover, and don't move, even if a snake is about to bite you. You have a better chance of evading them that way than running like a scared chicken. Is that clear?"

We were eleven men and two women, and we all nodded.

"Then let's go," he said and waved his hand as a signal to follow him.

It was late in the evening, hot and windy. We marched in tandem and followed our guide, barely keeping up with him, as it was not easy to walk fast on moving sand. The simple act of putting one foot after the other became a trying experience. I began to sweat. To make matters worse, a strong wind blew the fine sand into our eyes. Two times I had to stop, unable to see ahead.

As we trudged along, we heard a sound and we all hit the ground at the same time. With my belly pressing on the ground, I looked around for a sign of danger. Had the border guards detected us? Was my attempt to escape about to end in failure? Was it the Dark Cave for me, after all? Luckily, we didn't hear the sound again, there was nothing but blowing wind, and after waiting a little longer, we stood up and dusted ourselves, a bit shaken and somewhat ashamed. We never found out what caused the sound. Fleeing rabbits might have spooked us.

Sometime after midnight, we finally came upon the wire fence that separated the two countries and slipped under it.

For a moment, I lingered at the border, looking back at the country I had left. If only I could say farewell to my people, my clansmen, my wife and son. Choking with emotion, I turned around and ran after the group. Soon, the bright lights of Djibouti City were visible, glittering in the distance.

At the break of dawn, we sneaked into the city and quickly dispersed to blend in with the locals. I was alone in a city and among people I had never seen before. Our guide had told me which way to go to find my clansmen. I walked towards the southern part of the city, crossing several blocks, until I came to the Sudi neighbourhood. I had barely sat down in a teashop when a man approached me.

"What clan do you belong to?" he asked.

"Sudi," I answered.

"I know all the Sudi in Djibouti. How come we never met?"

"I just came to town."

Other Sudi men, who had heard our conversation, pulled their chairs closer. Soon I was surrounded by ten men, all eager to hear news about our people back home. The traditional hospitality of our people kicked in and they ordered breakfast for me.

Having had no proper sleep for two days, I could hardly keep my eyes open; but I couldn't disappoint them and started relating the story of our people and the dangerous situation they faced back home. They quietly listened, their anger and agitation palpable. They clenched their teeth, bit their lips, and twirled their moustaches. Djibouti was their home now, but they were Sudi and concerned about their kinsfolk. The misfortune of any Sudi person was their misfortune. The suffering of any Sudi clansman was their suffering.

I still had more tragic stories to tell about our people back home when I started to nod off and almost fell asleep on the chair. They took me to a room where I slept the rest of that day and the night.

When I woke up, I wanted to go out. But my clansmen told me it wasn't safe for me to be out during daytime. The Djibouti police could stop me in the street and arrest me. So I stayed in the room during the days and only ventured out at night.

Meanwhile, they went to work to finance my escape. Within a matter of days, my clansmen had not only managed to collect money from every Sudi man in Djibouti, but also got me a passport, a visa, and an air ticket to New York. How they made all this happen in such a short time, I would never know. When, late one night, four Sudi men handed me my passport and airline ticket, it was time to go.

I had to fly to Paris and from there to New York. The names of these cities were familiar to me from the accounts I had heard from my seaman cellmate in Hargis. I also heard them from the evening news on the radio. Two Sudi clansmen, Abdulla and Farah, accompanied me to the airport and showed me how to check in. With me was a small suitcase I had purchased, filled with some clothes donated by my hosts. At the immigration wicket, I handed my passport to the officer, while my friends waited at the side, in case anything went wrong. The officer started checking my passport while chatting in earnest with his fellow officers.

"You are a resident in Djibouti?" he asked.

"Yes," I said.

"Where is your family?"

"They are home. I will return in a month."

He flipped a few pages, then put a stamp on it and gave it back to me.

With my stamped passport in my hands, it was time to go. My two clansmen shook hands with me, embraced me, and left.

Having boarded the plane, I sat on a chair, excited and anxious. I had no idea that the inside of an airplane was so luxurious and large. Airplanes in the sky looked like birds with no hint of what was inside them. The plane took off with alarming speed. Higher and higher it flew. When I looked down from the window, I saw scattered clouds under me. I had never imagined in my wildest dreams that one day I would reach the clouds. Not only had I reached the clouds, I had surpassed them. I looked up. No clouds. I looked down. White clouds. It seemed as if the sky and the earth had switched places.

From the moment the airplane flew, I was missing something. The ground that had been under feet all my life was no more. Like a tree without roots or a house without a foundation, I felt unhinged and vulnerable. So many things could go wrong and my life was hanging on the balance. The airplane could plunge into a cloud of rain or smash into a mountain. The pilot could get lost in the sky, an empty space with no guideposts. And Allah forbid if that happened, whom could the pilot turn to and ask for directions? Angels in the sky? The falcons and the birds?

For the other passengers, it was a different story. They seemed to be enjoying the ride and having a great time. They acted as if they were in their homes. They shared conversations. They exchanged jokes and laughed together. Some stood up and walked around. A few even slept in their chairs peacefully. How could they feel so comfortable and relaxed while flying through the skies inside a big bird made by man? How could they be so complacent high up in the sky? Feeling sick and distraught, I prayed for a safe passage.

Fortunately, my worst fears didn't come true. The pilot didn't get lost in the skies. He did not smash the airplane into a mountain. Instead, he landed it safely at the Paris airport. The moment the airplane came to a halt, the passengers grabbed their bags and went to the front and down a ladder. I did the same, and what a relief it was when I stood again on solid ground and followed the other passengers into a big hall.

It was brilliantly lit and busy with people hurrying to and fro, many of them pushing carts of luggage. There were signs and posters everywhere, showing beautiful people. It was enough to make me feel dizzy. I drifted along in panic. Anybody I came across, I showed my ticket. They all pointed the same direction and I kept going. But then came a woman with long red hair who, through hand gestures, told me to go in the opposite direction. Not sure what to do now, I sat down on an empty seat, simply watching people go by. I had never seen so many white people before, though I had seen some in Djibouti.

Finally, a woman wearing all blue and a hat noticed my predicament and started to talk to me. I shook my head to let her know that I didn't speak her language. Luckily, she understood me, looked at my ticket, and signalled to me to follow her. We went to an office where they quickly took a look at my passport and ticket. Then she led me out of the building into the open, and towards an airplane, where people were already boarding. Another few minutes and I would have missed my flight and been stranded at the Paris airport.

The plane took off, and again I experienced that feeling of unease and foreboding, of being uprooted from the ground and the earth where I belonged. At least, on the previous flight, I could sometimes catch a glimpse of land when I looked down. This time a limitless sea lay below me. I never thought so much water and sea existed on this earth. What kind of rain pouring years and years could bring about all this water? No doubt the sharks that the seaman had told me about would be hiding in those waters. And Allah forbid, if the airplane crashed and plunged into that sea, the sharks would be there, waiting for me. How could one escape from their fangs? Not a tree in that sea to climb up to save myself. Not a rock to latch on to or mountaintop to seek refuge on. A woman in uniform came to bring food, but I only took the tea, which I found very weak, and a roll of bread.

After what felt like an eternity, the airplane started to descend. It was late in the afternoon. Down below, I could see land again. Farms, settlements, and big houses appeared. Trucks and cars sped on a smooth highway. It all looked so organized. And then came the tall buildings, a forest of them rising up, the like of which I had never seen but only imagined, after the stories told to me by the seaman.

The moment the plane hit the ground and came to a halt, I sighed with relief. I followed the other passengers out. No doubt, there would be more checking points and more immigration officers. I had to face them with a passport obtained through the work of my clansmen. It didn't bother me much. If I had survived those air flights, I could survive anything.

At the immigration wicket, I handed in my passport. The officer flipped the pages, and after a while stamped the passport and gave it back with a welcoming smile. I put the passport back into my pocket and went into a hall with moving counters that carried bags and suitcases. I spotted my small bag and was about to grab it when I noticed a man walking towards me. I immediately recognized him as a fellow Sudi. He had come to pick me up. The Sudi clansmen in Djibouti had contacted him so that he could help me out in New York. We exchanged greetings, then after a short conversation we walked together towards the exit.

As we got close to the glass door, it slid open. I looked around. Nobody stood there who could have opened it.

"Who opened the door for us?" I asked.

"A computer," said Ahmed.

I went back inside the building to see what happened. Again the door opened by itself to let me out, and I asked Ahmed, "Is Computer one of our Sudi clansmen?"

"No, a computer is a machine. It doesn't belong to any clan."

"But at least it knows that we are Sudi, doesn't it?"

"No, computers don't know anybody. They just do what they are supposed to do. They open doors for people. They have many other functions as well."

"What a nice fellow! If computers belonged to clans, this one would definitely be Sudi."

"Unfortunately, they don't."

For a while, I stood and watched other passengers coming out of the airport, and laughed with amazement every time the door opened with no human hand involved. They could call them computers or whatever they wanted. To me, this was magic and miracle put together.

I would have liked to watch this a bit more, but I didn't want to keep Ahmed waiting. So I left with him. When we arrived in the city and got out of the taxi, we stopped at a place where Ahmed received money from what looked like a wall. It was something so strange that I couldn't believe my eyes.

I said nothing and merely shook my head, wondering what else the computer could do until we reached his apartment. So many black Americans lived in the area around his apartment. They probably belonged to some weird clans I knew nothing about. In the sitting room of his house, we relaxed and ate rice and meat that Ahmed brought from a restaurant nearby. At the same time, we had a serious discussion about what I had to do from here onwards.

My clansman did most of the talking. He said that I had to make a decision and choose one of two options. I could claim refugee status in the United States or I could proceed to Canada and claim the same thing there. "You have better chances of being accepted as a refugee in Canada," he opined. He seemed to know what he was talking about, and I went along with him.

"How far is Canada from here?" I asked.

"Not far from us. Canada is just to the north of us."

"What language do they speak?"

"If you go to Toronto, they speak the English language."

The next morning, I left New York on a bus. Ahmed accompanied me. The bus was luxurious, unlike those I had seen in Hargis, and heated. We passed busy streets with all kinds of shops; I was aware that the buildings were tall, but I could not see the tops of them. Finally we were outside New York, and I was amazed at how wide the highways were, and how busy. I didn't see a patch of forest or desert, everywhere seemed inhabited. Once we reached the border, I said goodbye to Ahmed, who caught a bus that was heading back to New York. At the Canadian immigration desk, an officer interrogated me. I answered all the questions through an interpreter, after which she provided me with a document.

I could now enter Canada as a refugee claimant. I put the document in my small bag and took a bus to Toronto. There was no money in my pocket after paying the bus fare. Not even a cent. A small piece of paper in my pocket gave me a sense of security, though. It had the telephone number of two Sudi clansmen in Toronto. Ahmed gave the piece of paper to me before he bid me farewell and left me. My future in Canada depended on that piece of paper.

11

THE BUS ARRIVED IN TORONTO and pulled into a busy and noisy terminal. It had barely stopped when the passengers grabbed their luggage and headed for the door. I did the same. But what then? Where should I go and what to do?

I needed help getting in contact with my clansmen. So I took out the piece of paper with the telephone number from my pocket and showed it to the driver of the bus. He looked at it and said something. I shook my head and waved my hands to let him know that I did not speak his language. Somehow, he understood what I was saying. He stood up and walked to a nearby telephone location, the piece of paper still in his hand. He dialed the number and held the phone to his ear for some time, probably wondering how a man who couldn't make a telephone call would survive in this city. He remained silent for a long time. Apparently, nobody was answering the phone. After a while, he gave up. Flailing his hands, he handed the piece of paper back to me.

I nodded my head in appreciation for his efforts and left the bus station. Not knowing what else to do, I started walking down the streets. A feeling of apprehension and uncertainty weighed on me. I had to try to contact my Sudi clansmen again. But what if they had left the country or moved to another city in Canada? I was facing a situation I had never anticipated.

As I drifted through the cold streets, I saw people with different features, white, brown, black, all in a hurry. Where were they going? The hustle and bustle in the streets was mind-boggling. My eyes wandered in all directions, looking for my clansmen. As if I had a chance to find them that way in a city with more people than the Duki and Sudi clans put together! Never before had I seen so many people and felt so alone.

Once, I crossed a busy street at the wrong moment and a speeding car almost ran over me. Had I not jumped out of the way at the last moment, it would have been the tragic end of a Sudi clansman for nothing.

All of a sudden, cold white stuff started falling from the sky and my first day in Canada became more complicated. I looked up at the sky. It seemed to be disintegrating into small white bits. Apparently, this was the snow that the seaman had talked to me about, and it kept coming down. Never before had I witnessed anything like this. Back home, only rain fell from the sky.

Within no time, a layer of the white stuff blanketed the ground, turning it so slippery that the simple act of walking became a risky venture. I watched my steps and walked cautiously. As careful as I was, I slipped and fell flat on my face. I lay there for a while, feeling numb and disoriented. It took me some time and effort, but I finally managed to scramble on to my feet. Meanwhile, I cursed those who had caused me all this trouble—General Kahin and the Duki clan.

While the snow kept falling, the sun began to set and a cold night closed in on the city. The bitter cold and hunger were taking a toll on me and I started to shiver. My teeth chattered, my nose ran, and my feet felt numb. I had to find a way out of this predicament before I froze to death in this Canadian city.

To rest and collect my thoughts, I took refuge in a shelter beside a road. A bearded white old man with a tattered overcoat sat in a corner. He didn't even notice my presence, but kept humming to himself and making other noises. Suddenly he looked at me and said something.

I shook my head to signal to him my inability to understand his language. But he continued talking to me. It was no use listening to him and I looked away. He got upset and raised his voice. He probably thought I was ignoring him or something.

Other people came into the shelter, boarded buses that arrived, and left; but the old man and I stayed put. It seemed that neither of us had a place to go. Like me, the old man was down on his luck. Gradually, the crowds on the street thinned.

Once again, the old man spoke to me. But this time, his tone sounded sympathetic. He had probably figured out my inability to speak English and the fact that I had found myself in a world I knew nothing about. One desperate man to another and the empathy they had for each other came through. He stood up and gave me a signal to follow him.

I hesitated for a moment. It was hard to imagine how a man with tattered clothes and a shabby appearance could help me. He couldn't even help himself. But then, what did I have to lose? I followed him. Along the way, he stopped at an intersection and stretched out his hand to passersby, begging for money. I watched and waited.

The men mostly ignored him. He had better luck with the women. Two ladies felt sympathy for him and dropped a few coins in his hand. With the money, he went into a grocery store and bought a packet of cigarettes. He took one out, lit it, inhaled strongly and exhaled. Smiling for the first time, he resumed walking. I continued following him. When we had crossed two more streets, we came upon a grey, three-storey building. He went inside and signaled to me to come inside too. I did with utmost caution.

Inside, men in worn-out clothes, with disheveled hair and tired looks, sat and stood everywhere, even on the stairs. It seemed to be a place for the poor of the city, those with nothing of their own. A strong black man in his thirties was in charge of the place. When he found out that I could not speak English, he paid me special attention and allocated a bed for me in a room already occupied by six other men.

Without taking off my clothes or my shoes I snuggled into the warm bed. I had eaten nothing since my breakfast in New York. I was starving and my stomach growled: a cry for help that wouldn't be answered. Not until I found my clansmen in Toronto. Not with that cold freezing wind blowing outside. I continued to hear it slamming against the trees, hissing in the night. Gradually I drifted into sleep.

Sometime in the middle of the night, a commotion woke me up. I sat up on my bed, then went to the door and peeped out to see what was going on. The supervisor was engaged in a heated argument with another man. He tried to push him out of the building. The man resisted, and a scuffle ensued. A lot of shoving, kicking, and grunting. I watched the fight and wondered if the two men belonged to different clans. Then I recalled what the seaman had told me, that people in Europe, America, and Canada lived as free individuals and not as clansmen.

I slipped back into sleep despite the fact that the man on my right side was constantly moaning and the man on my left was having an angry conversation with himself. Early in the morning, a loud voice echoed through the building. It was the supervisor, telling everybody to wake up. The men didn't like it one bit. They cursed and grumbled. Where would they go at this early hour in the morning? It was still dark out-side. But they had no choice and dragged themselves out of bed, spitting curses; some even shouted back.

Nobody took a bath, nobody shaved, and nobody brushed his teeth. We went downstairs into a big room furnished with tables and chairs. Half asleep and yawning, the men slumped onto the chairs. Only when the breakfast—an egg sandwich and a steaming cup of coffee—was served did they fully wake up. I munched on the sandwich and drank the coffee, quietly thanking whoever provided us with this breakfast

After their breakfast, the men left the place and shuffled off in the direction of downtown, where the tallest buildings were. I didn't go with them, but approached the supervisor, who was standing in the corridor at the window outside his office. I had to make one more attempt to con-tact my clansmen. I prayed that it would work this time; I sure didn't want to sleep in this shelter another night.

For the second time, I took the piece of paper out of my pocket, and I showed it to the supervisor. I resorted to hand gestures and signals to make him understand what I wanted, and he understood me immedi-ately and dialed the number using the telephone next to him. Someone answered the phone and the supervisor handed it to me.

"Who are you?" the voice at the other end spoke, in our own language.

"I am a Sudi," I said, thrilled to hear my native language.

"And where are you?"

"I am here in Toronto."

"Where in Toronto? Do you know the address of the place you are calling from?"

"I am near a tall building."

The man chuckled. "There are tall buildings everywhere in Toronto. Let me talk to somebody who can give me the address, and we will come and pick you up from there."

I handed back the phone to the supervisor. They spoke together in English and he provided the address of the place. From there on, I just had to wait. I stood outside on the sidewalk. Not knowing which direction they were coming from, I kept looking both ways.

After two hours of waiting I saw them, two men coming towards me. I could tell they were Sudi. I could recognize a Sudi from a mile away. The mere sight of Mohamed and Jama, as they were called, warmed my heart. Like brothers who have not seen each other for a long time, we exchanged warm greetings; then we walked briskly together to a location where a lot of cars were parked.

I had no doubt in my mind that they would welcome me into their home and take care of me until I could stand on my feet. It was what one clansman did for another, particularly at a time when our clan was under the gun of the Duki clan. It was something we owed to one another. No longer would I have to worry about getting lost in the streets of this big Canadian city and starving to death.

But one thing they couldn't help me with was the freezing cold. I would often be shivering. "Why is this country so cold?" I asked them as I buried my hands in my armpits to keep them warm.

"Their sun is not strong enough. It is a weak one," Jama explained.

"They have a different sun from the one we have back home?" I asked, not sure what he meant.

"Yes, they do. Look up at the sky and see for yourself. It is nothing like our sun," Jama said and smiled.

I found it hard to believe that there was more than one sun in the world, but I looked up at the sky anyway. Not a trace of the sun anywhere. It was all grey and cloudy up there.

When my eyes came back to earth, I noticed that my breath was as visible as hot steam from a boiling kettle. The breaths of other people in the street looked the same. Somewhat alarmed, I turned to Jama once again and asked, "What happens to our breath? It is like we are all smoking cigarettes."

Jama chuckled. "Nothing to worry about. It is the cold weather turning everything white: breath takes the colour of smoke, water changes to white snow. Even people are not spared. Look at these white Canadians. You think they were like that from the beginning?"

"You mean they once looked like us? You mean the cold weather turned them white?"

"Yes."

"And why didn't you turn white like them?"

"You have to stay long enough."

We reached the car, which was a small red one, and I got into the back seat. Inside, it was colder than outside, and all my bones shook. "It will get warm soon," Jama said, and I felt warm air blowing at my feet.

Mohamed drove the car westwards on a busy road called Bloor Street. After we had crossed so many streets, he turned right, then left, and soon arrived at a four-storey building. He parked the car and we went inside and into a box called an elevator, which took us up to the second floor. Here we came out and walked down the corridor to the apartment where Mohamed and Jama had been living since they arrived in Canada a little more than a year ago. Like me, they had once been refugee claimants. The Canadian government had accepted their claims, and soon they would become Canadians. It was only a matter of time, they told me.

Before his arrival in Canada, Mohamed had gone to schools in the United States of America and learned a lot of things. He was also married, but hadn't seen his wife since he left our country. He expected her to join him soon. Jama, on the other hand, was a twenty-six-year-old free-spirited bachelor who loved to play tricks on people. He was also temperamental and unpredictable.

As soon as we entered the apartment, Jama proceeded towards the kitchen and prepared tea for us. As we sipped the tea and relaxed on big comfortable chairs, it was time we talked about the main issue on our minds, an issue more important to us than anything else. Mohamed and Jama could hardly wait to hear news about our clan back home.

I told them everything, starting from the day the Duki government killed all the Sudi politicians, and concluding by letting them know the circumstances that had forced me to flee our country. I also told them of my plan to return at the right time, not only to avenge the killing of my father, but to fight the Duki clan to the end.

Mohamed and Jama listened to me with grim faces. The anger churning inside them was almost palpable, their breathing audible. The suffering of every Sudi was their suffering; the loss of every Sudi life was their loss; and the pain of every Sudi was their pain. With heavy hearts, we went to bed late in the evening to get some sleep.

In the morning, Mohamed left early for work. He was employed in a garment factory. Jama accompanied me to the welfare office to help me apply for financial assistance. We took the subway train and got off at Dundas West, a block from the welfare office. For any new refugee into Canada who lacked financial means to support himself, going to the welfare government office was the first trip to make.

At the office we met a social worker, a young girl full of energy, who seemed born to help others, and things started happening quickly. Forms were filled, papers signed, a new file created under my name, welfare payments approved: money for accommodation, money for food, and money for winter clothes. The stark contrast between the Canadian government and the Duki government astounded me. How could you compare between day and night, good and evil, heaven and hell? Two governments who had nothing in common. How unjust that they had to share anything even something as small as a name—government.

But all that assistance didn't come without strings. The social worker demanded that I go to school and learn English. Learning English would help me integrate into Canada, she said. When I told her I was too old to go to school, she got serious and warned me, "You shouldn't miss these lessons, or the welfare cheque will be withheld."

Like any camel boy, I had never thought about schools and reading. They were not relevant to my life. But in Canada, I faced a new reality. I had to go to school and do what they asked me to do.

Learning the English language might not be such a bad idea, after all. I could understand the people of Toronto and the people around me. I could talk to Canadians, particularly to those women who bare their legs and half of their breasts too. I could find a job and earn money; not to mention that if I failed to go to school, the welfare cheque would be put on hold. I couldn't afford not to go to school.

In the evening, when Mohamed returned from work, having bought groceries, we prepared dinner together. Jama cooked the meat and rice. I sliced the vegetables and washed the dishes. In less than an hour, the dinner was ready: rice with lamb and vegetables. We would have that same menu every night. Not enjoying spoons and forks, we ate with our bare hands and licked our fingers.

After dinner we sat down together in the living room. It was time we talked once again about our age-old nemesis. I argued that we should have been fighting the Duki clan; we should already be engaged in an all-out war against them. "How could we allow ourselves to be slaughtered like sheep in prison cells and before firing squads? What has happened to us? In the past, we never refused or shied away from a fight, never allowed the Duki attacks to go unanswered. So why this time?"

"Why this time? This time, it's different," Mohamed argued back. "This time, they have deadly weapons they never had before. They have all the government power and the military in their hands. That is why! So let's wait until we have a better chance of winning."

Jama agreed with me, but didn't say much.

For days, I rarely went out of the house. The cold weather made me a prisoner inside, not to mention my fear of getting lost in the city. Only something as important as my English classes could force me to venture out, but they hadn't started yet.

Meanwhile, I was looking forward to my interview with the refugee office. To help me prepare for the interview, Mohamed put together an outline of my story. By now, he knew everything about me and I didn't need to tell him anything. I had only one misgiving about the way he framed my story. He forgot to mention my herd of camels that the Duki raiders took away from me. But even without that, I had a strong case and could hardly wait to prove it.

The Canadian government offered me more assistance. A lawyer, called AJ Clarke, was assigned to work with me and defend my refugee claim. A government so caring was something new to me and it all seemed too good to be true. The first time I went to see the lawyer, Jama accompanied me. He had to show me the office and help me communicate with the lawyer. The lawyer welcomed us in. As soon as we sat down, we started to discuss my refugee claim. The lawyer mostly listened and took notes as Jama relayed my story.

A week later, it was finally my day to face the Canadian immigration authorities. I woke up early and braced myself for the cold weather. Wearing my brown winter jacket, which I had recently bought, I took the subway to go to my lawyer's office. I got off at Bathurst and started walking east. Piles of snow that looked like small white hills lay beside the road. The barely visible ice patches posed the greatest risk. I learned this the hard way, when I stepped on hardened black ice, slipped, and fell flat on my back. Two boys laughed at me, but a man walking by came to my help. He asked me if I was all right. Somehow, I understood what he was saying and nodded in response; then I stood up, brushed my pants, and kept going. It was still early in the morning when I arrived at the lawyer's office.

We didn't stay too long there and left quickly in his car to make the appointment. The traffic was barely moving on the road and the lawyer got frustrated. He tried his best to drive faster. He slapped the steering wheel, he blew the horn, but nothing worked. By the time we reached the immigration office on University Avenue, it was past our appointment time. With a sense of urgency, the lawyer spoke to the girl at reception, and she called somebody on the phone. We didn't wait long before a tall woman with short blonde hair came looking for us.

She led us past many offices to the other end of the building, her high-heeled shoes clacking sharply on the floor tiles. The muscles on her legs, I thought, must be as strong and robust as that of any camel boy. I kept my distance from her, fearing that she might step on my feet with all that force.

We entered a well-lit office in which a tall and slim immigration officer welcomed us. A Somali man who turned out to be an interpreter sat beside him. I wondered what clan he belonged to. After shaking hands, the officer motioned us to take a seat. We barely sat down when the officer went right down to business and peppered me with questions: "Why did you leave your country? What kind of work did you do back home? How did you manage to travel all the way to Canada? Why are you seeking refugee status in Canada? Tell us the whole story." Even the interpreter had a difficult time coping with him.

Before I had a chance to say anything, my lawyer intervened. He didn't like something and raised his objection.

"To ask my client to tell his story in one big swoop like that will put him under undue pressure. He might skip an important point, or lose the chronological order of events," my lawyer said.

An argument soon erupted between my lawyer and the immigration officer. I had no idea what was going on and looked at the Somali interpreter for answers. He whispered into my ear once in a while to let me know what was being said.

Their argument sometimes grew heated and continued until the officer relented and even asked my lawyer to go first with the questions.

Mr Clarke began to present my story, one question at a time: a story of a man fleeing the government of his country in fear for his life, a story of the ultimate injustice. His questions covered most of my adult life from the day the Duki killed my father to the day I arrived in Canada. "What would happen to you if the Canadian government sent you back to your country?" was the last question.

"I will be a dead man," I said immediately. I didn't even have to think about it.

The immigration officer then took over. And one thing was pretty much certain to me: his questions would not be as friendly as those of my lawyer.

"You said you belong to the Sudi clan, and that the government dominated by the Duki clan would kill you if you went back to your country. Right?"

"Right."

"What for?"

"For being a Sudi clansman."

"They will kill you just because you are a Sudi clansman?"

"Yes."

"As simple as that?"

"Sir, it is not that simple from where I come. The clans are who we are. It is our big family and identity. It is our blood, our life, and our world. It is the reason we fight and kill one another."

"But there are many of your clansmen who still live in your country, are there not?"

"Yes, they are there, but they face arrest and death every minute of their lives."

"So you don't expect to go back?"

"Not as long as the Duki government is in power," I said, remembering how Mohamed had told me to answer such a question. Deep down, I knew this wasn't the whole truth. I would go back under the right circumstances. I would go back to fight the Duki clan and avenge the killing of my father. I had too much unfinished business back home.

"You said the government arrested you just because you yawned. Is that correct?" The officer asked, changing the subject.

"Yes, that is correct," I nodded.

"Did you appeal your case to the Supreme Court of your country?"

"No."

"Why not?"

"Because all the courts including the highest court are owned and controlled by the Duki clan."

"Did you complain to the Human Rights Commission?"

I had no idea what a Human Rights Commission was. After the interpreter explained it to me, I turned back to the officer and said, "We don't have such things back home. We know nothing about human rights. I don't think anybody back home would give a damn about it even if they knew it."

"Was there any authority in the country that you could appeal to about this injustice of going to jail for yawning?"

"No. All the power is in the hands of the Duki clan. The Supreme Leader is a Duki; the judges are Duki; the minister of justice is a Duki; the minister of defense is a Duki; the minister of foreign affairs is a Duki—"

"Okay! Okay! I get the point."

"Tell him!" I urged the interpreter. "Tell him that the whole government is Duki."

The interpreter shrugged his shoulders and merely said, "I am just the interpreter."

"So what! Interpreters don't tell the truth?"

"Truth or no truth, I am just interpreting what is being said from one language to another."

"Why are you so hesitant to tell the truth about the Duki government? Are you a Duki clansman?"

"No, I am not."

"You better not be or you will hear from me."

To resume his questioning, the immigration officer intervened. "You said most of the political prisoners were Sudi clansmen. Is that right?"

"Yes."

"Were they all in jail for yawning?"

"No, my clansmen stopped yawning after my arrest, particularly when the Duki security agents were around. The other Sudi prisoners were arrested for other things."

"Like what?"

"Like refusing to go to the Orientation Centre."

"What is an Orientation Centre?"

"A place where the Duki government cleanses brains."

"Have they cleansed your brain?" The officer smiled for the first time. He had no more questions and concluded the interview.

Feeling relieved, I said goodbye to the officer. I shook hands with Mr Clarke and thanked him when we stepped out of the office.

On the way back, I bought a notebook and a pen from a grocery store to prepare myself for school. I used to think that books and schools were nothing more than the leftover of British rule in my country and that a camel boy had better things to do. That was then; this was now, in Canada, and I had to get on with it.

12

THE NEXT DAY, I WENT to school and sat where no camel boy had ever sat before—in a classroom. The other students in the school came from different parts of the world and spoke their own strange languages. But we were all here for the same reason—to learn the English language. A teacher wearing a green jacket entered the classroom. Coincidentally he was called Mr Green. He began by explaining some points using a white board and a marker. It was time to learn and focus all my attention on the teacher. It was time to learn the most important language in the world. But my mind soon drifted away. I found myself thinking about my clan back home. Images of Duki soldiers arresting my Sudi clansmen on the streets and in their homes started to haunt me. It wasn't going to be easy to concentrate on the lesson. Still, at the end of the day I managed to learn the alphabet and a few words—"good morning" and "good night" among them. The help I received from other students made a difference.

Particularly helpful was a white woman in her late twenties who worked part-time in the school. Her name was Mary, and she was some kind of an administrator and assisted the teacher. She sat next to me once in a while, always in good mood, always patient with me. Her giving spirit encouraged and motivated me. For all I knew, she could have been an angel sent to me for a purpose. As the days passed, we became friends. One day, I even brought her to our apartment and introduced her to Mohamed and Jama.

On Fridays, the teacher gave us homework for the weekend. Mohamed and Jama helped me with these assignments. I was also practicing speaking English, sometimes resorting to unconventional means. For example, while walking in the streets, I would pretend to be lost and ask strangers for directions. My efforts paid off and within three months I could speak English reasonably well. I felt so confident that I began to search for a part-time job.

A company employed me as a security guard at a graveyard. At first, the whole notion of working in a graveyard sounded laughable and creepy to me, and I hesitated. But, surprisingly, it turned out to be a good job and an easy one. It was a very quiet place. Nobody screamed at me. Nobody caused trouble; there was peace and serenity everywhere. Dead people proved a lot more fun to be with than many living people.

In the six weeks I worked there, I barely spoke to anyone. One day, two men brought a large wooden crate on a truck and asked me to assist them in unloading it.

"What is in the crate?" I asked them, not realizing that it was a coffin.

"A dead body, what else," one of them responded.

"I am sorry. And you are burying the body in this graveyard?"

"No, we are doing cremation and we want you to give us a hand."

"What is cremation?" I asked.

"The body will be burnt," one of them said and looked at the other in surprise.

I had never heard of dead human bodies being burned. It did not make sense to me. I was appalled and disgusted. "You are burning a dead human body?" I asked, just to be sure that I heard them right.

"Yes," said the taller guy.

"Why not just bury it into the ground where we all came from?" I asked, hoping to change their minds.

"It's to be cremated," they said together.

Burning a human dead body in a blazing fire struck me as abhorrent and cruel. I cringed at the idea of taking part in such an activity. To me, it was like giving a taste of hell to the dead person before he even faced his God. Not even the dead body of a Duki deserved cremation. Had I known that this was part of my job, I would never have taken it.

The men were still waiting for me and I had to make a decision: either I had to help them in burning the dead body or walk away from my job. I chose the latter and strode off. I didn't even go to my employer to claim payment for the five days they owed me.

I started to look for another job. At the same time, I kept going to school four days a week.

At the end of classes, I usually left the school with Mary. It turned out that we lived in the same area. On our way home, we often strolled along Bloor Street until we reached the intersection of Bloor and Ossington where we said goodbye to each other and went our own ways.

A single mother, Mary lived in a two-bedroom apartment with her four-year-old daughter, a dog, and a cat. She had lived alone for two years and had neither a husband nor a boyfriend since her marriage ended in divorce. Why a woman as beautiful as Mary remained single for so long was a bit of a mystery to me. She had the perfect body, an angelic face, and a charming smile; not to mention her good nature.

On Fridays, when she wore her tight blue jeans, she looked especially attractive and drew a lot of attention. A guy followed us one day and kept on saying, "Work it, baby, work it."

"What work is he talking about?" I asked Mary.

"He isn't talking about work."

"So what is he talking about?"

"He is commenting about the way I am walking."

I stopped to confront the scoundrel. Mary tried to intervene, but I pushed her away, took a few steps in his direction and shouted angrily, "Mind your own lame and bumbling walk and leave the lady alone or I will slap you in the face."

"Take it easy, dude. I am just cheering for her," the guy said as he backed off quickly and left us alone.

Somebody should have taught him a lesson a long time ago on how to show some respect for the women walking in the streets.

As time went by, Mary and I became close friends. Her warm and intimate hugs put in motion waves of desire inside me. Her magic smile and kisses on my cheek left me drooling for more. I couldn't wait to take her to bed one day and make love to her. It would be a night to remember. A night when no amount of Canadian snow and ice could dampen my spirits. It would be a night when I could forget everything else, even my sworn enemy—the Duki Clan.

But I could see a problem that might spoil and torpedo our budding friendship. She had a dog at home, a dog she called the best friend she had ever had. It was as if she was talking about a boyfriend. I wondered what she saw in an animal that should have stayed in the wilderness where it belonged. Like my people, I could never imagine having anything to do with a dog or a wolf or a lion. We feared all meat-eating animals. Nothing could bring us together. We hated them, particularly dogs, which we considered to be the lowest of the low. Any animal that could eat us dead or alive struck fear in our hearts and friendship with them was out of the question.

But all my fear and hatred of dogs didn't stop me when one day Mary invited me to her apartment. She offered to help me with my lessons on the weekend. So that I wouldn't get lost, she gave me directions on how to find her place. God knows I had more than lessons and books on my mind. The opportunity I had been waiting for had just presented itself without much effort on my part. That whole day, excited about the oncoming get-together, I couldn't help checking the time every few minutes.

It was just after sunset on a mild Saturday when I arrived at her apartment. I cautiously knocked on the door and Mary soon opened it. She welcomed me with a big smile. Then she led me into her living room where I eased myself into an armchair. The moment I sat down, Mary excused herself to go to the kitchen.

I looked around the living room. It was tidy, well-kept, and smelled good. It was the kind of home every man wanted to come to in the evening after a long day at work. A well-kept home had always been the hallmark of a fine lady. And Mary was one of the finest. I had known this from the day I first met her in the classroom.

As I waited for her to come out from the kitchen, the dog appeared out of nowhere and proceeded towards me. It was a big one, the kind I feared most. If it started barking in a threatening way or touched any part of my body, all bets would be off. I knew where the door was to make my escape. To keep a good distance from it, I moved away. But the dog would not take the hint, and came closer until it sniffed my shoes. I couldn't have been in a more tense situation.

Just when I needed her, Mary returned from the kitchen and served me a cup of tea; then she sat between me and the dog. The dog retreated, its eyes still focused on me.

Embracing her dog, Mary turned to me and said, "What do you think of my dog?"

"It is a big one . . . I mean, it is good," I mumbled.

"Isn't he beautiful?"

I did not know what to say. I never imagined that a dog could be beautiful. To me, dogs were just dogs, dangerous beasts, with neither beauty nor any other redeeming value in them. So I answered her with another question. "Why do you keep a dog in your apartment? Why do all Canadians have dogs in their houses?"

Mary giggled in disbelief. She never expected to answer such a question. She thought everyone in the world loved dogs and that my question was a bit weird. "Don't you like dogs?" she asked me, knitting her brows.

"No, I don't. I don't like dogs or any other animal that eats meat. And neither do my people. The animals that eat grass, that is our thing," I said.

Mary had nothing more to say for a while. She was taken aback and merely smiled in disbelief and shook her head.

As if I had not already said enough about my hatred and fear of dogs, I added, "Let me give you an example: if I am riding in the subway train and somebody with a dog sits near me, I leave my seat and move away to a different location. I might even get off the train."

Unable to remain silent any longer, Mary snapped at me, "What is your problem with dogs? Why don't you like such nice animals?"

"I don't know. We just don't like them."

"Do you like cats?"

"No."

"Do you like birds?"

"No."

"Do you like flowers?"

"No."

"Do you like going to the beach, swimming in warm waters, and lying on clean sandy beaches?"

"No."

"How about going out with friends on a weekend, having a good time, drinking red wine, eating a delicious dinner of shrimp, and so on? Do you like that?"

"No," I said, not even sure what a shrimp was.

"Is there anything in this world that you like?" Mary said raising her voice, her eyes wide with disbelief. She probably never imagined in her wildest dreams that a normal human being would answer those questions the way I did.

"Yes, there are things I like."

"What do you like?"

"I like my clan," I said and added quickly, "We all do."

"What else do you like?" Mary probed.

"My sub-clan."

"Okay, what else?"

"My sub-sub-clan."

"Anything other than the clan and sub-clan and so on?"

"You," I smiled and we both broke into laughter.

"So I am in fourth place after the clan and the sub-clan and so on," she said, sounding and looking incredulous.

"Trust me, where I came from, that is not a bad position to be," I said and patted her on the back.

At that point, her young daughter interrupted us. She had been asleep in the other room. Our conversation and laughter probably woke her up. At first, she looked a bit scared of me, a stranger in their house. But after her mother had introduced me, she relaxed. Pretty soon, she was cheerfully playing with me. She made fun of my accent and the way I pronounced English words. "Mama," she said, "I am only four years old, and I can speak English better than Ali. Is he crazy or what?"

"No, sweetie, Ali is not crazy," Mary told her. "He came from another country in a distant part of the world. That is why he has a unique accent. He started learning the English language not that long ago."

"Why did he leave his country?"

"He had a problem with the government over there."

"They didn't like him?"

"Yes, they didn't like him and he left them."

"Why didn't they like him? Is he a bad man?"

"No, sweetie, Ali is not a bad man. They have a bad government in their country that doesn't like some of the people."

"Does our government like him?"

"Yes, it does."

"Why?"

"Because we have a good government in Canada with good laws that protect all the people. Now can you please go and play with your cat?"

The young girl went away reluctantly to play with the cat.

After she left us, it was time for some meaningful conversation with Mary, time for some romantic talk. But just then a hockey game came on the television. Mary started watching and cheering for one of the teams, the Maple Leafs. From that moment onwards, she got hooked and nothing could take her eyes off the screen. All my plans for the night came crashing down. She had no time to help me with my English lesson. Any chance of romance and good times also evaporated.

Disappointed, I watched the game with her for a while. Even though I knew nothing about the teams, I cheered for the Maple Leafs. I had to take her side in this game, where grown men skidded and slid on ice while chasing a small round thing. Luckily, her team had the upper hand, which put her in a good mood. The game continued for a long time and seemed endless. After about two hours, I had had enough and said goodbye. There was always the possibility of a second chance. I wasn't giving up on Mary.

In fact, she invited me back into her home a week later. She probably felt guilty that she didn't get a chance to help me with my lessons the first time. So the moment I arrived, we got down to business. She explained to me some English grammar, the relationships between nouns and verbs, and other things. She covered a lot and I learned much. After the lesson, I didn't leave. I had a lot more in mind than nouns and verbs. I stayed with her until late into the evening. By then, Mary's daughter had already gone to bed. Even the pets had settled down. And there was no hockey game on television.

It was a good time to make my move and take a chance. I started touching her in all the right places. Mary didn't disappoint me. Excited and all smiles, she went along. A God-sent song came on the radio at the right time and nudged the mood in the right direction. As I later learned, it was Marvin Gaye singing, and Mary sang along with him: "Baby, I can't hold it much longer . . . It's getting stronger and stronger . . . And when I get that feeling, I want sexual healing."

By the time the song ended, a wave of sexual desire took hold of us. For an instant, my wife back home came to my mind. I should have felt a sense of guilt and betrayal. Strangely enough, I didn't. It was as if nothing would stop me. Forces more powerful than marriage vows took hold of me.

I pulled Mary up close and kissed her on the cheek. She reciprocated and kissed me back not only on the cheeks, but also on the lips. Within no time, sparks were flying; the temperature rose, and we both felt the heat. It was sexual passion at its height, and at its best. Her decorated beautiful hands explored every part of my body. I reciprocated and reached for places I used to consider out of limits. As the sexual foreplay gathered momentum, we had to get on with it. Mary switched off the television and we hurried towards the bedroom.

She barely reached the bed when she started stripping herself of her top, her bra, and her pants. She tossed them away, here and there, and all over the floor, as if she getting rid of a burden. If only she had waited for me to undress her. Back home, only a prostitute would undress herself so readily. I had never seen a woman so butt-naked, even my wife. The glare of the light didn't help either. I was accustomed to making love in a semi-dark room to keep it sweet and secret. The bright light in Mary's bedroom stopped me in my tracks. I couldn't take off my clothes and almost froze. To do something about the bright light, I looked around for the electric switch to turn the light off.

"What are you doing?" Mary intervened.

"I am switching off the light. It is too bright."

"Are you out of your mind? It will be pitch-dark, and we won't see each other."

"Don't worry about that. We will see each other. With that naked white body of yours in the room, who needs artificial light?"

She thought I was joking and giggled, telling me once again to leave the lights on.

I relented and came back to bed. She undressed me slowly and kissed me in all the right places. She sure knew how to get a man going. My body yearned for a piece of her and we soon melted into one, hips slamming into hips, chest grinding chest, muscles pumped up and going all the way, the faculty of speech mutating into mere grunts and groans, hands reaching out and touching, two naked bodies quivering with desire. What a feeling! What a joyful moment! Like I had found a new world without the Duki clan! The climax of all climaxes was about to unfold. The juices were about to flow. The world stood still for the coming.

Suddenly, it all went haywire. The dog in hot pursuit of the cat barged into the bedroom, jumped on the bed, and started sniffing my bare back. I freaked out and almost fell off the bed. No way was I going to tolerate a dog touching my bare body! For all I knew, it could bite me to death. It could lick my bare body and stain me for life. I reacted so abruptly that one minute I was making love on the bed and the next minute I was standing at the far end of the room. The cursed dog spoiled everything.

How awkward it all looked, my sexual desire at its peak and my penis pulsating. I didn't know what to do. I had to keep my distance from those cursed animals. Even the cat forgot about the dog and eyed my genitals. Anything about a certain size and moving could only mean a mouse and fair game to the stupid cat.

The bedroom looked like a war zone as the dog barked and the cat mewed, and Mary had to do something about it. She finally stepped in to take charge and deal with her pets. But first, she asked me to get back into bed. I would have none of that as long as the dog and the cat were in the room.

"Take it easy, Ali," Mary said. "These are only pets. They are not going to eat you."

"I don't like coming near dogs and cats when I am fully clothed. And when I am naked, forget it," I said. "Take them out. Then and only then will I come back to bed."

In her effort to calm down the dog, Mary kissed it on the mouth.

"What are you doing?" I asked, not believing my eyes.

"I kissed the dog," she said with the utmost indifference and innocence.

"How can you do that? I never kissed my camels and you kissed a dog? On the mouth!"

"Yes I did. So what?"

Without another word, I grabbed my clothes, the pants in one hand and the shirt in the other, and stormed out of the bedroom. The woman making love to me had kissed a dog on the mouth! Touching the dog wouldn't have bothered me; but a kiss, mouth-to-mouth, with a dog! I felt disgusted. She had gone too far. Beautiful Mary was no longer beautiful to me.

I rushed through the living room, not even stopping to put my clothes on. I ran for the door, naked. Along the way, I could hear Mary calling to me, "Where are you going?" I didn't answer. I didn't look back. I picked up my shoes as well and barged out of the apartment, mumbling to myself, "She kissed a dog on the mouth! She kissed a dog on the mouth! And if she thinks a Sudi clansman and a dog are going to share a woman, she is damn wrong. Who does she think I am? Another dog?"

I exited the door straight away. Only then did I stop to put my clothes on. It was late in the night, probably close to midnight, and I took it for granted that nobody would be around. I could have been wrong and given somebody the biggest surprise of his life. Luckily, nobody saw me. After zipping my fly, I hurried home.

I walked briskly, almost jogging until I came at the Bloor and Ossington intersection. The streets were almost empty. A drizzle had driven people into their homes. A wasted, drunken man stood there alone, as mad as hell, and screaming. "I don't like you all, the prime minister of Canada, the parliament, and all the judges in your courts! You are all corrupt sons-of-bitches! You are all crooks and you make me sick!" he shouted in a wild rage.

Like all raving maniacs in the streets, he had no idea what he was talking about. He was just spewing a lot of nonsense. He would certainly have second thoughts about the Canadian politicians and judges had he been a Sudi clansman under the government of the Supreme Leader for one day.

On the other side of the street, a woman lingered. She wore a miniskirt and appeared to be a prostitute. For a while, I could not take my eyes off her. The flames of sexual desire cut short by the stupid dog and cat were still warm, yearning for a second chance. But I didn't go for it and restrained myself. For one thing, I had no money to pay her. Not to mention my fear of this deadly disease, AIDS, that I had heard about on television. I wouldn't risk my life for that kind of sex even if I had money.

On the streets, cars sped and roared past me. I had to be careful when crossing the streets until I arrived at our apartment. I opened the door slowly, careful not to make the slightest sound, so as not to wake anybody up. But the old door squeaked. Both Jama and Mohamed heard the noise and woke up.

"Where have you been?" Jama asked, coming out from his room and covering his eyes from the glare of the light.

"I was at Mary's apartment," I admitted, and scratched my head like a young boy caught in a mischievous act.

"What time is it?"

"I don't know. It is close to midnight."

"Why didn't you sleep there if you stayed that late?"

"Long story."

"We have time for it."

"Not really a long story. There was just a problem and I had to leave."

"What problem?"

"She kissed her dog."

"So what if she kissed her dog? They all kiss their dogs."

Not interested in an argument about kissing dogs, I didn't respond and merely spit in a trashcan. The image of Mary kissing the dog on the mouth still horrified me.

"So what did you do when she kissed the dog?" Mohamed appeared out of nowhere and interjected, making the most of an issue I would rather forget.

"I ran out of the apartment. What else would you expect me to do? I did not even put on my clothes until I left the apartment. When she kissed the dog on the mouth, I just lost it and ran for the door," I said and went into my room, slamming the door behind me.

Falling asleep didn't come easily. I stayed awake for more than an hour, Mary and her godforsaken dog still on my mind. It could have

been the best of nights, and it had turned out to be a big disappointment. The kiss on the dog destroyed not only a good opportunity, but a
sincere friendship too. Not a chance that she would ever invite me into
her home again.

In the morning I woke up late, dragged myself out bed, and checked
the mailbox. And there it was—the letter from the immigration authorities that I had been waiting for. It would change my status in the country
one way or another. I opened it quickly and read it.

It was good news. The Canadian government had accepted me as a
refugee. My mood changed in an instant from despondency and disappointment to elation and excitement. I could now sponsor my wife and
son to come to Canada. Now we could be together here in Toronto, until
such time when I could go back home. How I wished to see them again,
after all those long years.

I didn't go to my English class that day. Instead, I headed towards the
immigration office on University Avenue to file for the sponsorship of
my family. I arrived there early, and yet there was already a long line-up
of people in front of the building, all of them waiting to get in. They had
been there for hours, signs of a sleepless night obvious on their haggard
faces. It would be a long wait.

It was one of those hot days in Canada. Something they called humid-
ity made things worse. I sweated profusely and could barely stand in the
line. I never thought it could get this hot in Canada. Where were the
freezing snow and cold arctic winds when I needed them? Within a span
of a few weeks, the weather had gone from one extreme to another. I
made a quick dash to a grocery store to buy a bottle of water.

My number finally came up and they led me into a cool air-condi-
tioned office where a middle-aged female immigration officer welcomed
me. She asked me questions about my family—their names, their ages,
and their education—and filled a form. I answered all her questions and
signed the form at the bottom. That was all she needed and I thanked
her and left.

On the way back home, I took the subway. It was the evening rush
hour and not one empty seat was available on the train. I stood near
the door, holding on to a post for support as the train lurched from side

to side. A bit exhausted, I yawned. Immediately, alarm bells went off in my brain. I looked around warily; then quickly reminded myself that no Duki policeman hiding among the Canadians in the train was going to jump on me and arrest me. Flashbacks of that infamous day had followed me all the way into Canada.

Inside the train it was eerily quiet; as quiet as the graveyard I had worked at as a security guard. Not a peep of sound anywhere other than the rumbling of the speeding train. No one initiated a conversation; nobody even looked into the eye of the man or women facing them on the seat across. Back home, we talked with one another wherever we met, complete strangers arguing like old friends. No introductions needed. Initiating a conversation with another person was never a problem. A man would just brag about the fighting prowess of his clan or sub-clan. That would set off a heated argument. Others would respond and challenge him. Sometimes their heated arguments remained no more than verbal exchanges; other times the shouting matches led to a fight, even to murder.

At Bathurst station a passenger came on board who was a stark contrast to everybody else on the train. He was in his late thirties with a receding hairline, unshaven beard, and a big smile on his face. As soon as he saw me, he approached and we shook hands. He certainly looked like somebody who would inject life into this boring subway ride. I might even learn a few English words from him in the process.

"Guess who I saw today?" he asked, still sporting the big smile.

"The prime minister of Canada," I said and smiled back at him.

"No, think again. I am talking about somebody a lot more important than the prime minister of Canada," he chuckled, and gave me a conspiratorial wink.

"Who is more important than the prime minister? In Canada, he is number one, isn't he?"

"Jesus Christ is more important than anybody else, here in Canada and anywhere else. Jesus Christ is number one."

"You saw Jesus Christ?"

"Yes."

"I did not know Jesus Christ was in Canada," I responded, somewhat taken aback by the enormity of the man's claim.

"Forget about Canada, he is here in Toronto with us. I saw him on Yonge Street," the man said and burst out laughing.

The other passengers were now fully awake, keen to hear the story about the sighting of Jesus Christ in their city. Books and newspapers were quickly put away. They knew that the spectacular event could possibly happen sometime in the distant future, but here and now, and on Yonge Street? They were not going to fall for that; yet, they eagerly waited to hear the story. Some smiled while watching from the corners of their eyes.

I did not believe him either. But I would rather talk to a crazy man than suffer the silence of the rush-hour train. So I asked him, "What is Jesus Christ doing on Yonge Street?"

"He is saving us."

"Saving you from whom? We are all safe here in Canada."

"Jesus! Should I have to tell you that? Where have you been? He is saving us from ourselves. We got lost in a world of sin. Satan led us astray. We don't go to church anymore. Wives and husbands cheat one another. Sons murder their mothers and priests abuse children. It is about time Jesus came back to earth. It is about time He saw all this with his own eyes."

"Why only Jesus? Why not all the prophets? Jesus, Moses, Mohamed and all the rest," I argued back. "Let them all come back and see what is going on. They killed my father, raided my herd of camels, and put me in jail for yawning. The prophets should know that too."

By now, I understood where my new friend was coming from. Too much religion had got into him and driven him into la-la land. We had our own religious fanatics back home too. Ours had gone one step even further and equipped themselves with guns and knives, ready to kill. How ironic that too much of a good thing could be dangerous, like the life-sustaining water that turns into a killer flood. If only they had taken things in moderation, even something as sacred as religion.

After mumbling some kind of a sermon to himself for a while, my new friend turned to me and asked, "Who put you in jail for yawning? That is crazy. That is insane." Suddenly, after hearing that someone had gone to jail for yawning, he seemed to have regained his sanity.

"The Duki government back home put me in jail," I told him.

"Jesus! Why did they arrest you for such a thing? That is no crime. What is wrong with them?" His eyes scanned the other passengers, searching for their reaction.

"I am a Sudi clansman," I said, as if a Canadian with mental problems would understand what that meant.

"So what?"

"They hate us, and we don't like them either."

"You obviously have a problem with this other clan. Why don't you settle your problems in peace?"

"I don't know. Ask Jesus the next time you see him on Yonge Street," I said and stepped out of the train at Ossington subway.

13

Neither Mohamed nor Jama was at home when I arrived back in our apartment. Tea cups on the living-room table showed that they had just left, probably to go buy groceries. I took the empty tea cups to the kitchen and waited for them. I was watching the evening news on the television when they came back with bags full of groceries.

"Did you have a good time in Big Uncle John's meat market?" I asked, in an attempt to make fun of them.

"Yes, we had a good time, but not because of buying groceries from the supermarket," Jama shouted while on his way to the kitchen to unload the bags.

"What else was there? Don't tell me that you found girls over there!"

"We heard good news from back home, the kind of news you would like," Jama said as he came out from the kitchen and changed the television channel to MuchMusic.

Not taking him seriously, I asked, "Where did you get the good news? From Big Uncle John?"

"Not from Uncle John, but from my cousin Ahmed in Saudi Arabia. I spoke to him on the phone just before we left."

"Tell me! What did he say?" I asked eagerly, realizing that Jama was not kidding. Any news from back home always had my full attention in an instant.

"They did it. They finally did it."

"What? Who did what?"

"War! I am talking about war. Our clan finally took up arms and started fighting the Duki clan and its government."

"When did this happen?"

"Yesterday."

"Yesterday! This is the best news ever, brother! How did it start?" I had to know everything. My heart raced, my body shook with excitement.

"How it started is not important. What is important is that we are fighting their government now," Jama said proudly and nodded his head a few times for emphasis.

"I can't believe that after hearing such wonderful news, you just went to the supermarket and the meat store," I hissed, a bit disappointed.

"What did you expect us to do?" Jama retorted.

"To wait for me and tell me this good news a lot earlier."

"We had no food in the apartment. Don't you want something to eat?"

"I would rather have the news than all the food in the world."

"You know what! Forget about it. Instead of being thankful for the good news, you are whining like an upset kid."

"Don't get sore, Jama. I just wanted to hear it a bit earlier. You know what I am thinking about now?"

"Celebrating the start of the war? Perhaps taking another shot at Mary?"

"No, not that. For heaven's sake, Jama, get serious and forget about that thing. This is no time to fool around. I am thinking of going back to our country."

"When?"

"Now. What am I waiting for? I have to join the fight. It is about time the Duki paid a price for what they have done to me and to all of us."

"You can't go back now!" Mohamed shouted from his room.

"Why?"

"Do you have a travelling document? I mean a passport?"

"No. The only passport I ever had was taken away from me when I applied for refugee status."

"Without a passport, you can't go anywhere."

"How can I get it? Mohamed, you know these things."

"To get a Canadian passport, you have to be a Canadian citizen. You are not a Canadian. So you can't get it."

"How long will this take? When will I become a Canadian citizen?"

"Three years from the day you were accepted as a refugee and got the residence permit."

"Mohamed, all your education in America can't find a way for me to go back to our country?" I said, greatly disappointed.

"I wish I could help you. I can't. Only a government can issue a passport."

"What if I ask the Canadian government to deport me? What do you think of that?" I suggested.

"They will deport you and you know where the airplane will land? At the airport that is still in the hands of the Duki government and their forces. Do you want to go there?"

"No, I don't want to go there. I want to fight them, not to surrender to them," I sighed in disgust and sat back on the sofa. The opportunity to take my revenge on the Duki was right there. And yet I felt helpless because of a damn passport. If only I could find a way to get back home. If only I could join the fight.

"Look at the bright side," Jama said, trying to cheer me up. "At least we are now fighting back. The days when they used to kill us in their jails and before firing squads are over. Everybody reaps what he sows. It is about time the Duki got a taste of the fruit from the tree they themselves planted."

It didn't happen often, but once in a while, Jama came up with words of wisdom. I couldn't have agreed with him more. The Duki had a lot of blood on their hands, our blood. It was time they paid a price for it.

How long had I waited for this day? How long had I wished that the Sudi clan would take up arms and fight back? The payback time had come and a sacred war had started; a war to right the wrongs; a war to make the killers and criminals face justice and pay a price for their actions. Along the way, there would be a lot of suffering and destruction. There would be bloodshed, death, and mayhem. But in the end we would march into victory. No doubt in my mind.

From that day on, I became obsessed with the war. Nothing else mattered to me. Nothing else got my attention. I talked about it in the daytime. I dreamed about it at night. One way or another, our fight and struggle against the Duki was always on my mind. I lost interest in learning English. I walked away from a temporary job in a warehouse where I used to stock cartons and boxes in shelves. I didn't like the guy I was

working with, anyway. They called him a supervisor. I called him a con-
niving, smooth-talking hypocrite and a conman who borrowed money
from all the male employees and never paid them back. He even took
bribes from one of the married female employees. With his dick. Like
the Duki.

To get the latest information about the war, we made expensive telephone calls to Sudi people we knew in England, Saudi Arabia, and Abu
Dhabi. I had to know about every attack waged, every battle won or lost,
and who did what. Even rumours helped to make my day.

Every day, I went to the doughnut shop at Bloor and Ossington. I
sat there by myself, but sometimes Mohamed and Jama joined me and
we drank one cup of tea after another as we talked about the war. We
discussed tactics. We predicted what moves our side would make and
where they should attack. We argued about what we should do after winning the war.

Meanwhile, we waited for the arrival of Mohamed's wife. Her sponsorship process had succeeded. We expected her to arrive in Toronto
within days. She would provide us the latest news about the war. The day
her flight was scheduled to land, I accompanied Mohamed to the airport. The flight was delayed a bit and we loitered inside the airport area
until the airplane finally landed.

"How is the war going?" I asked Amina, Mohamed's wife, the instant
I set my eyes on her, not even allowing the married couple to complete
their greetings.

Caught off guard, Amina turned to her husband. "Don't we have to go
home first?"

"No, go ahead. Ali can't wait. We all can't wait for the news," he said
and we all sat down in the airport lounge and listened to her with rapt
attention.

"It all started when a man by the name of Mohali and ten other Sudi
fighters attacked a military base," she said. "I guess you all heard about
him, didn't you?"

"Yes, we did," Mohamed replied.

"Mohali and his small team of armed Sudi launched the first attack,
killed five soldiers, and destroyed two military vehicles." Amina stopped,

as if talking about the war was too much for her.

"Then what happened?" Mohamed said, encouraging her.

"After that, hell broke loose," Amina said in a low voice. "The Supreme Leader's response came fast and furious. He unleashed all the military forces. They had the big guns, the armoured tanks, the jet fighters, the heavy artillery, and they used them all against us. They stopped at nothing. They bombarded our villages. They burned our houses to the ground. They shot fleeing women and children. The dead bodies lay in the streets and on the outskirts of the town. The sight of decomposing bodies and the stench was everywhere. Nobody had time to bury them. And who would care about the dead when the living fared no better?"

"But our clansmen are fighting back, are they not?" I interjected, after her grim and heart-wrenching account of the war.

"Yes, they are," she said. "Mohali's small fighting group grew overnight into an army of thousands of Sudi fighters. Every day, they are launching counterattacks. They are hitting the Duki government hard. They have already claimed the liberation of a portion of the countryside."

I thought about the people I knew back home and wondered if they were still alive or had perished, particularly Koosar. Even an old man trying to survive by selling dead people's clothes couldn't be safe from them. Isman, my second cousin, also came to mind and I wondered if they had snuffed the life out of him before he had a chance to escape to the countryside. I felt pessimistic about Jiro. He was a disaster waiting to happen; he just couldn't help doing and saying the wrong things. They probably shot him at the outset along with thousands of fellow Sudi men and women.

The image of families bombarded in their houses, roofs collapsing on them, kept going through my mind. It depressed me and upset me. What government would go that far? What kind of revenge-seeking, hate-filled government would shoot fleeing children and women? The Duki government, for sure.

The bloodshed continued unabated for months. There was no end in sight to the war. Death and destruction scourged the land; too many tragic events unfolded. But despite all of that, my enthusiasm for the war never waned. The cruelty and evil actions of the government strengthened my resolve. This was no time to waver, no time to dither.

The arrival of Mohamed's wife forced us to make some changes in our living arrangement. Mohamed needed to live in a separate place with his wife. It was the right thing to do. Jama and I decided to leave the apartment we had shared with him. We looked for a new place and found a basement apartment two blocks away to the west.

The night we moved to the new apartment, I was exhausted. Loading and unloading the rented truck had taken its toll on me. It was the kind of night you would expect to get a good sleep. But I didn't and stayed awake for hours, distraught and angry. Images of airplanes bombarding our villages continued to haunt me. I tossed and turned on the bed. To fall asleep even for a few hours became impossible. Finally I gave up and sat up on the bed. It was well past midnight. I got up and knocked on Jama's door. No response. I knocked again, this time a bit harder. At the same time, I started calling him to wake him up.

Jama opened the door. He looked so shocked and confused to see me that I almost felt a sense of guilt. "What happened? What is the matter?" he asked me furiously.

"I had to talk to you," I said.

"About what?"

"I am thinking of going back home."

"Now?"

"Yes."

"Haven't we discussed this matter before?"

"Yes, we have."

"I thought we agreed that you had to wait for a passport."

"I have a new idea."

"What new idea?"

"I want to walk."

"Walk to where?"

"Walk all the way to Somalia. In that case, I won't need any passport."

"You want to walk around the world to go to Somalia?"

"Yes."

"For what?"

"What do you mean for what? To take my revenge on the Duki clan!"

"You filed sponsorship for your family. Are you not waiting for them?"

"I have to join the fight. I have to avenge the killing of my father. That is more important than anything else."

"So you insist on walking all the way to Somalia?"

"Yes."

"Do you even know which direction is Somalia? I mean, will you go eastwards or westwards?"

"We are closer to the sun than Canada. So I will go towards the direction of the sun."

"The morning sun or the evening sun?"

"The morning sun."

"So you will go east?"

"Yes."

"You can't do that. You can't walk all the way to Somalia."

"Why?"

"Have you ever seen the map of the world?"

"I don't care about maps. I will ask the people along the way for directions."

"There are no people along the way. The only thing there is a big ocean and you can't walk on that ocean. If you can swim like a fish, you can cross the ocean that way. Can you do that?"

I remembered how, when I flew to New York from Paris, all I saw below was a vast ocean, and how nervous I was.

"No, I can't swim like a fish, but can I walk around the ocean?"

"You can't do that either."

"Why?"

"Because the ocean stretches from one end of the world to the other. Now, can we go back to sleep?" he said in a sour mood, slamming his door shut behind him.

Disappointed, I returned to my room and sat on my bed. As I sat there, I remembered the last thing Koosar had told me just before I left Somalia. He said I could come back from the farthest corners of the world within hours. He had good intentions and didn't want me to fall into the claws of the Duki government. But his words sure didn't measure up to reality. There were all kinds of obstacles to going back. Like the victim of a trick,

I felt bad about my gullibility. I lay down on the bed to try to get some sleep. Dawn was breaking when I dozed off into a restless sleep.

Late in the morning, I woke up with a severe headache. I slowly dragged myself out of bed and took a bath. Jama had already left and I was alone in the apartment. To make myself a quick breakfast, I poured cornflakes into a bowl, added milk and drained it within minutes; then I hurried towards the doughnut shop. It had been wet and rainy for two days and streams of water were flowing in the streets. Regardless, I walked along Bloor Street in the pouring rain.

By the time I reached the doughnut shop, I was soaking wet. Water dripped from my clothes like I had taken a shower fully dressed. But that didn't bother me a bit. I had always considered rain a blessing and cherished it. Anybody who grew up in a country that didn't get much of a rain throughout the year would know where I was coming from. Definitely not the Canadian customers in the doughnut shop, who looked flabbergasted. I was probably the strangest and oddest sight they had ever witnessed. They stole quick glances at me and shook their heads. They whispered with one another and suppressed laughter. I thought of giving them a piece of my mind. I thought of saying to them, "It is just rainwater. Nothing more. It is just nature giving me a bath." In the end, I just ignored them. I had better things to do. At the counter, I grabbed a cup of tea and made my way to the table where Mohamed and Jama were sitting. It was a long weekend and neither of them had gone to work.

"You can get sick from that." Mohamed pointed his finger at me.

"From what?" I looked sideways, trying to figure out what he was talking about.

"From being soaked wet."

"What are you talking about? Only Allah can inflict me with sickness," I shot back, dismissing his warnings.

"Anybody who walks in that cold rainy weather is asking for the flu, and Allah will give it to him."

"Allah knows what I ask him every day and want from Him. And trust me, it is not flu."

"What do you want from Him?"

"What do you think?"

"I think you want Him to give you a lot of money, to make you a millionaire."

"Wrong."

"To take you to Paradise?"

"Wrong again. Paradise can wait."

"So what is it?"

"To help us defeat the Duki government. That is all I want from Him now."

"Maybe your prayers are working because we had a bit of a victory yesterday."

"What have you heard?" I put down the cup of tea and looked at Mohamed with intense anticipation.

"Our fighters attacked a prison in which many Sudi prisoners were held. They took it over, and freed all our men in there."

"And the prison guards?"

"They killed the Duki prison guards. And the others, they just kicked them in the butt and let them go."

"This is good news. I am telling you, guys, my prayers are working. We need to pray some more," I said and beamed with glee.

"Unfortunately, there is some bad news as well," Mohamed added in a sad tone.

"Bad news?" I echoed his words, hoping that I didn't hear him right.

Mohamed hesitated, then went on reluctantly. "After our fighters who had carried out the operation had left, Duki soldiers arrived. They rounded up all the Sudi nomads in the area, accused them of harbouring the 'terrorists', and shot them one by one. Thirty Sudis were killed in one spot."

That news hit me hard. I could think of nothing to say. Mohamed and Jama also remained silent.

To break the silence, Mohamed cleared his throat and spoke. "We are engaged in a critical struggle for our survival and freedom," he said. "So many other people in the world found themselves in this situation and travelled this same difficult road. I give you an example: the Americans. You think they were always big and powerful as they are now?"

"You mean they were once like us? Desperate and fighting for their rights and freedom?" I asked, unaware that America used to be a colony of the British like we used to be.

"Yes, there was a time when they were the underdogs struggling for their independence. They were outgunned and outnumbered. And when their ragtag militia faced the army of the British, thousands of them perished in a cold snowy winter. They suffered heavy losses. And yet they continued fighting under the command of George Washington. They didn't give up and fold; they didn't raise the white flag and surrender. Every time they suffered a setback, they quickly regrouped and fought back until they won and the United States of America was born."

That was an encouraging story and certainly the Americans deserved praise for their struggle for independence. But Mohamed got one thing wrong and I took issue with him immediately. I said, "Mohamed, you owe an apology to the British."

"Apology! Why?"

"You compared the British government with the Duki government," I shot back. "You equated them. That is wrong. It is more than wrong. It is heresy."

"I didn't equate them."

"Yes, you did. The British people were good people. They ruled us for decades. They drank the milk of our camels and liked it. They never tortured us or bombarded our villages like the Duki do. They never killed innocent Sudi clansmen looking after their camels or arrested us for yawning or laughing or refusing to go to an Orientation Centre."

"Yes, indeed, that is like comparing day and night," Jama remarked, taking my side.

"Wait a minute! You are missing the point here," Mohamed scrambled to defend himself, a bit flustered. "I only meant to say that the Sudi clan is an underdog like the American people were. I never equated the British with the Duki clan. Nobody said they are similar."

After backtracking a bit and clarifying his statements, Mohamed stood up to go home. His wife was waiting for him. Jama and I also left and headed for our apartment. We barely spoke to each other. We quietly watched a beautiful sunset. A gloomy day had ended with a nice and colourful evening.

If only the war would end as beautifully as that day was ending. But it didn't and raged on. Days turned to weeks and months and the bad news kept coming: Sudi clansmen overrun by military tanks, children and women hit by mortars while hiding in their homes, girls and wives raped in front of their fathers and husbands. There were signs of genocide everywhere.

The gut-wrenching news from the war could turn the hair of a baby grey. But I never lost hope. My strong faith in my clan kept me going. Throughout our history, my clansmen were known for their tenacity and gallantry. Although we never looked for war, we never rejected it either. No matter how long it took and how bloody this war got, we would one day prevail. We had revenge to take, a cause to fight for, and our honour to uphold.

On a cold windy day in Canada, my clan proved me right. It was the day they finally came through, upheld their honour and took their revenge. Not knowing what a special day this was going to be, I woke up late once again and arrived at the doughnut shop in the afternoon. Mohamed and Jama were there in an exceptionally boisterous mood. Their cheerful mood radiated towards me from afar. They must have heard the ultimate good news, I thought. Nothing else could have made them so happy. I regretted having gotten up so late and hurried towards them without even picking up a cup of tea from the counter.

"What happened? What have you heard?" I asked, before I had even reached their table.

"We won," Jama said with a grin that exposed all his white teeth from ear to ear.

"The war?"

"What else?"

I jumped up from the chair in jubilation and started chanting. "We won! We won! The Sudi clan won." Nothing had made me so happy before. It was the best news I ever heard in my life. I shook hands with Mohamed and Jama, not once, not twice, but three times. Our laughter and rejoicing rose to a high pitch. Our joyous screams became a nuisance to the other customers, but we couldn't have cared less. We not only ignored them, we defied them. Nobody could tell us to shut up on the day our clan had successfully toppled the Duki government.

"Hey, John, give all customers in the shop a cup of coffee and a dough-nut. I will pay for all of them," I shouted to the man behind the counter.

"What is the occasion?" John inquired.

"The Sudi clan has won the war."

"Who are the Sudi clan?"

"The good guys," I said.

"And who are the bad guys?"

"The Duki and their government!"

"There are no good guys and bad guys. There are only good ideas and had ideas," said a customer wearing a black jacket and glasses that gave him the look of one of those educated folks who teach in schools.

"You know nothing about what I am saying. So keep your opinions to yourself," I snapped at him.

The man shrugged his shoulders in a dismissive manner and winked to his friend sitting across from him. They laughed and resumed their conversation. But they lowered their voices and I couldn't hear them anymore.

"Hey, John," I called the owner of the doughnut shop again. "Give a cup of coffee and a doughnut to everybody except the guy over there, the one with the black jacket and his friend."

"Why not for those guys?" the doughnut shop owner asked, apparently eager to sell as many cups of coffee and donuts to shore up his bottom line.

"They are supporting the Duki clan, and I am not paying for them. Let the Duki clan buy them coffee and donuts," I responded, and turned to Mohamed to continue talking about the war and how we won it. "Mohamed, where were we when this guy interrupted us? Yes, talk to me about how we won the war. Tell me everything."

"I got the news from Samater, my cousin in England," Mohamed said and added, "He called me a short while ago."

"And what did he say."

"At first he said nothing and just kept laughing. Then he told me that we defeated the Duki government and that the Supreme Leader was no more."

"But how? I want to hear how it all happened."

He said the Duki government had been getting weaker and weaker and we stood a good chance of defeating them. But then something else came out of nowhere that sealed the fate of the Duki government. The Tuwi joined the fight on our side. They had been sitting on the fence far too long. And when they started shooting the Duki government soldiers from the rear, it was all over. The enemy forces didn't have a chance.

For a moment, I fell silent, basking in the news of the victory. The dictatorship of the Duki government had come to an abrupt end. The age of darkness had slipped into history. A bright sun had arisen and ushered in a new period. Good riddance to General Kahin, the man who had called himself The Supreme Leader and the great everything, when he was nothing but a clan warrior masquerading as the president of a country. Where would he and the members of his government go? They must have grabbed their kids and whatever they could take from their homes and fled to the region of their clan. They wouldn't be safe anywhere else.

To savour the moment, I recited an old poem written about a Sudi victory over the Duki clan forty years earlier. Then, I remembered something I should have asked Mohamed before anything else: is the Supreme Leader still alive? Do we know what happened to him? Did they get him?

"No, they didn't get him and he is still alive," Mohamed said. "He fled with his clan."

I looked out into the street, a bit disappointed. But the thought of the so-called Supreme Leader, the man who used to roar like a lion, now running for his life like a scared chicken soon put a grin on my face. He no longer amounted to anything. He wasn't even worth talking about. Better to forget about him and not waste my time. We had a future to build and better things to do. But before anything else, we had to celebrate. To do that, we left the doughnut shop and headed towards downtown, the best place to celebrate our cherished victory.

Along the way, we had a serious discussion about our future and where to go from here.

"What can we do to prevent another General Kahin taking over our country and forming another Duki government?" Jama asked, raising an important issue.

"Yes, how can we make sure that a Duki clansman never rules us? That is the question," Mohamed responded.

"I say we separate from them. We make our own separate country. That will be an ideal and permanent solution. How about that?" Jama suggested.

"You are the wise guy today, Jama. Where did you get all this wisdom? I like your idea. I like what I am hearing from you," I laughed and added, "We will establish peace in our new country. Moreover, we will make a government as just and as neutral as the traffic lights of Canada. Have you seen these traffic lights? They stop everybody and give the same time to all people. No one gets the shaft. No one gets special favours. I like those traffic lights."

"You yourself are talking some wisdom today, Ali. Let us form a government as fair as the traffic lights. I can't wait for that to happen," Mohamed said and we all shook hands.

The subject of secession from Somalia had been on the mind of some of my clansmen for some time. It made a lot of sense to us. No Duki clansman would ever rule us again. No Supreme Leader would ever get an opportunity to kill us by the thousands. And besides, we had been a separate country before, under the British. There was no reason we couldn't be a separate nation once again.

At Yonge and Bloor, the centre of Toronto, if not of the whole world, we got off the train. We walked south for a few blocks and entered a bar on the eastern side of Yonge Street where the sounds of raucous customers greeted us. An empty table was hard to come by in such a crowded place. We waited, and soon a table was found for us.

Mohamed and Jama ordered beer. I opted for a cup of orange juice. On a normal day, I would never have allowed myself to sit in a place where they served alcohol. But this was the day we had defeated the Duki government. Not a normal day by any standard. It was a day of celebration, a day when only our Sudi clan mattered and nothing else.

When the waiter served us, we clinked glasses, swigged our drinks, and we sang. Before long, we were chanting wildly:

No more Supreme Leader!

No more General Kahin!

From here to eternity,
no more Duki clan!

We emptied our glasses and asked for refills. "One more for the Sudi clan," Jama shouted to the waiter.

Jama hadn't drunk much before he got out of control and started acting a bit crazy. I couldn't tell if it was the beer or the joy of our victory that had affected him and made him behave this way. He encouraged the other customers to cheer along with us, "Long live the Sudi clan! Long live our victory!" Most of the other customers, who were partly drunk themselves, cheered along, just for the heck of it, until the chorus rang out from the bar. The manager finally intervened to restore order and told us to knock it off. We calmed down a little, but we continued to drink and laugh till the wee hours of the night.

The next day Mohamed did not go to work. And neither did Jama. They declared it Freedom Day for the Sudi clan and went back to bed.

When I woke up that morning, I started thinking about my father and if I would ever avenge his killing. I had to go back to Somalia. The overthrow of the Duki government gave me an opportunity. And the sooner I acted, the better. The Duki clan would be there, out of power and out of luck. I knew where to find them.

14

AFTER THE LONG DESTRUCTIVE WAR, we thought that peace would prevail in our country for the foreseeable future. We believed that everything had changed, that people were tired of war and conflict. Too much blood had already been shed. Too many fathers lost their sons, too many wives their husbands. Unfortunately, it didn't work out that way. With each clan aspiring to sit on the throne and rule the country this time, peace prospects soon evaporated. Any chance of consensus among the clans became impossible. The Duki had set an example others wanted to follow. "It is our time" was the new rallying cry.

A vicious war soon raged between the Tuwi and the Duki. The Tuwi started it and waged an all-out attack on the Duki, hoping to knock them down completely. Only then could they claim their authority to sit on the throne. But the Duki regrouped and stood their ground. They had hopes of taking over the government once again. They tasted power and liked it. They couldn't live without it. The other clans had their own dreams too.

Amidst this chaos, the elders of the Sudi clan convened a hasty meeting to make a decision about our future. They decided to secede from the rest of the country. We had to chart a new course and create our own new country. We called it the Somaha Republic. It was a drastic decision but a popular one that set off celebrations in every part of our land. The freedom and honour of our clan should never be compromised again. The formation of the Somaha Republic gave us a sense of security and pride.

At the same time, our elders formed an interim government, which quickly established peace and order in our territory within a short period. On the other hand, the war between the Tuwi and the Duki continued and turned vicious. The Tuwi had no intention of stopping their attacks on the Duki and inflicted upon them horrific acts of violence. But the Duki refused to surrender, and the war dragged on. The whole world watched and wondered about the never-ending civil war until a powerful man couldn't watch it anymore and decided to do something about it. The president of the United States ordered the US military to intervene and restore order and stability. It was a humanitarian gesture.

The Tuwi had reservations about the intervention of a foreign power into their land and their war. They thought they had a good chance of defeating the Duki clan once and for all. To make matters worse, the Americans made an attempt to arrest or kill a Tuwi warlord, Colonel Musa. This was the last straw for the Tuwi clan. They took up arms to wage a holy war against the Americans. Thousands of Tuwi slinging AK-47s engaged the American military and their black helicopters in the narrow streets of their city. They were ready to defend their warlord and die for him. No matter what he had done, he was their clansman. Nobody could take him away from them.

The Americans were caught off guard. They never expected the extent of the furious reaction of the Tuwi clansmen. Outnumbered and outflanked, they were soon taking fire from all directions. The hostile environment worked against them. They could barely see anything—the smoke, the dust, the narrow streets and the barriers on roads where the Tuwi fighters could be hiding. Two helicopters crashed in the middle of a street and the American soldiers tried to save the pilots. They fought against all odds to reach them, braving a rain of bullets and suffering more casualties on the way. In the end, they were pushed back and had to retreat to their camps, leaving their comrades behind.

After two weeks, the Americans had had enough. They declared the mission hopeless and gave up. They packed their bags and left the country in the middle of the night.

The Tuwi celebrated their victory over the Americans, claiming to be the new Viet Cong. But the way they celebrated caught the attention of the world. It was no way to celebrate anything. They tied dead American soldiers on tops of cars and drove down the streets as though displaying trophies. Even the other battle-hardened clans were shocked at this sight.

Days after the American military operation ended in failure, I was sitting in the Bloor doughnut shop with Mohamed and Jama when I noticed a Tuwi clansman walking in. I knew him quite well and waved my hand to attract his attention, playfully remarking, "Why are you swaggering like a superpower?"

"I am a superpower. I am a Black Viet Cong. Who do you think you are talking to?" the Tuwi crowed defiantly.

"You can brag all you want, but let me tell you something: The Americans were just trying to help you," Mohamed said.

"Who asked for their help? Tell me. Nobody needed anything from this hollowed giant depleted by overreaching, arrogance, and special interests," the man answered.

"Why are you so pissed off at them? I don't understand it," Mohamed shot back.

"Why should I not be? They barged into our town with their marines and their air force. Nobody was fighting them. Nobody gave them a visa to come into our land. They just crashed into our party like a crazy intruder. And what was the first thing they did? They denounced our warlord and were out to kill him."

"Come on! Get a grip on yourself. So they made a mistake, a lapse of judgement, and tried to get rid of your warlord. So what? Give them a break. They had good intentions, for heaven's sake," Mohamed tried to reason, but it wasn't working.

"They sure made a mistake. And talking about mistakes, how is the Somaha Republic doing these days? Is it working for you?" the Tuwi asked, pushing a sensitive button that he knew would definitely get us going.

"Wait a minute," I quickly chimed in. "How can you call our Somaha Republic a mistake?"

"Because you are dividing the nation."

"We were a nation? Like Canada?"

"Yes."

"When did we become a nation? This is news to me. You were always a Tuwi, I was a Sudi, and a Duki was only a Duki. And now that we are separating from you guys to form our own separate country, all of a sudden you are saying we were a nation before."

"You don't believe in Somali nationhood? You are denying . . . " The Tuwi trailed off and looked from one of us to the other, amazed by how alienated we had become from them.

"Why didn't you tell the Duki clan about this nationhood that you have just discovered when they were killing us by the tens of thousands?" I retorted angrily.

"I understand where you are going with this. Terrible things happened and I hear you. But things will change. There will never be a Duki government again," the Tuwi said.

"You are wasting your time," I said. "You should have done the right thing a long time ago."

"What thing?"

"You should have minded your own business. You should have made your own republic in your own region like we did. But then again, maybe the famous poet had a point when he depicted you guys as hopeless slackers."

"You should not say that, Ali. That is an insult."

"No, that is no insult. We are just telling you to make your own separate republic as well and forget about us."

"And the Duki clan?"

"Who cares about the Duki clan! They can make their own republic too. Or they can go to hell as far as I am concerned."

"Ali, can't we let bygones be bygones? Can't we move on? A tragic thing happened. But that doesn't mean it will happen again."

"And forget about all that happened? Nobody spills the blood of Sudi clansmen and gets away with it," I said, sticking to my guns.

"Come on! You can't separate. You can't leave us," the Tuwi said.

"Can't separate? We already did. How many times do we have to say goodbye to you? We are telling you in your face: we don't want you."

"Okay, okay, I know what you are trying to do, but . . . "

"No buts and no ifs. You have to face the reality and get on with it or you can keep on dithering till another General Kahin comes along."

"I guess you made up your minds and there's no turning back."

"We sure did," I said and leaned back on my chair.

"But not so fast, Ali. You have a long way to go before you have your own separate country. You still have no diplomatic recognition. No government has yet recognized your newly-invented republic. Don't count your chickens before they hatch."

With that, he stood up to leave us.

Jama, who was exceptionally quiet that day, smiled and remarked, "He didn't even finish his cup of tea. You chased him away."

"Jama, nobody can chase away a Black Viet Cong," Mohamed said and they laughed.

I didn't laugh, still bothered by the notion of diplomatic recognition and what it meant for us. Turning to Mohamed, I asked, "Is what he said true? Do we have to get some kind of recognition and approval from the other countries before we become a separate country?"

"Yes," Mohamed responded calmly.

"Doesn't our clan have the right to separate from the other clans and form our own new country if we want to?"

"We can separate, but the separation is not complete until recognized by the United Nations and the international community. It is something important and critical. It is something we have to get," Mohamed said and smiled impishly at me.

His condescending smile didn't offend me. I let him have fun at my expense, at a camel boy trying to make sense of world politics. This diplomatic recognition was bad news to me, a kind of red flag down the road. It could endanger our future and our newly-formed country. Getting impatient and worried, I asked him again, "Are you saying that diplomatic recognition is a must? I mean, is there any way around it?"

"No, there is no way around it. We have to get it. It is the way the international politics works. We need recognition from the other countries in the world," Mohamed responded firmly.

"Why do we need recognition?"

"To join the world community. We are talking about the United Nations here."

"That is not fair."

"Who said international politics is about fairness?"

"What is it about, then?"

"It is about the national interests of the various countries coming head to head with one another. It is about power, both military and financial. It is about who you are and what you can bring to the table," Mohamed explained what sounded to me like the embodiment of brute force and injustice.

"Probably these countries don't know what happened to us. Maybe, if we tell them what we had been through at the hands of the Duki government, they would be more sympathetic to our cause."

"That is what I am saying. That is the whole point. Engaging and communicating with other countries is something we have to do. It is called diplomacy."

Mohamed might have told me about the reality out there, but the idea of diplomatic recognition still seemed irrelevant and unfair to me. How could foreign countries determine our future? Who gave them the right to stand in our way and to reject our desire to form our own separate country? What do they know about us anyway?

I also wondered if there had been a precedent for when the people of a country couldn't get along and the only option for them was to separate from each other. To find out that out, I asked Mohamed, "Are you telling me that in the history of the world, no country has ever been split into two parts for one reason or another?"

Mohamed thought for a moment and said, "No, I am not saying that. There have been a few cases. Bangladesh used to be part of Pakistan."

"That means we have a chance." The precedent of other countries who went through a break-up revived my sinking hope.

"Of course, we have a chance. I never said there is no chance. We just have to work for it and earn it."

"And how can we do that?"

"First of all, we have to establish a democratic government and show the world that we are a real functioning country. At the same time, we have to play the game of diplomacy."

"What do you mean by 'play the game of diplomacy'?"

"Befriending other governments, adopting good public relations with them. That is what I mean by diplomacy. And once we convince one country to extend political recognition, the others will soon follow suit. That is all."

"So one country recognizes us and opens the door for us, and others will do the same. Is that what you are saying?"

"Pretty much."

"That shouldn't be difficult. That shouldn't be a problem. Of all those hundreds of countries in the world, we can't win over one country? I think we can. I think we can find one country that will do us favour. We can't be at odds with the whole damn world."

"Is there any country you have in mind?"

"How about France?" It was the first country that came to mind.

"We don't have a chance with the French. You can rule them out."

"Why?"

"If you don't speak the French language, you are out of luck with the French."

"Wow! They love their language that much?"

"As much as their women, maybe even more. And nobody has ever said that French men don't love their women."

"That doesn't make sense, Mohamed, but let us move on. How about Canada? Canadians helped us as refugees. Can they do a little bit more and become the first country that recognizes us?"

"No, Canada won't be the first one. Canadian foreign policy is too cautious. It lacks that maverick streak that goes the extra mile; that aggressive cutting edge that breaks new ground."

Through the window, I could see Canadians walking in the street, all bundled up with their overcoats, hats, and gloves to fight off the freezing cold. I shook my head, feeling a bit sad, and said, "Without a doubt, Canadians are one of the most decent and civilized people on earth. It is a fact. But there is that one thing holding them back."

"And what is that?" Mohamed inquired.

"It is that damn snow falling on them day after day, month after month and season after season. It is their Achilles' heel. It is their Duki clan. It dampened their spirit and slowed them down. Look at them. I bet the only thing on their mind is how to survive this winter and make it to the next summer. The deadly blasts of the Arctic winds and the snowstorms took a toll on them. I wish I could bring the sun a bit closer to them."

"There you go. You can blame the weather for losing Canada," Mohamed remarked as he watched the people walking in the street.

"What do you think of the United States?" I asked with a tinge of excitement. "From what I hear on the news, these guys are not as cautious as the Canadians. They jump on everything. They go everywhere in the world with guns blazing."

"The United States is upset with us. Forget about them too." Mohamed's answer was forceful and blunt this time.

"The Americans are upset with us! Why?"

"Because of what the Tuwi clansmen did. They dishonoured the dead bodies of American soldiers. It was terrible."

"But it was the Tuwi clansmen who did that, not us."

"The Americans don't know the difference between the Sudi and the Tuwi clansmen. They just see us as one nation."

"What nation! They went to the moon and they don't know that we are just clans? They can't differentiate between a Tuwi, Sudi and Duki clansman?"

"No, they can't differentiate. Maybe they should have learned more about the earth and our clans before they flew to the moon."

"How about England? The English people sure know us. They once ruled us and they owe us a favour for old time's sake," I said, fully confident that I found a winner and the right country.

"England is also upset with us."

"Even good old England is upset with us! Why? What have we done to upset them?"

"We rejected their advice when we took our independence from them."

"And the advice was?"

"That the Sudi clan become a separate country and join the commonwealth."

"That was good advice."

"Indeed, it was. We should have listened to them and taken their advice. We lost our mind and joined all those other clans to form one big country."

"We really blew it and made a stupid mistake. That commonwealth thing was a good deal. How about if we apologize to England now and ask them to give us a second chance? We will be nice to them. What do you think of that?"

"I don't think they will give us a second chance. It is too late. They will just say to us: 'I told you so.'"

For a moment, we both fell silent as I struggled to come up with another country that might extend a helping hand, the countries I heard about from the television and radio. "How about China?" I finally blurted out.

"The Chinese government don't do favours."

"Never?"

"Never."

"Why? That is not good."

"They are reducing their own population. So why would they do favours to other people? You know how big their population is?"

"No."

"More than a billion. Had there been ten more countries in the world with that kind of population, we would have reached the stage that Dr Malthus had warned us about. The earth's resources would be exhausted. No clean water to drink. No food to eat, nothing. And people would have no option but to eat one another. And if that happens, you can forget about getting help from anybody."

"I know nothing about Dr Malthus and his gloomy talk; but how much is a billion?"

"One thousand million."

"And how much is a million?"

"Ten hundred thousand."

"I can't even imagine so many people in one country. How many clans do they have over there in China?"

"I am not sure. Probably one big clan, the Chinese clan."

"That is one hell of a clan. I wish the Sudi clan was as big as the Chinese clan. Oh man, what we could do to the Duki clan."

"What do you mean? What do you have in mind?"

"Imagine this possibility. Imagine all Sudi men and women, old and young, more than a billion of us, coming together; men on one side and women on the other side. Imagine we all piss at the same time in the direction of the Duki clan settlements after drinking as much tea and camel milk as our stomachs can take. What do you think the result would be?"

"A stinking mess, of course."

"It would be a lot more than a stinking mess. It would be raging floods of urine the likes of which the world has never seen before. It would be like the juices of hell on a rampage, bearing down on the Duki clan settlements. They see what is coming towards them from a short distance. No Duki clansman is safe and they all start screaming. Their only hope is to outrun it and get out of the way, but they can't. They are doomed. And lo and behold, the torrents of urine sweep them off their feet. Their heads pop in and out a few times before they all drown with their camels and sheep as we watch them from a distance, jeering at them and savouring the moment."

"That would be too risky for us. He would attack us," Mohamed said curtly. It seemed that he had a counter argument for every statement I made.

"Who would attack us?" I asked, somewhat befuddled.

"The American president."

"Why?"

"For using weapons of mass destruction."

"What weapons of mass destruction?"

"He would say that urine in big quantities is tantamount to weapons of mass destruction. He would say it is a breach of international law."

"I can't believe this. Do you really think he would attack us for pissing?" I asked him, finding it hard to believe what Mohamed told me.

"Yes, I do. But first he would set the stage for war and take the issue to the Security Council of the United Nations, asking them to pass a resolution against us. That resolution would be just a cover to despatch the US Marines, US army, and US Air Force. It would be 'Shock and Awe' all over again. Look at what happened to Iraq. And they didn't even pee at anybody."

"This doesn't make sense to me. How did this man, who is attacking people for ridiculous reasons, become the president of America?" I asked, putting our issue of political recognition on the back burner for a while to understand how the president of the United States of America could go so wrong.

"They elected him. He won the election."

"You mean they voted for him?"

"Yes, they did."

"What were they thinking when they cast their votes for this man?"

"The right to own guns, abortion, and school prayers. That is what they were thinking about. These are their favourite issues."

I didn't know what to say and remained silent.

"Hard to believe, isn't it?" Mohamed continued, "You would think that the self-proclaimed 'Greatest Nation on Earth, the Home of the Brave, the Land of the Free, and the prophets of exceptionalism' would do better than that."

"The Americans made a mistake in electing this guy. No doubt about that. He is probably their Supreme Leader. You think they will repeat that mistake in the future?" I asked.

"Who knows? It might even get worse. Next time, they might elect a buffoon with an ego."

"Let us forget about the Americans too. We are looking for political recognition, not the American military bombarding us. Now let me think of another country. What do you say about that country that successfully separated from Pakistan?" I asked, trying my luck with a country that I had just heard of from Mohamed.

"Bangladesh?"

"Yes, Bangladesh. They have been in our shoes. They know what it is like to be looking for political recognition."

"I don't think Bangladesh can help us in any way."

"What do you mean?"

"In the general scheme of things, Bangladesh is not a big player in the world. They are too poor and too inconsequential. The only time you hear from them is when a natural disaster hits them."

"That is not fair, Mohamed. Shouldn't all countries be equal? Why are you dismissing Bangladesh as inconsequential?"

"Nobody is equal to nobody. There are the big and the powerful countries that make things happen and rule the world; and then there are the nobodies that are just poor and desperate."

"I guess we are one of the nobodies?"

"Yes, we are. You are damn right."

"Like Bangladesh."

"No. Worse than Bangladesh. At least, Bangladesh has a stable government."

I wasn't convinced and had my doubts about Mohamed's statements; but I moved on to look for another country and asked him, "How about the Arab countries?" As the story goes, the Sudi clan had some roots in the Arab countries and we always considered them as distant relatives. Like we were the lost black cousin of the Arabs! It was time these guys did something for us and helped us.

"Have you heard the saying 'those who help themselves can help others'?" Mohamed asked.

"Yes."

"I rest my case."

"What is that supposed to mean? That they are too weak to help anybody?"

"If they could lend a hand to anybody, they would have helped the Palestinians."

"Okay, forget about the Arab countries too." I was running out of countries; but then I remembered one more. "How about Iran?" I blurted out another Muslim country that had often been in the news lately.

"The Iran of Ayatollah Khomeini?" Mohamed asked, a bit surprised.

"Is there another Iran?"

"Now you are getting desperate. Forget about Iran. We don't need their help. It will make our case a lot worse."

"How can Iran make our case a lot worse? I don't under-stand it."

"Because the Americans are allergic to Iran. They are against everything and anything that Iran is involved in. It is like waving a red flag to a bull. They will oppose us and use their veto power if they have to. In any case, the Iranian government will never support us for anything. They are Shiite and we are Sunni. And believe me, they don't like the Sunni

Muslims. They hate us. To them, we are the junior infidels."

"Infidels? Where did they get that from?" I interrupted him.

"I don't know. All I know is that the Iran government has a hand in every conflict between the two sects of the Muslim religion anywhere in the world. They are waging a crusade against the Sunni Muslims. So forget about them."

"Okay, okay. Let me think of another country. How about Ethiopia? Don't tell me that America is allergic to them as well."

"Ethiopia should have recognized us long time ago. It is in their political interest. But here is the problem . . . "

"Mohamed, you are in a negative mood and see a problem in every country," I pushed back at him, raising my voice in frustration.

To defend himself, Mohamed embarked on a long tirade about the fact that the third world countries and particularly Africans always expected the Europeans and Americans to take the lead on every issue, even on an issue so important to them and so close to home.

With a bit of desperation, I pointed out other countries that could help us and extend political recognition to us, countries I had heard about from the news, like Germany, Japan, and Pakistan. For each country, Mohamed came up with some political interest that could deny us their recognition.

Finally, Mohamed decided that we had had enough discussion about international politics for one day. He paid for the tea and went home.

I left the donut shop with Jama, who had quietly sat with us the whole day. And even on the way home, he seemed to be in some kind of meditation. He was suffering from a bad flu that day, not to mention that he was also busy finding a one-bedroom apartment to rent. Now that the sponsorship of my family had been successful, he knew that the arrival of my family into Canada was just a matter of time. And the moment that happened, Jama was ready to leave the apartment for me and my family. I could not have been more grateful to him.

15

AFTER RECEIVING THEIR VISAS FROM the Canadian Embassy in Ethiopia, my family was ready to fly to Canada. In a telephone call, my wife gave me the day and time they were expected to arrive in Toronto. Two hours before their arrival time, I took the airport bus from Kipling subway station. Mohamed and Jama had to go to work and didn't accompany me.

At the airport, I sat in the arrivals waiting area, my eyes focused on the gate. After an hour, a long line of people streamed out into the big arrivals hall. There was no sign of Fatima. I began to worry about them when, finally, Fatima and Dagaal came through, looking tired and dazed. They had yet to see me in the waiting crowd and their eyes scanned all directions looking for me. Didn't she recognize me, I wondered? It had been a long time since we last saw each other.

"Fatima, Fatima!" I shouted to attract her attention and reassure her that I was here while pushing my way through the crowd to get closer to them. It was only when Fatima heard my voice and saw me that I felt relieved and calmed down. Dagaal kept staring at me. A son and a father seeing each other for the first time, what an occasion! He slowly shuffled forward as he held his mother's hand.

They were late coming out because they had to register with Canadian immigration first. For some reason, the questioning had been intense, as though Fatima was an imposter, and her luggage was checked thoroughly. Why they targeted my family, I had no idea. In the end, the officer found nothing wrong with the documents and luggage of my family and let them go. My wife and son stepped out, free to enter their new country and meet me. I hugged both my wife and my son, one after another.

"How are you? Are you all okay?" I asked.

"We are fine. Only tired after the long flight," Fatima said.

Dagaal merely nodded without showing much excitement in meeting his father for the first time in his life. He looked at me as if I were a stranger and not his father. How could I blame him when I had never been part of his life and never told him what he meant to me? He needed time to know me; time to get over the lingering effect of an absentee father.

Even my relationship with my wife seemed distant. For too long I had been an absentee husband. Nine years had passed since the day my wife last saw me in a prison cell with my face beaten and bloodied. How I had waited for this moment. How I had waited to see her again and hold her. We could now begin our life as a husband and a wife, and as a family. Nobody could separate us again. Not a government of an enemy clan or anybody else. Outside the airport, we took a taxi and headed for our apartment.

As the taxi raced along Highway 427, we barely said anything meaningful to each other. Fatima and Dagaal sat in the back seat, their attention focused on the sights of Toronto—the tall buildings, the wide highways, the multitude of cars on the road. Their eyes feasted on the plentiful grass in the parks and lawns. "There is grass over here, but there are no sheep or camels grazing. Why is that?" Fatima inquired.

"It is a public park. It is for people to sit and rest. There are no camels here in Canada," I explained to her. "And sheep are in farms, outside the city."

"What a waste to leave all that green grass untouched," she remarked.

We reached home just before lunch time and sat in the living room. There was a lot of catching up to do, much to talk about. But first, I went into the kitchen and warmed the rice and chicken that had been in the refrigerator. I served them the food and tea afterwards. All along, Fatima watched me with a mixture of amusement and surprise. It was the first time she saw me, or any man, go into the kitchen and serve her food while she just relaxed in the living room. The look on her face said it all.

In Canada, more surprises awaited her over the days and weeks—the culture, the language and, above all, the cold weather. Coming to a new country had its difficulties, as I well knew. Riding the subway train and shopping in the mall posed a challenge; she made great efforts to cope with all that and even went to a night school to learn English. Dagaal fared better. He was a young boy with an open mind. It didn't take him long before he adjusted to the rhythms and nuances of life in Canada.

At the beginning, my wife looked to me for assistance in almost every-thing and justifiably so. She needed me to go with her to the grocery store. My son expected me to take him to school every morning. I had to be there for them. But something always pulled me to the Bloor dough-nut shop. I had to go there to meet Mohamed and Jama at least once a day. I was eagerly anticipating news about a second meeting of the Sudi elders, which was to be convened to form the government of the Somaha Republic. Sometimes, Mohamed and Jama provided me the latest news.

The first government had been a provisional one, to rule the country for a short period. In this meeting, the Sudi elders would elect a new president who would stay in office for four years. We couldn't hold a general election in which everybody voted, which might have been a lot better. Our young country lacked the financial means and expertise to hold fair elections. So we let our elders do the electing for us.

For about a week, we followed with great interest the developments of the meeting. We couldn't wait to know who the new president of the Somaha Republic would be. Our feverish anticipation kept us on our toes. Unfortunately, the meeting didn't go well. A big hurdle stood in the way. The sticking point was the election of the president. Each sub-clan insisted that one of their own be elected president. And with that, the possibility of a quick resolution and consensus evaporated. Fractious disputes led to heated arguments. Scuffles broke out between represen-tatives of the sub-clans, threatening to derail the whole process. The meeting was about to end in disaster until in the final session, a majority decision was reached. Mr Moge was elected president.

Our new president had a dubious past. He had once worked closely with the deposed Supreme Leader. Also, he hadn't taken part in the Sudi war against the Duki government; he had not answered the call when his clan needed him. And yet we elected him president of our new country. It was ironic and even downright wrong. But the fact that he belonged to our clan trumped everything else. Somehow, we felt safe with any

Sudi leader, even one with such a past. We had to forgive him and stand behind him. But after only two months, I began to have second thoughts about the man.

President Moge formed a new government dominated by his Lulu sub-clan. This was the first worrisome sign of things to come. He had certainly started off on the wrong foot. And things got even worse. He made bellicose speeches against what he called the enemy within, swore to root them out with fire and fury. His speeches sounded familiar; they reminded me of General Kahin, the Supreme Leader and a Duki.

Our newly formed, war-ravaged country had to be rebuilt. Our wounded freedom fighters needed care and rehabilitation. Political recognition for the new country needed to be sought from foreign governments. Mr Moge had a lot on his plate and a worthwhile mission to carry out. But as far as he was concerned, none of that mattered. What mattered to him was to settle scores with other Sudi sub-clans. What mattered to him was to pick a fight with one sub-clan in particular, the Nunu.

In no uncertain terms, he depicted the Nunu as the enemy of his government. He threatened to annihilate them. Nothing was more important to him than to defeat them and shed their blood. It seemed that he would do at the sub-clan level what the Supreme Leader had done at the clan level.

It was early Saturday morning when President Moge ordered his militia to wage a full-fledged assault on the Nunu. He unleashed his forces just as we anticipated. It didn't surprise anybody.

President Moge had no doubt that he would be victorious in a matter of days. He counted on the full and unqualified support of his own sub-clan and he got it. Not one Lulu expressed dissent. Not one inquired why the Nunu sub-clan had to be attacked. Out of loyalty, they grabbed their guns, ready to kill or be killed.

To strengthen his hand, President Moge began to look for allies. He needed more than his sub-clan to wage this war. So he approached the Juju sub-clan and invited them to join the war on his side. The Juju sub-clan didn't need much convincing and quickly struck a deal with him. They had a long-standing quarrel with the Nunu that had been simmering for generations. The Juju had yet to forget the war between them and the Nunu that occurred sixty years earlier, caused by a fight between two teenagers over a waist belt. For them, this war was an opportunity to fight the waist belt war all over again, an opportunity for revenge. With two sub-clans and the Somaha government behind him, President Moge was confident that he had enough forces to crush the Nunu once and for all. But something was missing. He had never articulated any justification for this new war. Maybe, he had none. Maybe, he had just deep-seated hatred for the Nunu sub-clan. Whatever the reason, his timing was terrible. We had barely emerged from the brutal and bloody war against the Duki government when he ignited a new conflict between the Sudi sub-clans.

The Nunu sub-clan, to which I belonged, faced formidable forces. They attacked us on two fronts, the east and the west. The attacks came fast and furious, day and night. My sub-clan had to fight back or perish. Somehow, they managed to stand their ground and succeeded in pushing back the attacks. We were outgunned and outnumbered, and yet we survived the first armed confrontation.

This second war between the sub-clans couldn't have come at a worse time. The Somaha Republic, our new country, would suffer a setback in so many ways. It might not even survive as a separate country. And my plan to go back and avenge the killing of my father would have to be delayed. Where would I go now even if I had a passport? I would be arrested the moment I landed at the airport.

For hours, I would not say a word to anybody and merely listen to the radio. Inside my apartment, an uncomfortable silence prevailed. Even my young son understood the gravity of the situation and turned his full attention to the news.

As I followed the war, I racked my brain to figure out why President Moge had attacked us. There was no current issue to pit the Sudi sub-clans against one another; no dispute to warrant an armed conflict. True, skirmishes had erupted among our various sub-clans in the distant past, disputes over a water well, a girl, a waist belt, or a camel. But I couldn't fathom why a conflict had to happen at the present time, especially after the long and destructive war against the Duki, in which we had all suffered. Especially when we had to build a new country and a new future and to show the world that we were ready to govern ourselves. Nothing had happened this time that could lead to any sort of conflict. President Moge had just launched this war for no apparent reason.

The war spread beyond the two biggest towns in the Somaha Republic. Thousands of militias died on both sides, including my oldest second cousin, Farah. A telephone call to a fourth cousin in Dubai confirmed his death. He died for his sub-clan, and so did many others.

On the second day of the war, I listened to the news in the morning. Then I dressed and left home to go to the doughnut shop to see Mohamed and Jama. Neither of them belonged to the Nunu sub-clan and I could well anticipate their position concerning the war. Part of me wished they would prove me wrong, but I knew better. Mohamed belonged to the Lulu sub-clan, and Jama, the Juju. In fact, Mohamed and President Moge were distant relatives.

Feeling somewhat subdued, I walked slowly into the doughnut shop and saw Mohamed and Jama sitting in a corner. I joined them. The cool reception and the evasive glances I received spoke volumes; things would never be the same between us again. This meeting had the look of turning out to be our last one.

For a brief moment, none of us uttered a word as I faced the two of them across the table. Mohamed fidgeted and Jama looked away. But their unease could not stop me, and I raised the issue upfront. "You must have heard what President Moge has done, haven't you?" I asked.

"What did he do?" Mohamed responded, pretending he didn't know what I was talking about, the war that his sub-clansman president had started.

"What do you mean 'what did he do'? He attacked the Nunu and you know it," I said.

Mohamed squirmed and struggled to come up with an answer. I waited for him patiently to tell me why President Moge had attacked my sub-clan, to justify the unjustifiable.

"The president just attacked a group of bandits, that is it," he finally blurted out.

"Yes, they are bandits," Jama agreed with him.

Their answers confirmed what I had suspected all along. My former allies and clansmen, the two guys who had helped me settle in Canada, were now my enemies. Given the new reality, I weighed my words carefully and asked, "Do you remember what the Duki government used to call us when we were fighting them?"

"No." Mohamed shook his head.

"You don't remember the word *bandits*? Doesn't it ring a bell? That is exactly what General Kahin used to call us. It wasn't right then and it isn't right now."

"The government is just attacking a group of bandits and we are not like the Duki clansmen," Mohamed said angrily, taking the comparison as an insult.

Ignoring his anger, I shot back, "No amount of cheap insults can change the reality. You can call us all the names you want. You can come up with all sorts of excuses. But here is the truth: President Moge and your people started this war and attacked my sub-clansmen, my brothers and sisters, flesh and blood."

"They may belong to your sub-clan, but they oppose the Somaha government, and that makes them bandits," Mohamed reiterated.

"That's right," Jama said, taking his side one more time.

I ignored Jama, considering him an annoying sidekick, and directed my attention at Mohamed. "The Nunu haven't opposed anything. And even if they opposed your uncle, so what? Don't they have the right to do so? Or is it that anybody who happens to be against your uncle automatically becomes a bandit to be attacked?"

"The president of the Somaha Republic is not my uncle," Mohamed snorted, his nose twitching.

"He is your uncle and your beloved sub-clansman. And you would support him even if he . . . " I paused for a moment.

"Even if what?" Mohamed said.

"Even if he burned a mosque in broad daylight."

"So what if I support him? We all support our sub-clans. That is what you are doing yourself just now."

"At least I am not supporting my sub-clan for all the wrong reasons. Besides, whatever happened to the principles of democracy and justice that you used to talk about when we were fighting General Kahin and his clan? Do you espouse democracy and justice only when you are the victim?" I argued, knowing that I had the high moral ground and raised an indisputable point.

"I can believe in democracy and justice and support the president of the Somaha Republic at the same time. The two are not mutually exclusive."

Jama nodded his head to indicate that he concurred with Mohamed's view. He was agreeing with him about everything. It was as if they were thinking using the same brain. Once again I ignored him and directed my reply at Mohamed.

"Maybe, you can also bring the sky and the earth together and fuse them into one. Why not do that as well?"

"That is not a correct analogy," Mohamed said.

"Yes, that is not a correct analogy," Jama echoed.

"Why don't you say something for yourself," I finally lashed out at Jama, having had enough of him. "You are simply repeating whatever Mohamed says. And why are you supporting President Moge, anyway? You are a Juju, not a Lulu. You should have been neutral about this war."

"We are all fighting against bandits," Jama said defiantly.

"Get real and stop that nonsense about bandits. We all know what is bugging you, Jama. It is all about that stupid belt our two sub-clans fought over sixty years ago. As the folks down here say, that left a chip on your shoulder, a chip you have been carrying for the last sixty years. You take offence when nobody offends you. You pick a fight when there is no reason to fight. What do you want from us? The waist belt? Is that what you are after? After all these years and decades? After tens of thousands of people died on both sides for that damn worthless belt? What should we do to make you get over this? You want the belt, you got it. Here, take those ten bucks and buy a new one from the store right across the street. And you can keep the change," I said, throwing a ten-dollar bill at him.

Jama said nothing and ignored the bill, which fell on the floor under him.

After a moment of silence, Mohamed intervened, "Let us calm down here. Nobody has a chip on his shoulder."

"Yes, he has. And you too, Mohamed. I can't believe this. It is as if I am dealing with the Duki clan all over again. Whatever happened to our talk of forming a government as fair and just as the traffic lights of Canada? What is this? Re-fighting some of our ancient wars? And if that is the case, you guys have a problem. There is no other explanation."

"The only problem is that President Moge is waging this war to save the Somaha Republic. He is my president, and he is your president, Ali."

"No, he is not," I objected.

"Since when?"

"Since he attacked my sub-clan. From now on, I am just a Nunu, no more and no less."

I had stopped identifying myself with the Sudi. Even the Somaha Republic I had embraced earlier no longer meant anything to me.

"You are making too much out of this attack on a group of bandits."

"Don't you ever call my sub-clan bandits," I warned him, wagging my finger at him.

"They are bandits, and only bandits," Mohamed repeated the word one more time, almost taunting me.

The insult had barely come out of his mouth again when I lunged at him and punched him in the face. To avoid the blow, Mohamed jumped backwards. But it was too late. His nose bleeding, he fought back. He got help from Jama, who started hitting me from behind. I had to fend off blows from both front and back. Like my sub-clan, I was fighting on two fronts at the same time.

Our fight turned the small doughnut shop into a chaotic battleground. Tables and chairs got overturned; cups of tea and coffee fell on the floor; beverages were spilled. The sounds of things breaking and the screams and shouts of people filled the room. The war among the Sudi sub-clans back home had crossed the ocean into Canada.

The owner of the doughnut shop was frantic; he could do nothing to stop the fight. Stationed behind the counter, he kept pleading, "Guys, guys! Please get out of my shop, and do your fighting outside. You are destroying my business. Stop it now or I will call the police."

Nobody listened to him. The customers, who were caught in the middle of a fight, ran for their lives and rushed out the doors, except for a group of four men sitting at a table. The four men decided to take matters into their own hands and intercede. They threw themselves into the fray. They tackled us one by one. It didn't take long before they succeeded in stopping the fight. The owner of the shop couldn't have been more grateful to them, thanking them over and over.

With the four men between us, we could no longer reach each other. But we could still hurl insults, not personal ones but insults directed at our sub-clans, which were more hurtful than anything else. "You are a wild hyena like your people," Mohamed screamed at me, gasping for air.

"You are a tricky cat, Mohamed," I hurled. "And you are a fox, Jama, and not even a clever fox."

Then I stormed out of the doughnut shop. I had to leave before it was too late. The police would come at any moment. To remain in the vicinity wasn't a good idea.

As I was walking away from the scene, I felt pain in my lower back where Jama had hit me with something. I touched the aching spot a few times, my fingers lingering upon it. Blood also dripped from an injury above my right eye and I wiped it with my hand. I could have sought medical treatment for those injuries, but they didn't seem too serious. So I headed towards home.

Along the way, I had second thoughts about going home. It wasn't such a good idea, after all. It would be disconcerting to Fatima and Dagaal to see me in the shape I was in. I needed to sit down in a place by myself for some time to cool off, wash my face, and ponder about what had just happened and where to go from here.

A place that looked like a coffee shop caught my attention and I went inside. The lights were so dim that it looked a bit strange, though it had tables and chairs and a serving counter. I proceeded cautiously and looked for the washroom to take a look at the injury on my face. After washing my face and coming back from the bathroom, I found a vacant table.

As soon as I sat down, I realized that this was no coffee shop; it was a bar serving alcohol. Under normal circumstances, I would have bolted and asked forgiveness from Allah for having entered such a place. But there was nothing normal about the day they attacked my sub-clan. I was angry and distraught. I was ready to defy all the conventions I had grown up with. So I decided to stay. The joyful mood of the customers and the soft music playing in the background easily put me at ease.

On my right, a man and a woman were holding hands. They tickled each other and laughed together. They were having the time of their lives and obviously living in a different world, one a lot better than mine. On the other side, four men were engaged in a loud conversation punctuated with roars of laughter.

I wondered if drinking alcohol would make me forget about the Lulu and Juju sub-clans and make me as happy as these folks in the bar. Never before had I entertained such an idea. In my religion, drinking alcohol was a big no-no, a sinful act. The Surah in the Quran declaring the prohibition didn't mince words. I might have already crossed a line by just sitting inside a bar. But the attack on my Nunu sub-clan eclipsed all those religious directives and prohibitions. It was the only thing on my mind. I cared about nothing else and feared nothing. Not even hell with its scorching flames.

I didn't wait long when a smiling bartender came over and asked, "What would you like to drink?" At the same time, he put a small bowl of peanuts on the table.

I hesitated for a few seconds. At the back of my mind, I could hear voices warning me not to have anything to do with the Satanic drink or I would burn in hell. I ignored them and asked the bartender, "Can I have a glass of alcohol?"

"What do you want: beer, wine, rum, whisky?" The bartender read a list of all the various alcoholic drinks available in the bar, as if I could tell one from the other.

"Just give me one of them. Anything that gets me drunk and makes me forget President Moge and his sub-clan is fine with me."

"You have to tell me what you want. I can't choose for you," the man insisted, his smile fading.

"Give me the first one."

"Beer?"

"Yes, beer."

I had heard the name of this drink a few times and thought it might be the best. With my elbows perched on the table and the attack on my sub-clan still on my mind, I waited for the drink. If only somebody could tell me why President Moge waged the attack on us. If only somebody could explain why he did what he did. Not giving up, I tried in vain to find some logic in a war that didn't make sense.

The bartender served me a glass of beer and was about to turn when I asked him, "Hey, do you know why President Moge and his people attacked my sub-clan?"

"What sub-clan?" He stopped and stared at me.

"Never mind," I said and turned my attention to the glass of beer in front of me. A thick layer of bubbles covered its surface. It reminded me of the time when I owned sixty camels, and every morning drank fresh camel milk with bubbles covering its surface. Could beer be the milk of other animals, I wondered. But the only animals I had seen in Canada were dogs, cats, and cows. This was no cow milk. So could it be that of dogs or cats? The mere thought of that possibility alarmed me.

To get some clarification, I called the bartender back to my table and asked, "Tell me! How do you make this beer? Is it some kind of milk?"

"Milk! This is no milk. It is made from crops and fruits. What are you talking about?"

He bristled and looked at me in a strange way, probably thinking I was a bit crazy, if not downright mad.

Relieved, I smiled at the bartender to calm him down and cautiously took my first sip. And what a strong, sour taste! I didn't like it and almost threw up. Cursing the bartender and anybody who had anything to do with alcohol, and beer in particular, I called the bartender back to my table once again. While I waited for him, I wondered why they didn't do something about its taste and make it sweeter.

The bartender finally had time to answer my call. He looked a bit irritated. "What can I do for you?"

"Can I have some sugar," I said, still reeling from the unpleasant taste of the beer. If I was going to hell for drinking this stuff, it had better be tasty. It had better be sweet at least.

The bartender didn't ask any questions. He obliged and brought me some sugar in a bowl. I put more than two spoonfuls of sugar into the drink, but nothing changed. It still tasted sour.

I called the bartender once again. When he came over, I said, "Even sugar can't make this stuff taste better. What the hell is this? I put in all the sugar and it still tastes sour."

"You put sugar into the beer?" he asked.

"Yes."

"What for?"

"To make it taste sweet."

The customers in the bar who were listening to our conversation suddenly burst into laughter all at once. But the bartender was not amused. He just stared at me, an incredulous expression on his face. "What a strange thing to do! I can't believe you put sugar in beer. This is not tea or coffee," he said, and added, "This is not what normal people do. Where are you from, anyway?"

"I am a Nunu sub-clansman," I said loudly, so that all the customers should know who I was.

"Nunu sub-clansman! What is a Nunu sub-clansman?" the bartender asked with a penetrating look in his eyes.

"You don't know the Nunu sub-clan? You never heard of them?" I shot back in defiance.

"Should I know them?"

"Yes. Everybody should."

"Why?"

"You see the big bright sun in the sky that rises every morning?"

"Sure."

"Who do you think it rises for?"

"I guess it rises for the world?"

"No, it doesn't. It rises for the Nunu sub-clan only. And if you think it comes out for anybody else, think again."

"You can't be serious."

"And do you see those millions of stars that shine in the sky at night?" I went on, without missing a beat.

"They shine for the Nunu sub-clan as well?" he said sarcastically.

"You better believe it," I said with all the self-confidence of a camel boy.

"Okay, let us forget about the sun and the stars. What do you want now?" he asked.

"Bring me the other thing—whisky."

After giving me a long hard look, the bartender took away the half-empty glass of beer to the counter. He came back after a while with a glass of whisky. "No more sugar, please," he said, "I don't want any war taking place between the sugar and whisky like the sub-clans you were talking about."

I sipped the whisky cautiously. It didn't taste as bad as the beer. And for some reason, the more I drank, the better it tasted. Within a short time, I had drained the first glass, called the bartender, and ordered three more glasses of whisky. The pain on my back was long gone and so was the slight bleeding on my forehead.

"Three glasses of whisky at the same time?"

"Yes," I said and nodded.

"Are other people coming to join you?"

"No, nobody is coming to join me. I am drinking all by myself. A Nunu can take three at a time."

"Why don't I give you one glass now, and as soon as you drink that one, I will serve you another, and then another," the bartender suggested.

"No, I want all three glasses at the same time."

The bartender relented, shaking his head. He probably feared that I might cause another incident.

He came back with three glasses and put them on the table. As he turned around to go, I said, "Do you want to know why I ordered three glasses at the same time?"

"Yes," he said and stopped a few feet away from me.

"My sub-clan is fighting against three groups—the Somaha government and two sub-clans. Each glass of whisky stands for one of them. If my sub-clan can fight three groups at the same time, I sure can handle three glasses of whisky. Now, do you see where I am going with this?"

"Not really. Why is your sub-clan fighting all these people, anyway?"

"I told you. They just attacked us."

"But why?"

"I wish I knew. All day long, I was asking myself that same question:

Why did they attack us? Don't have the answer yet, but if there is one, I will find out."

"Good luck," the bartender muttered and walked away.

The customers in the bar stole curious glances at me and whispered to one another. They obviously perceived me as an odd character. There might be some truth to that. I couldn't blame them. They had no idea where I was coming from and what I was going through. Feeling self-conscious, I tried not to attract any attention to myself at first. But after draining three glasses of whisky, I couldn't care less. In fact, I wanted to engage them and challenge them. I wanted to bare my soul to them and tell them about President Moge's unprovoked attack on my sub-clan.

Come to think of it, they could help me understand what was going on back home and why President Moge attacked us. Canadians knew everything that happened on the surface of the earth. Nothing was hidden from them. Their computers told them. It was why they kept looking at these computers, in their offices, in their homes, and even in libraries. They could see everything in them. All I had to do was to ask the question. I stood up and walked unsteadily to the nearest table.

The man and the girl saw me coming towards them and stopped their conversation. They looked away and tried to ignore me. They thought I would leave them alone. They couldn't have been more wrong. Towering over them, I asked the man, "Why did they attack us?"

"Who attacked you?" the man turned and stared at me in a hostile manner.

"The Lulu sub-clan, the Juju sub-clan, and the Somaha government, all of them," I said.

"I don't know what you are talking about," he responded with a flash of anger; then he tried to resume his conversation with his girl.

"Why did they attack us?" I raised my voice to make it quite clear to him that I was not going anywhere until I got an answer.

"Why did Lee Harvey Oswald kill John F Kennedy?" the man shot back.

"I don't know."

"And I don't know why they attacked your sub-clan."

"Who was John F Kennedy?"

"He was the president of the United States."

"Was he a bad one?"

"No, he wasn't. He was a good president."

Killing a good president didn't make sense to me. I could understand getting rid of a bad one, but killing a good president!

I returned to my table and took a sip from the last glass of whisky, the drink of Satan as my sheikh would call it. Then I came right back to the same man. Something needed to be clarified about the killing of President Kennedy. "If President Kennedy was a good president as you say, why kill him?" I asked.

"I don't know. Nobody knows why Oswald killed him," the man said and glared at me.

"Not even the American police?"

"No."

"And you are sure he wasn't a bad president?"

"Yes."

Not interested in talking to me anymore, the man turned to his girl and they took up their conversation from where they had left off.

All of a sudden, a big man sitting near the counter proclaimed in a loud and pompous voice, "Every society gets the leader it deserves."

"Nobody deserves the likes of General Kahin and President Moge. So you better shut up!" I shouted back at him. Then I went back to my table and took a few more sips of my whisky while still on my feet. I did not want to sit down anymore. Once again, I went towards the man at the next table.

As soon as he saw me take a step in his direction, the man snapped. "Why don't you sit down and leave us alone? We don't know why the hell they attacked your whatever. And frankly speaking, we don't care," he said, and turned his attention back to his beautiful girl.

I didn't back down. Instead, I stood my ground and hollered, "Tell me! All of you in this place! Why did President Moge attack my sub-clan? And while you are at it, you can also tell me a few other things: why do you always have good presidents and we have bad ones? Why are you always the haves and we the have-nots? Why you and your science make machines, cars, computers, and we make nothing? Why are we always the desperate refugees and you are not? Why do you go forward and we go backwards? Why are you always the winners and we are the losers?"

By the time I was finished with my outburst, there was a dead silence in the bar. A few customers shuffled their feet. Nobody had anything to say. Nobody had answers to my questions, except the big man at the counter who shouted, "The sun rises for you and you are a loser! The sun must be disappointed in you." Then he gave a raucous laugh.

I took two steps towards him. "You go to hell," I said to him. He didn't take me seriously and started sniggering. He was strong enough to beat me up, but I didn't fear him. I was ready to challenge him to a fight.

I wobbled back to my seat to drain the last of my whisky. Along the way, I tripped on something and fell flat on my face. That triggered riotous laughter from the customers.

Upset about the laughter and the jeering, I scrambled to my feet and banged my fist on the table. Two glasses tumbled to the floor and broke into a million pieces. "I am a camel boy and a Nunu sub-clansman," I stood tall and shouted at them. "And nobody and I mean nobody laughs at a Nunu sub-clansman even when he is down and out; even when he has failed to avenge the killing of his father."

The laughter quickly died down. Only a few smiles lingered on some faces.

The next thing I knew, a large man in a black suit came out from behind the bar and called all the bartenders together. He appeared to own the place and I could hear him telling them not to serve me any more liquor. "He might hurt one of the customers or he might hurt himself," he said. From then on, it was only a matter of time before they kicked me out of the bar.

Not even five minutes had passed when I had a confrontation with my bartender. He told me to leave.

"I am leaving your place. You think I want to stay here? But you can't push me or touch me," I said to him, determined to leave the place on my own terms. It was a matter of honour for me. After making my statement and refusing to be pushed around, I staggered out into the street. I had no money left in my pocket to buy more whisky anyway.

At the intersection of Bloor and Ossington, I watched the traffic go by in all directions. A bone-chilling cold wind was gusting from the north. It was the Arctic wind, the one that made the hated snow look like a mere harmless inconvenience. Shivering, I cursed the frigid weather and put my hands in my pockets. My light brown jacket, the only one I owned, didn't help much. I had worn it every day throughout fall, winter and spring. I couldn't go anywhere without it. It had become a part of me. In fact, some people called me "the man with the brown jacket."

Cursing the weather, I looked at the people in the street, still convinced that the Canadians out there could tell me why my sub-clan was attacked. They had everything that happened in the world at the tips of their fingers with their computers and all. No doubt in my mind. I only had to ask them. One way or another, I had to find the answer. I had to seek it from the Canadians out there.

A taxi cruising down the street caught my attention. The driver would have been going around the city all day long, shuffling people from one part of the city to another and chatting with them. He definitely knew what was going on around the world. I waved my hand at him as soon as we locked eyes. At that he swerved in my direction so quickly that he crashed into a small grey car on his right. Both drivers jumped out to examine the damage. People stopped and gathered around to look.

"What the fuck were you thinking?" the owner of the small car, a strong white guy, screamed at the taxi driver, who looked like an Indian to me. He could have been a Pakistani for all I knew. I could never differentiate an Indian from a Pakistani. They look alike and talk alike, almost like identical twins. Who said people from these two countries don't belong to the same clan?

The taxi driver denied any wrongdoing and stood his ground. "It wasn't my fault. So watch out your language," he shouted back at the other guy with an accent that had the rhythm of an African drumbeat. He had to defend himself. To accept fault would cost him a lot of money that he had worked long hours to earn. Money he had crossed oceans for.

Furious, the white guy lunged at him and had to be restrained. Meanwhile, traffic had come to a standstill on both sides of the street, causing chaos and gridlock. More people gathered and the crowd was thick. The two men had stopped shouting at each other. Suddenly, the taxi driver changed his tune and accepted his fault, realizing that the police could come at any moment and things would get more complicated. They struck a deal and exchanged telephone numbers, after which the white guy drove away, still looking pissed off.

The taxi driver also wanted to leave the scene, but not before he had picked up the fare he thought he had been trying to secure when he bumped into the grey car. "Where is that person who was stopping me?" he asked.

"I am here," I raised my hand.

"Come on! Where are you going?"

"I am not going anywhere," I said.

"So, why were you stopping me?"

"I just wanted to ask you a question."

"You wanted to ask me a question?" He repeated my words as if he hadn't heard me right. "For that you stopped me?"

"Yes," I said.

"And what is the question?"

"Why did the Lulu and Juju sub-clans attack my sub-clan?"

"What the hell are you talking about? Are you drunk? Or are you just dumb? What is wrong with you? I am a taxi driver on the road and you stopped me for such a stupid question like that?"

The taxi driver kept hurling insults at me. I didn't respond to him and just walked away. I had no interest in engaging in a fight with a taxi driver in Canada. I had more deserving enemies to worry about.

Down the road, a beautiful girl was walking towards me. Her angelic face, long legs, and shapely body stood out among all the people in the street. Even her walk had the rhythm of music. Any other day, my eyes would have reveled in her beauty; my mind would have imagined things. But not this day. Not the day when my sub-clan had been attacked.

Just as she was about to pass me, I tried to engage her and asked, "Hey, you girl, yes you with the red hair, do you know why they attacked my Nunu sub-clan."

She heard me loud and clear. I knew she did. Yet she pretended that she didn't. Obviously she had no intention of answering my question. Not even one word. Not even a glance in my direction. She just picked up pace and hurried away as if she was scared of me.

A young boy carrying a hockey stick was standing in front of a store not far from me. He looked not more than twelve years old. But young people had their own computers too and knew as much as anybody. So I approached him and asked, "Hey, do you know why President Moge and his sub-clan attacked us?"

Like the girl, he didn't want to answer me and went into the store like he wanted to buy something. He did this to escape from me. His parents probably told him not to talk to strangers. Good for him.

Then along came an old white man carrying a walking stick and wearing a big hat that covered part of his forehead. I had the question ready for him and asked him. Like a man hearing voices from outer space, he frowned and narrowed his eyes. He peered at me for some time. When he still couldn't figure out what I was talking about, he shook his head and shuffled along.

Every time I failed to get a response from the people in the street, my frustration went up a notch. But I didn't give up and continued to look for an answer to a question that seemed to have no answer. No way was I going to concede failure and throw in the towel. I might be unable to do much for my sub-clan back home while so far away from them; but at least I had to know what was going on.

I continued walking west. On Dufferin Street, a policeman was marching towards me. The swagger, the official uniform, and the pistol dangling on his right hip exuded power. Just the sight of him sent a serious message to all criminals and evil-doers in the world. He was there to protect justice and the rule of law. He had sworn to keep the peace. He feared neither killers nor any other kind of criminals. Nobody could intimidate him.

From that infamous day back home when they arrested me for yawning, I had developed a kind of unease about all government security forces, with or without uniform. Even in Canada they reminded me of the interrogation and the torture I had suffered back home. I tried to avoid them. But on this day when my sub-clansmen were under attack, something changed inside me. No government officer of any kind could scare me or remind me of anything nasty. I was ready to confront the policeman and waited for him until he was close. "Why did they attack my sub-clan?" I suddenly blurted out the question and at the same time grabbed his left hand.

"What sub-clan are you talking about?" the officer inquired, easily freeing his hand.

"My sub-clan back home in the Somaha Republic."

"And who attacked your sub-clan?"

"The Lulu and Juju sub-clans and their government."

"I know nothing about the sub-clans and the attack you are talking about," he said and gave me a long hard look.

"You are a policeman. You know about crimes and criminals. So how come you know nothing about the attack on my sub-clan? That is also a crime, the worst of crimes, is it not?"

"I told you I know nothing about these attacks and these sub-clans. And, frankly speaking, it is none of my business," the policeman said, his tone showing a bit of irritation and impatience.

"What is your business?" I shot back.

"My business is to protect the citizens of Toronto."

"I am a Toronto citizen."

"So why are you talking about some goddamn sub-clans attacking each other in some foreign country? Has somebody attacked you here in Toronto?"

"Yes."

"Who attacked you?"

"Those who attacked my sub-clan."

"Don't talk nonsense. Nobody attacked you," the policeman said, now apparently intent on concluding the discussion and walking away.

"Mr Policeman, if my sub-clan is attacked, I am also attacked. I am my sub-clan and my sub-clan is me. We are one and the same. If they are at war, I am at war too. If they are at peace, I am at peace. Wherever they go, I go with them. We laugh together and cry together. We live together and die together. I feel their pain, and they feel mine, even though we are thousands of miles apart. Without my sub-clan, I am nothing. What will I do without them? Where will I be if they are defeated?" I pleaded.

"I am telling you that nobody attacked you. You are just drunk and crazy. So stop this nonsense about sub-clans and go home. And no more drinking. Do you hear me?"

The cop's indifference to my problem felt like a slap on the face. I followed him in the street, shouting, "If you don't know why they attacked my sub-clan, you know nothing. You know nothing about crime and criminals. You caught no murderers and thieves. You are just big and tall. And as they say, the bigger they are, the less they know."

The policeman didn't respond to my verbal attack. He continued walking down the street until I gave up on him and walked westwards along Bloor Street.

I was getting sober; the effect of the whisky was fading. And with that came remorse and regrets. I drank alcohol, the stuff Allah warned me about. How would I face Him on the day of reckoning? How could I expect to be admitted into his cherished paradise? I had to repent and seek forgiveness before it was too late. After drinking a cup of tea in a Tim Hortons and spending the last dollar in my pocket, I headed towards a mosque that I knew was located nearby.

The evening prayers were already in progress when I reached there. The Quran echoed from one corner of the mosque to the other. I fell on my knees, faced the qibla, and started praying. I recited the prayers in their proper sequence. But to my surprise and horror, the sacred words sounded empty and devoid of any spiritual content. Something wasn't right. My mind wandered off. I didn't know what to make of it. After a lot of soul-searching, it dawned on me that this was no time for prayers. I had to postpone my repentance for another day when nothing was troubling me, a day when I could pray without distraction. There was a time for prayers and a time for war. This was a time for war.

I was about to step out of the mosque when an intriguing idea hit me and I stopped in my tracks. Why not ask the question of why they attacked us to Allah, I thought to myself. After all, I was in a mosque, a place of worship, the place to communicate with the Great One. And unlike the taxi driver, the policeman, or the men in the bar, Allah was Allah. He knew everything, the good and the bad, the big and small, and everything in between. Nothing was hidden from Him.

I looked up at the ceiling and murmured, "Allah! Why did they attack my sub-clan? Why did they wage war on us?"

I waited patiently for an answer, not knowing how long it would take to get a response or how the answer would be transmitted to me. Somehow, I thought the answer would come through the ceiling and kept looking at it. Ten minutes, twenty minutes, thirty minutes, an hour passed. I detected no writing on the ceiling. No heavenly voice sounded from above. Due to my constant gaze upwards, my neck muscles and my eyes started to ache. I repeated the question a little louder. Still no answer. I thought that maybe if I identified myself, I might have a better chance. So with my eyes still glued to the ceiling, I said, "Allah! I am Ali, a Nunu sub-clansman and I have only one thing to ask today: I just want to know why they attacked my sub-clan."

People praying close by turned in my direction with curious looks. I ignored them and kept my focus on the ceiling. When another hour had passed with no answer or response from Allah, I finally gave up and came out of the mosque, disappointed. I wondered what went wrong. Was the one and only Great One upset with me because I had drunk the whisky and sinned? Or was He just telling me that the Nunu could defend themselves and not to worry?

It was getting late and I walked back to my apartment. By now the crowds in the street had thinned, though some people had lingered for last-minute shopping, braving the cold wind that was gusting with deadly force along Bloor Street. The terrible cold had frozen the small puddles on the sidewalk and seemed like it would freeze bare skin. Just to rest in a warm place, I entered a coffee shop and sat there for an hour or two. The attendant there kindly placed a cup of hot coffee before me.

By the time I reached my apartment, it was close to midnight. My son had already gone to bed. Only Fatima sat in the living room, waiting for me. The instant she heard the knock on the door, she opened it. And was she in a bad mood. "What time is it? Do you have to come so late?" she scolded me.

I slumped on the sofa quietly and made no attempt to justify myself. I didn't want to have any conversation about what I had been doing all day. The less she knew what I had been up to, the better. On the television, the late-night news was on and I watched it while I ate a dinner of rice and mutton that Fatima had warmed up for me. During the brief commercial promotions on the television, I exchanged a few words with her about the attack on our sub-clan.

Fatima didn't show much interest. She was too sleepy and kept yawning in reply. The only thing she was interested in was why I had come home so late. I mumbled something about hanging around on Bloor Street. To tell her that I drank alcohol was out of the question.

When the news ended, Fatima switched off the television and made her way into the bedroom. She was tired and upset. I had never seen her in such a sour mood. Following her to the bedroom, I had no doubt that there would be no pillow talk that night.

And sure enough, Fatima fell asleep the minute she covered herself with the blanket. I wished I could do the same. But I stayed awake, my eyes wide open. My mind refused to ease into sleep. My heart drummed inside my chest. I felt cold at a time when the heat of my body could have fried an egg. I tossed and turned, I struggled with the pillow and the blanket.

Inches away from me, it was a different story. Fatima lay fast asleep, as innocent as a baby, her bosom heaving up and down in a gentle rhythm. She seemed to have no care in the world. As if the attack on our sub-clan had never happened. As if our sub-clansmen were not dying in a barren blood-stained battlefield. Her carefree attitude on such a night didn't make sense. It irritated me.

The more Fatima slept peacefully, the more questions popped up in my mind: How could she remain so calm and carefree at a time when the Nunu sub-clan was under attack? What was wrong with her? Had life in Canada spoiled her so much? Or did she know something I didn't? To get to the bottom of this, I decided to wake her up. "Fatima," I said softly.

She did not respond.

"Fatima," I said louder, and touched her.

Instinctively she rubbed her shoulder where I touched, as if brushing away an insect; then she rolled over to the other side, still fast asleep.

I was losing patience. Her lack of sensitivity and empathy at such a critical time defied everything we stood for. She had to explain and justify her behaviour. So I grabbed her hip and shook her violently to wake her up.

Fatima stirred, gradually awakening. Still half asleep and a bit confused, she opened her eyes. Then she smiled for the first time that night. I immediately understood why. She thought I wanted to make love to her. Before I could say anything, she flipped on her back, eased out of her nightgown, and whispered, "What got into you so suddenly at such a late hour?" Under the blanket, she lay naked.

"No, not that, not the night our sub-clan is under attack," I whispered into her ear. Sex was the last thing on my mind. Any other night, I would have been grateful and eager as a kid being offered a candy, but not that night. To engage in sex when my Nunu folk were dying in the battlefield would be crazy; it would be immoral. And even if I tried to do it, I wouldn't be able to perform. The mood was not there.

"Then what is your problem?" she asked, fully awake now. She put her legs together and wrapped herself in her nightgown, embarrassed at the appearance of initiating sex, something she had never expected to do.

"The problem is that our sub-clan is under attack, and no Nunu man in his right mind will indulge in sex tonight. You can touch my penis and see for yourself. There is nothing there. It might be in a state of mourning," I picked up Fatima's hand to make her feel my penis.

She pulled her hand away, as if she had touched a snake. "You still haven't told me why you woke me up in the middle of the night, and it had better be a good reason," she muttered, after making perfectly clear that she had no intention of touching "that thing," as she put it.

"We have to talk," I said.

"Talk about what?"

"I have a question."

"A question at this time of night? I think the snow has gone into your head. What time is it?"

"I don't know, probably sometime before dawn."

"The question could not wait until I woke up in the morning?"

"No."

"And what is this very important question that couldn't wait?"

"Why did they attack our sub-clan?"

"You don't know?"

"No, I don't."

"Did you ask Mohamed and Jama?"

"They said we are bandits. That is how they depicted us. Can you believe it?"

"And what did you say to them?"

"There is nothing to say to them anymore. I had a fight with them."

"You fought with the only Sudi clansmen we know in Toronto?"

"Forget about Sudi. That was when we were fighting the Duki clan. Now, they are Lulu and Juju, and we are Nunu. Now there is nothing but war between us."

"I know we are not bandits, but I don't know why they attacked us. I am a woman; it is you men who are fighting and making wars, and therefore it is you who should know why they attacked us."

"What do you think?"

"I think Satan got into them."

"What Satan?"

"The one mentioned in our religion. The one who caused Adam and Eve to be ejected from Heaven, remember?"

"Waw! Is that one still around?"

"Yes, what did you think?"

"I thought he died."

"Satan never dies. He doesn't even get sick. Have you ever seen his burial ground?"

"No."

"That is why. He just changes into different forms and shapes. Sometimes, he comes as wind, or an animal, or a person, or a disease, and so on."

I fell silent for a while, pondering about what she had just told me. It certainly wouldn't be easy to pin down something that transforms itself from a person to an animal to the wind that blows. If Satan was the one behind the attack, then it could get more dangerous for us.

"What are you thinking about?" Fatima looked at me and asked.

"I think Satan got promotion. He is no longer an animal or a disease or wind."

"So what is he now?"

"The president of the Somaha Republic."

Fatima laughed, then rolled on the bed to go back to sleep.

"Just let me ask you one more question. You can go back to sleep then," I pleaded with her.

"What is it?"

"Why did they listen to Satan?"

"Why did Eve listen to him?"

"Allah was leading her astray."

"You can say the same about them."

"You can go to sleep now," I sighed, knowing that she had a point there. Not much hope for me to fall asleep that night. If only I could forget about the attack on my sub-clan for a few hours.

16

In the morning, I dragged myself out of bed, cranky and exhausted. The brief hectic sleep late at night hadn't helped much. As I stood up, I could hear noises from the kitchen It was Fatima, bustling from the living room to the kitchen and back again. She was washing dishes and cleaning up the place.

After taking a quick shower, I sat in the living room where Fatima had already put my breakfast. I had just taken my first bite of an egg sandwich when the Somali language edition of BBC news came on the radio. The lead item of the news: the war between the sub-clans in the Somaha Republic. I stopped eating and listened intently, my whole attention focused on the news.

The reporter described a series of battles that had taken place on the eastern front. Casualties had mounted on both sides, he said. Every attack elicited a counter-attack, every offensive a solid defense. Despite all the forces stacked against them, my Nunu sub-clan had held their ground. They had managed to persevere and survive against the odds. Feeling proud, I started chewing my food again.

President Moge had a plan to drive my sub-clan out of the towns and into the jungle; a plan to humiliate us and hurt us. So far, it hadn't worked and had failed miserably. The war had degenerated into a stalemate with neither side defeating the other. President Moge should have known better. My sub-clansmen, who had their settlements deep in the southern part of the Somaha Republic, had always been a force to be reckoned with. There was a reason why the Duki clan called us the Naked Infidels, a reason why we had earned their respect in the battlefield. For anything else, we could be outmaneuvered and outwitted, but when it came to war, we always defended our turf come hell or high water.

When the news ended, I left the house—but not before checking the mailbox beside our door. There I found a letter from the Canadian citizenship office. It was a letter I had been eagerly awaiting for some time. I opened it quickly and read it. The immigration office had set a date for my citizenship test. It would be held in four days. To become a Canadian citizen, all I had to do was to pass that test.

There was a time when I could hardly wait to acquire Canadian citizenship and become eligible for a passport. But with the new war going on back home, things had become more complicated. My plan to travel back to the Somaha Republic was now in limbo. If I passed the citizenship test and got a passport, where would I go? The security forces of President Moge and his sub-clansmen could arrest me at the airport and kill me.

I decided to take the test anyway. President Moge's war couldn't go on forever. Sooner or later, it would come to an end. He might not even stay in power for long. He would definitely be thrown out if he didn't win this war.

To prepare for the test, I read a small book they had sent with the letter. The answers to all citizenship questions could be found in that book, they told me. Not to take any chances, I read the book three times. Still, I feared that I might flunk the simple test. From the day I heard about the attack on my sub-clan, my life had changed in a dramatic way. Not an hour passed when I didn't think about my people. Terrifying nightmares kept me awake at night for hours. I hadn't had proper sleep for many days. This could have an adverse effect on my ability to think straight and answer the questions correctly.

On the day of the test, I listened to the BBC morning news once again. I wasn't going to miss it for the world. Nothing much had changed in the war. The fighters of my sub-clan had held their ground, not yielding an inch. Their strategy of fending off the attacks and then immediately counter-attacking had worked well for them. At the end of the news, I hurried to the citizenship court, a bit apprehensive about my chances. I barely made it in time.

Just as I sat down in the waiting room, the girl at the reception called my name. "Judge Ramon will see you now," she told me, pointing her finger down the corridor. I went where she indicated and knocked on the judge's door and stepped inside. A beaming elderly man welcomed me into his spacious office with a warm handshake. I was feeling jittery and nervous, but the judge's warm greeting helped to put me at ease.

While he organized the papers on his desk, I looked around the office. Pictures of two men were hanging on the wall behind the judge. I didn't know who they were. They must have been important men in Canada in the past. Perhaps previous prime ministers.

No sooner had he finished with his papers than he started the test, asking me questions. How many provinces are there in Canada? Which province has the biggest population? Who is its premier? Who was the Canadian prime minister who repatriated the Canadian Constitution from the United Kingdom and when? Who was the first prime minister of Canada? The questions followed one after another in quick succession like bullets from a machine gun. But I managed to respond with quick, short answers. I was holding my own and doing fine. My memory didn't fail me and came through, except for the last question: Who was the first prime minister of Canada? I tried hard but couldn't recall him. It was the only thing standing between me and my Canadian citizenship.

I had this false notion that the leaders who had governed the country in the distant past didn't matter. I considered it an old story that had no value at the present time. After all, they had been dead for many years. This was a mistake.

"Haven't you read his name in the book?" the judge asked.

"Yes, I think I did. I just can't recall his name," I said, apologetically.

"You have to remember his name. If you want to be a Canadian, you must know the name of our first prime minister, the founder of this country."

Once again, I racked my brain to remember the name upon which my Canadian citizenship depended.

"Let me give you a hint," the judge suggested benevolently and said, "fast food, fast food, fast food . . . "

"Mr Cheeseburger," I blurted out.

"No."

"Mr Hamburger."

"No."

"Mr French Fries."

"No."

"Mr Ketchup."

"No."

"Mr Big Mac."

"You tried hard and came up with truly odd names. But some would say that you came close to it in the end. Maybe we should have called him 'Mr Big Mac'. His name was Sir John A McDonald," the judge said, smiling as he folded and set aside the paper from which he was reading the questions.

"But, judge, the man who founded this country can't be alive. He must have died a long time ago," I remarked sheepishly as a last-ditch attempt to make an excuse for my failure to recall the name.

"Of course he died. He founded this nation more than a hundred and fifty years ago."

"And you are still talking about him and remember him after all these years?"

"You bet we are. He was a good leader and the father of this nation. And you can't forget such a man," the judge said. To further explain the importance of the first Canadian prime minister, the judge added, "Almost every country in the world had at least one exceptional leader in its history. America had George Washington, Thomas Jefferson, and Abraham Lincoln; England had Winston Churchill; Turkey had Kamal Ataturk; India had Mahatama Gandhi; South Africa had Nelson Mandela, and so on. These leaders are all dead and yet their people still remember them. Why? Because they are respected and loved for their political visions and their contribution to the well-being of their nations. Don't you have in your country a leader who served your country and your people exceptionally well in his time, and don't you remember him for that?"

"No, judge, we don't," I told him. "We never had a good leader. I don't think we even had someone you can call a leader."

"You never had a leader?"

"No."

"So what did you have?"

"Warlords."

"And these warlords do what?"

"Wars. That is what their name says, isn't it? They just wage attacks on the clan or sub-clan that they consider to be their enemy."

"That is very unfortunate. I am sorry to hear that. What are you fighting over, anyway?"

"Judge, we fight over everything: water wells, girls, camels, waist belts, to name just a few. Lately, we are fighting over power and government, which has made the situation a lot worse. It has got so crazy and dangerous that sometimes I don't even know what we are fighting about."

"Sometimes you don't even know what you are fighting about?" the judge repeated, arching his eyebrows.

"Yes. Two sub-clans waged an attack on my sub-clan a week ago and I don't know why."

"Perhaps I should not be surprised. If you fought over a waist belt, you could fight over nothing," the judge remarked, feeling sorry for me and my people. Then he paused as he reflected deeply upon what he had just heard, and said, "It must be the nature of your clan culture that is causing you all these social and political problems."

I didn't know what to say, whether to agree with the judge or not. So I just looked out of the window.

Judge John Ramon, a former university teacher and politician, was a man of wisdom, as I soon realized. He frowned and said, "How can you tolerate these warlords?"

"Judge, we don't tolerate them. Some of us resist them and wage war on them. But how many warlords can you fight? When we fight one warlord and defeat him, another one comes along. General Kahin took over the government in a military coup. He was a Duki clansman who looked upon our Sudi clan as an enemy to be crushed. From the day he came to power, he started killing us. His fellow clansmen cheered him, supported him, and stood by him. They agreed with him on everything. For them, it was an opportunity of a lifetime, an opportunity to defeat their historic enemy once and for all, an opportunity to take their revenge on us."

"Is General Kahin still in power in your country?"

"No, Judge, my clan finally deposed him and brought his government down in a guerilla war."

"So there is peace now?"

"No, there is no peace. Another war just started."

"And who is fighting whom now?"

"President Moge and his sub-clan attacked my sub-clan a few days ago."

"You mean the war between the clans is replaced by a war between the sub-clans."

"Yes, Judge. We fought and shed a lot of blood to get rid of a government by a clan and for a clan. And what did we get? A government by a sub-clan and for a sub-clan."

"It seems that you are back to square one and nothing much has changed. Is that what you are saying?"

"Yes, Judge. That is what I am saying. Nothing much has changed."

"This is a mess. In fact, it is more than a mess. It is a tragedy. But do you know where you went wrong and why things didn't get any better?"

"No."

"You fought and shed blood for the wrong cause. You fought for a clan. That was the wrong cause. That is why you are back to square one. What you should have done is to fight for a higher cause. Then you wouldn't be in this situation now."

"A higher cause? Like what?"

"Like equality and justice for all. Like individual rights and the rule of law. These are the higher causes that are worth fighting for. That is what you should have fought for. You didn't. And you know why?"

"Not really."

"I will tell you. There is a culprit out there that is always leading you in the wrong path, a culprit that is behind all your problems."

"You mean the warlords?"

"No, these characters are merely a symptom and a by-product. The basic culprit behind all your political and social problems is your culture, your clan-based culture. It is the blind loyalties that you have for your clans and sub-clans. That is the real culprit. That is the underlying cause of everything that went wrong in your society and your country.

It is an easy issue to understand. A total blind loyalty to any group takes away your freedom, your independence and your basic humanity as individuals. Let's face it. You are not a free people. You are in bondage to your clans or sub-clans or whatever, and subservient to them emotionally and psychologically."

"What does that mean, Judge," I asked, not quite clear about his strong statements.

"It means your people lack complete individual freedom and that is what is holding you back. That is your problem. Free individuals think rationally. Free individuals make decisions on the basis of their conscience, upon the facts of the issue, upon what is right and what is wrong. Free individuals ask questions—the why, the what, and the how. In contrast, people who have a blind loyalty to a group just go along with the group, no matter what. That kind of mentality always leads you on the wrong path, with catastrophic results. You don't ask questions; you don't seek the facts and the truth; you just take a gun and fight for your clan or sub-clan and lay down your lives for them like a properly trained pet.

"Erich Fromm, a well-known psychologist," the judge continued, "in his book, *Escape from Freedom*, explains how people in tribal-based cultures shrink from individual freedom, renounce their individuality, and bond with a group—a tribe, a clan or a sub clan—that can give them protection. As babies, we all need protection which we mainly get from our families—from our mothers and fathers. But in these clan-based societies like yours, when the baby outgrows from his mother and father, he still feels insecure as a man."

"Judge, are you saying we feel insecure like babies?"

"Yes, that is exactly what I am saying. You feel vulnerable and in need of protection like a baby. And there is a reason for that."

"What is the reason? This is really getting more complicated."

"No, it is not complicated. I will explain. In your country, you probably never had a proper government that enforces law in a just way, to create a safe environment for all its citizens. That is where the insecurity comes from. That is what forces you to cling to a clan or tribe that would give you a sense of belonging and protection. You trade your freedom for security—but freedom is the most valuable thing any human being could have—a total freedom.

"But you can do something about it," the judge went on. "You can fight your inner demons and free yourself from clan bondage. You can seek a better future by embracing individual freedom like we do in Canada. But to do so, you need to make fundamental changes in your culture. Change is never easy. We all know that. It needs hard work and determination. You can't reach the top of the mountain unless you climb the steep rocks. Good economy, education, security, and the rule of law are the tools that will take you there."

Stung by the judge's criticism of my people in his long speech, I couldn't remain silent anymore and said, "Judge, you think a Nunu subclansman is not a free person?"

The judge smiled, somewhat amused, and said, "None of you is free. A person who is absolutely loyal to any group can never be a free person. He can't be. Period. He becomes a tool for the group, an abiding henchman as observed by Eric Hoffer. In his book, *The True Believer*, Mr Hoffer wrote about the fanaticism inherent in group politics in its different forms: nationalistic, racial, tribal, or clan-based, and I quote, 'When we renounce our individuality and become part of a group, we not only renounce the personal advantage, but also rid ourselves of personal responsibility. There is no telling to what extremes of cruelty and ruthlessness a man will go when he is freed from the fears, hesitations, doubts and the vague stirrings of decency that go with individual judgment. When we lose our individual independence, we find a new freedom—freedom to hate, bully, lie, torture, and betray without shame and remorse.'"

The judge paused again for a moment to drink water, then resumed his long monologue. "When I was a student," he said, "I read the novel *Zorba the Greek*, written by Nikos Kazantzakis. This man, Zorba, was asked what he did for his people. He said, 'There was a time when I used to say: That man is a Turk, or a Bulgar, or a Greek. I have done things for my country that would make your hair stand on end, boss. I have cut people's throats, burned villages, robbed and raped women, wiped out entire families. Why? Because they were Bulgars or Turks and so on.

Nowadays I say this man is a good fellow, that one's a bastard. They can be Greeks, or Bulgars or Turks, it doesn't matter. Is he good? Or is he bad? That's the only thing I ask nowadays . . . '"

Like a teacher in a school, the judge rambled on. "All these authors and thinkers are in one way or another talking about the same thing—the sinister herd mentality that not only causes clan and tribal conflicts in your part of the world, but also ultra-nationalistic fervor and racial bigotry in other places. It all starts by one group demonizing, dehumanizing, and vilifying another group. They call them names. They call them villains, lowdown degenerates, barbarians, monsters, and terrorists. The self-serving malicious propaganda is put in high gear. Like psychopaths, they can't wait to see blood flowing like rivers. Reason, common sense, and logic become a rare commodity. So-called intelligent human beings suddenly turn into the most clueless and vicious animals on earth. Another Holocaust, another Rwandan tragedy, another Darfur genocide unfolds. And they won't rest until they step over the dead bodies of the 'enemy' and realize what we call 'victory'.

"And one more thing you need to know," the judge added. "Government is a complex organization. To make it work, the citizens of the country have to be politically mature. And it seems to me that your people lack a lot in that field. You had no political philosophers as we had over the centuries. You had no John Locke who wrote the Second Treatise of Government. You had no Edmund Burke who, due to the difficulties and complexities of the art of government, preached prudence, reason, deep reflection, and utilitarian pragmatism. You had no John Stuart Mill who championed individual liberty. You had neither Montesquieu nor Voltaire nor Diderot, who believed in the rights of the individual. The fact of the matter is that your political culture and society has to undergo a fundamental change to become more seasoned and more accommodating for the practice of good politics. With your political culture as it is, you can't improve your economy; you can't attain progress; and you can't create a real democratic government. It is as simple as that. For liberal democracy to work, the society must be predominantly composed of educated, fair-minded, free people. In essence, a real nation consists of free individuals. A nation of clans and not of free individuals is not a nation. A government based on a clan or a sub-clan and not on ideas and the rule of law is not a proper government. It is bound to fail sooner or later. It is like a house without a solid foundation."

I thought this judge might be talkative by nature and would never stop. My mind wandered. The judge noticed and said with a smile, "Anyway, you have passed the test for Canadian citizenship. Come back in three weeks for the citizenship ceremony. Or do you want to remain a Nunu sub-clansman?"

"Thanks, Judge. I want to be a Canadian and a Nunu sub-clansman at the same time," I said and left with my head spinning with his ideas and slogans.

I took the subway and got off at Christie station. As I walked towards home, I came across a small park. Exhausted, I sat on a bench. Not far from me, an old man was playing with his dog. He appeared to be retired and had no care in the world. His sub-clan is not under attack, I thought to myself, and stood up to resume my walk. I should have gone home and tried to get some sleep, but I didn't. Instead, I slipped into the same bar to which I had gone before. It was nearly empty this time.

The bartender who had served me the previous day greeted me with a guarded smile and said, "Who am I looking at here? The camel boy? Is that you again?"

"Yes, it is me."

"How are you doing today?"

"Not good," I mumbled.

"What is the problem? You still don't know why they attacked your sub-clan?"

I was surprised that he remembered. "Not yet," I told him.

"Oh, no. You are not going to ask us that thing again?"

"No, I am not. I just came for a drink."

"What are you drinking?"

"The same one I had yesterday."

"Whisky?"

"Yes."

"No trouble-making, now. You got to promise."

"I promise."

Satisfied, the bartender served me a glass of whisky. I thanked him and started sipping it quietly. Some of the things the citizenship judge talked about in his long speech still echoed in my mind. He had made statements which annoyed and intrigued me at the same time. He depicted us as some kind of slaves to our clans and sub-clans. How insulting! But he had also said things that made sense when he talked about the tragedy of a government based on a clan or a sub-clan and nothing else. As a Nunu sub-clansman, I had to agree with him about that, every word of it.

Unlike the previous day, I kept to myself and had no interaction with the other customers in the bar. I just drank one glass of whisky after another until I had spent all my money, the twenty dollars I had taken from my wife. With no more money to pay for the drinks, I left the bar on my own. Nobody kicked me out this time.

Out in the street, I walked unsteadily, sometimes bumping into passersby. I didn't go home and just lingered around in the area until I felt sober. As soon as I realized that the effect of the whisky had ebbed away, it was back to the feelings of guilt. I had drunk alcohol and sinned again. I had to pray and repent. Day after day, I continued doing so.

How long could I go on this way, I wondered. How long could I keep drinking first and repenting later? It didn't make sense. This was no way to live. My sinful ways were getting out of control and I had to quit drinking once and for all. But no matter how much I tried and swore not to drink one more drop of alcohol, in the days that followed, I found myself returning to the bar. It was the attack on my sub-clan that made me do it. I couldn't help myself as long as the attack on my sub-clan continued.

My wife soon discovered my newly-adopted drinking habit and things went from bad to worse. Upset, she reminded me of my responsibilities as a husband and as a father of our young son. She warned me about the consequences. "You have a choice between good and bad, right and wrong, and sin and virtue," she told me angrily.

It was good advice and words of wisdom. I couldn't have agreed more with her. And yet, I failed to change my ways and frequented the bar until I came home one night in a bad shape. It must have been very late at night, certainly past midnight. My wife opened the door, saw me swaying from side to side, and slammed the door in my face. I cursed her at the top of my voice and pounded on the door with all the force I could muster.

She opened the door again, furious and screaming. "I don't want you here. So get out of my life."

"Where should I go? This is my home."

"No, this is not your home anymore. Your home is where you drink alcohol. That is the home of all losers like you."

"I am a loser? Is that what you think? How dare you!"

"Yes, you are a loser. Where were you all day long?"

"I was in Dufferin Mall," I lied.

"That is a lie. Dufferin Mall closes at 9 o'clock in the evening."

"I was sitting in a doughnut shop," I said, coming up with a new one.

"Go back to the doughnut shop or wherever." She almost broke down with emotion. "You don't have a regular job anymore. You don't give us money. We can't go on living on a welfare cheque. I want a man who takes care of his family, not a loser like you. I have had enough of you."

"I am a bit messed up now. It is a difficult time for me and for all our people. You know what we are going through. Let me get in and we will talk."

"Talk about what? Talk about a war you can't do anything about? I have nothing more to say to you. I don't even want to be your wife anymore. It is time we go our own separate ways."

The talk about ending our marriage hit me hard, even though I was somewhat drunk. To point out my failures and shortcomings in such difficult times was one thing. To threaten me with divorce and separation was another. She went too far and I had to do something. She was no longer the woman I married twelve years ago. Not even close. She had watched too much Canadian television and got new ideas. I had to take a firm stand and fight back. I had to assume my position as the head of the family. So I glared at her, and said, "Let me get this straight: are you saying that you no longer want me as your husband? Is that what you are saying? Is that your final decision?"

"Yes, that is exactly what I am saying. You heard me right. A man who has nothing to do but drink alcohol is not good enough for me as a husband," she said in a calm voice.

"How dare you say something like that to me?" I yelled at her angrily and pushed her out of the way. In the heat of the moment, I grabbed a plate from a table and threw it at her. It missed her and hit the wall, breaking into pieces.

My wife ducked, but didn't back down or get scared. Instead, she stood her ground, looked me in the eye, and said, "I can talk to you and tell you the truth. Where do you think we are? This is Canada." She then picked up the phone and called 911.

I never thought she would take such a drastic step and call the police. I regretted throwing the plate at her.

The police came over within minutes, put me under arrest, and took me to a police station. Over there, they asked me a few questions. When I answered them all, they told me that I was drunk and abusive. Then, they locked me in a cell where I sat on the floor for a long time. I might have dozed off for an hour or two.

The next day in the afternoon, they released me, but with conditions and limitations. I had to stay away from my wife, my son, and my home. I shouldn't bother them or cause them any trouble. If I went back there, they said, I was breaking the law.

In essence, I was a homeless man when I walked out of the police station. The family and place I used to call home were no longer mine. So I just drifted from one street to another until late in the evening. That night, I ended up sleeping in a small park east of Ossington subway station. The next night, it got cold and I had to go to a shelter, the same one where I had stayed my first night in Canada. I never thought I would ever see that place again. But then, who among us can tell what tomorrow will bring?

A few days later, I came across Mohamed and Jama on Bloor Street. I didn't even greet them, let alone ask them for help and a place to sleep. I just passed them by as if we had never met before. As long as the war between our sub-clans continued, we had nothing to say to each other. Like enemies, we had drawn a line on the sand; a line none of us had any intention of crossing.

During daytime, I usually hung around in the western part of the
city, close to my family's apartment. Sometimes, I lingered near Dagaal's
school to get a glimpse of him when he left in the afternoon and went
home. Just to see him from afar gave me solace and a lot of satisfaction.
His classmates often accompanied him and I watched him from a distance until he reached home safely.

Sometimes, though, I ventured into the downtown area and walked
all the way to Yonge and Bloor instead of taking the subway. By doing so,
I saved some fare money; not a lot, but it made a difference to me.

One day, on a cold afternoon, I reached Yonge and Bloor after a long
walk. Tired and a bit tipsy, I entered a small coffee shop on the northeast
end of the intersection. Before I sat down, I picked up a donut and a cup
of tea from the counter. As I was having my donut and sipping my tea,
a Somali man I had never seen before came in. We exchanged greetings
and I invited him to join me.

"My name is Farah," he said, as he sat down.

But I needed more than his name and asked, "What clan do you
belong to?"

"I am Duki," he said.

For the first time, I was seeing a Duki clansman in Toronto. It didn't
surprise me, though. After they were defeated in the war and their government collapsed, many Duki fled the country seeking refugee status
all over the world. The fire they had ignited caught up with them and
burned them as well. How ironic to see a Duki clansman seeking refugee
status in Canada. On what basis would he claim refugee status? A refugee from himself and his own actions?

Shaking my head about the new turn of events, I asked one of the
waiters in the coffee shop to bring us a knife and a cup of tea. The knife
was for me, the tea for the Duki. I wanted Farah, the Duki clansman, to
have his last cup of tea.

"What do you need the knife for?" the waiter looked at me, a bit curious and intrigued. After all, I was eating a donut, not a beef steak.

"I need it for the donut. It is a bit hard," I said, and then turned to the
Duki clansman, identifying myself as a Rori clansman. I had to put him
at ease and catch him off guard.

The few minutes I waited for the knife felt like a year. Meanwhile, I tried to engage the Duki in conversation. It was not easy. I didn't know what to say and where to begin. My mind just went blank. What could you say to an enemy that turned your life upside down?

The waiter finally came back with a small knife. I was counting on a bigger and a longer one, the deadly type. I grabbed it anyway and lunged at the Duki before he had even finished his tea. I had to drive the knife through his chest and into his heart.

He fell backwards and instinctively raised his hand to shield himself. His quick reaction probably saved his life. The knife slashed his right arm but came short of reaching its intended destination. He was still within reach though. Once again, I threw myself at him, determined to do the job properly this time. I thought I had got him when, out of nowhere, two men grabbed me from behind and pulled me back. One of them was white and the other black; and they were stronger than me. They held me tight and knocked the knife out of my hand. It didn't surprise me when they turned out to be policemen in plain clothes.

A few feet away, the waiters and a group of customers were helping the Duki fellow, trying to stop the blood gushing from his arm. I knew he would recover. I might have squandered my last chance of avenging the killing of my father. A feeling of shame and sadness came over me.

Wailing sirens approached from a distance. It didn't take long before multiple cars with flashing lights were all around the area. With his pistol drawn and ready to shoot, a uniformed cop rushed into the coffee shop. He was taking no chances. Once he realized that he faced no danger, he put away his pistol and handcuffed me. Two other cops arrived and directed the paramedics towards the injured Duki while the first cop led me out to a police car. He kept me locked inside while he and his partner spoke to witnesses. Then two of them got into the car and drove me away.

The police car drove eastwards along Bloor, lights flashing, then turned north and soon entered the parking lot of an impressive redbrick building. It was a police station and very busy inside. After I was registered at the reception desk, my fingerprints and mugshots were taken, and I was locked in a small prison cell in the basement at the end of a long corridor. Nobody shared my cell with me. The next day I was taken back downtown to an old court building. Here a judge heard my case from the two plainclothesmen who had disarmed me in the coffee shop, and one of the officers who had arrested me. The judge ordered me to stand trial and I was taken to an old prison building and put in a cell. In this new prison, again I was alone.

About five days had passed when a guard led me out one morning and took me to an office where a man in a suit was waiting for me. He turned out to be the lawyer who had been assigned to defend me in court and had come to discuss the strategy we should be adopting for my defense.

I had no illusions about my situation. The case against me couldn't have been more serious. I had attempted to kill a man and had no intention of denying it. In the eyes of the police, I was a dangerous criminal who had to be put away for years. No hope of being acquitted even with the best of lawyers. So many people had witnessed what I had done and had no regrets at all. How could I have any regrets when I was only seeking justice? Justice for my dead father, whom they had murdered. I had a valid reason to do what I did, something that could pose a solid defense of my case in court.

The lawyer started with exploratory questions, asking me about my family and their names. Gradually, his tone shifted and the questions became more serious. He wanted to know why I had attacked the man with a knife.

I didn't beat about the bush and gave him my motivation, why I tried to kill the man. I had to explain to him that I was merely taking my revenge on the clan that had murdered my father. I had to tell him that it was all about justice and nothing else. I said, "They started this. They killed my father in cold blood. So I wanted to get even and take my revenge on them. That was all. That is why I wanted to kill this guy."

The lawyer started shaking his head, as if he was hearing the most bizarre thing in the world.

"Is the guy you tried to kill the same guy who murdered your father?" he asked me.

"I don't think so, but he is a Duki clansman," I shot back.

"How many Duki clansmen are there in the world?"

"I don't know. I didn't count them. Maybe about a million."

"And you want to kill any one of those million people in order to avenge the killing of your father?"

"Yes," I said and nodded.

"But they can't be all guilty, can they? I mean, you could kill an innocent man."

"They killed my father and that makes them all guilty. None of them is innocent," I stated firmly.

"How could a million men be all guilty for the murder of one man?" he demanded.

"Duki clansmen are all the same to me. They are all Duki clansmen. If I see one of them, I see them all. They all have the blood of my father on their hands."

"This is insane. And you know what? Now I know how to argue your case. We are doing an insanity plea."

"And who is insane?"

"You," he replied and looked at me without batting an eye.

"I am not insane," I protested, fuming at the insult. "We all do that— the Duki clansmen do that. And so do the Sudi clansmen and the Tuwi clansmen. Are we all insane? Is the whole country insane?"

"Anybody who thinks like that is either insane or lives in the dark ages. It is one or the other. Take your pick!" He put it bluntly and made it quite clear that he would only defend me on the basis of insanity.

I thought it was time I took matters into my own hands and do without this lawyer. I stood up to bring an end to the discussion. He had shown no respect for me and my people. I didn't need his help. Enough of his insults and his lawyer talk. I could defend myself in the court. After all, it was my case and my story. I knew it better than anybody else.

"I don't need your defense," I said to him and ended his service before it had even started.

I was in jail for a long time, awaiting my trial. Weeks passed. I was kept by myself because they thought I was insane and dangerous. I could go out to walk in a yard, where some other prisoners played basketball. I was shown the library but I could not read. In the mess hall, I ate alone. Once I was visited by a man and woman, who asked me many questions about myself and wrote down my answers in a notebook.

Finally, I was taken to face a judge and a jury in a court. It was a Thursday morning. The judge opened the proceedings by telling the prosecutor to make his case.

The prosecutor stood up, and told the jury what had happened. He described the scene and called me a potential murderer and a dangerous man. Then the prosecutor called on his first witness, the waiter in the coffee shop who had brought me a knife upon my request. He also called on two people who had been sitting close to me and observed what had happened. Next, he called on the two men who had saved the Duki by holding me back.

All the witnesses described what had happened carefully. The judge asked if I had any questions to ask the witnesses who testified against me. I didn't contradict them on anything and let their statements stand. As soon as the prosecutor had finished with his witnesses, I told the judge I had something to say about what happened. Here the judge called the prosecutor to his bench and spoke with him. Then he looked at me.

"Mr Ali. In the absence of a lawyer, and seeing that you are not familiar with the proceedings of a trial, and have dismissed the lawyer assigned to you, I will ask you questions, and you can answer them to give your version of events to the jury. Is that agreed?"

"It is agreed, Judge," I said solemnly.

The judge proceeded.

"Mr Ali, did you attack with a knife a young man by the name of Farah inside a coffee shop on February 10 of this year?"

"Yes, I did," I admitted.

"Had you met the victim before?"

"No."

"Did you know him personally?"

"No."

"Had Farah done anything wrong to you?"

"No."

"So why did you attack him with a knife?"

"He belongs to the Duki clan. He is a Duki clansman."

"And so?"

"The Duki clan killed my father. That is why."

"But Farah didn't kill your father, did he?"

"No, he didn't. What I am trying to tell you, Judge, is that he belongs to the clan that killed my father."

"You tried to kill an innocent person who had done nothing to you and was not threatening you in any way."

"My father was also innocent, as innocent as anybody. And the Duki clan killed him."

"So you believed you would serve justice by killing another innocent man?"

"Yes, I do believe that. They killed my innocent father. Killing one of them is an act of revenge and an act of justice at the same time."

"You are wrong. The killing of your innocent father was a crime. Killing another innocent person is not an act of justice; it is committing another crime. You are adding one injustice to another. Two injustices don't equal to justice."

"Judge, about fifteen years ago, a group of armed Duki clansmen tracked down my father, caught up with him and killed him. He did nothing to them. He was just looking for his lost camel and they killed him just because my father was a Sudi clansman. No other reason whatsoever. They didn't stop there, they also raided my camels. They took away everything dear to me. I should have done something about it, shouldn't I? I had to take my revenge on those who had murdered my father, hadn't I?"

"What happened to your father is terrible and unfortunate. But do you think that gives you justification to do what you did?" the judge asked.

"Yes, it does. I was the only son my father left behind. I have an obligation to avenge his killing. I had to shed their blood just as they shed the blood of my father. If not me, who? No one! They took away from me a wise and loving father, the only parent I had ever known. What should I have done? Forget about my father? Be a coward and allow the Duki clan to get away with the blood of my beloved father?"

The judge said, "Again, we are sorry that your father was killed. But here in Canada, we believe a person is innocent until proven guilty. That means only the man or men who killed your father are guilty of that crime. All other Duki clansmen are not. The man you tried to kill was innocent even if his brother killed your father—forget about the entire Duki clan. That is the basis upon which our justice system, our society, and our culture are built on. Let me repeat: only the person who committed a crime is responsible for his action, not his brother, not his father, not his cousin and certainly not a person who only belongs to the same clan. No one should die and pay a price for a crime he didn't commit."

I was taken back to the prison. The next day, I returned to the court. The judge asked the head of the jury to announce their decision. He did. The jury had found me guilty of attempted murder. It was their law, not mine. They recited the reasons and justifications behind their decision. They said I shouldn't have taken the law into my own hands. They said I shouldn't have attempted to kill an innocent person even though he belonged to the Duki clan. After the jury spoke, the judge announced the sentence—fifteen years in jail without parole.

It was at this time that I saw Fatima in the audience. My wife looked sad. She had tears in her eyes, and I knew that she had forgiven me for my drinking and wanted me back home. I knew that she understood the reason behind my actions. Dagaal looked devastated, as though he had just heard of my death. He sobbed quietly. But did he understand? To see their faces made me feel a lot worse than the jury's guilty sentence.

For the second time in my life, I was on my way to a prison. The circumstances couldn't have been more different though. The first time had been for yawning; this time it was for trying to take revenge. As the police car sped towards the prison, I remembered the citizenship judge, and his unforgettable lecture came to mind. He had said, "A society and a government based on clans and sub-clans, and not on free individuals and the rule of law, are bound to fail sooner or later." The truth of that statement echoed in my mind. My personal experiences could vouch for it. I had the scars to prove it.

Who knows? Maybe the Canadian judge who sent me to jail had a valid point when he said, "A person is innocent until proven guilty that he himself and only himself committed the crime, and no one should die and pay a price for a crime he didn't commit."

And then, there was that overarching question at the back of my mind, the question of whether good government, peace, and justice will ever prevail in our land. Like in Canada. Like in most other countries in the world. As they say, time will tell.